The Eternal Trust

The Eternal Trust

Melinda Rucker Haynes

Five Star • Waterville, Maine

This novel is a work of fiction. Names, characters, places and incidents are either the product of the author's imagination, or, if real, used fictitiously.

Five Star First Edition Romance Series.

Published in 2002 in conjunction with Melinda Rucker Haynes.

Set in 11 pt. Plantin by Myrna S. Raven.

Printed in the United States on permanent paper.

Library of Congress Cataloging-in-Publication Data

Haynes, Melinda Rucker.
    The eternal trust / by Melinda Rucker Haynes.
        p. cm.— (Five Star first edition romance series)
    ISBN 0-7862-4208-6 (hc : alk. paper)
    1. Time travel—Fiction. I. Title. II. Series.
PS3608.A96 E84 2002
    813′.6—dc21   2002023086

For
Buzzy and Binky
We're together again for another adventure
in eternal Love.

Prologue

Taintinain, China
August 1945

Rockets screamed overhead, falling ominously silent just before the impact that rolled thunderous shock waves across the land. Smoke shrouded the Japanese garrison set ablaze in the Russian infantry's attack. The deadly hand-to-hand combat that followed swiftly routed the occupying Japanese, sending the few survivors to scramble away with the Chinese civilians trying to escape the Russian invasion.

The Japanese commander couldn't breathe for the chalky dust of the parade ground clogging his mouth. As he lifted his face out of the dirt and raised himself to his elbows, acrid smoke stung his eyes and he choked, spitting red into the soil. Using his sword to crutch himself to his knees, Baron Fusao Tsuji blinked down at the blood spreading across the chest of his khaki uniform. The next explosion blew him backward and he briefly lost consciousness again.

Knifing pain prodded Tsuji to turn away from the brilliant white light overwhelming the darkness before him. He opened his eyes, hearing sobbing gasps as she struggled to drag him to shelter. Do not fear, dear one, he thought groggily. I live still. This is not the time.

In the shadow of a mountain of rubble that had been their quarters during the long years of the Imperial Japanese occupation of China, his baroness knelt over him. Her beloved, tear-streaked face convulsed with grief.

"Fusao? Fusao, hear me. You must release the sword," his

wife whispered inches above his lips. Her delicate fingers entwined with his on the handle of the samurai sword he clutched to his chest. "I know now to whom I must take it. That means this life is ending. Let it go, my love. I will take the sword to him. We will be separated only a moment then the sword and I will return to you. Like always."

His hand tightened on the sword. He couldn't give it up. Not again.

"Please, Fusao, I do not have much time left. I must do this. You know I must," she pleaded, her voice breaking.

As he died, the last thing Baron Tsuji saw was his cherished wife's desperate face, but his last thoughts were only of the sword she took from his limp hands.

Explosions rocked the temple, splintering the carved wooden beams supporting the gabled roof. Red tiles crashed into the courtyard, pocking the brick pavement already cluttered with the debris of war. Three men dashed through the boiling dust into the smoky interior of the temple.

"Set up the radio!" U.S. Navy Lt. Martin Everly ordered in Mandarin dialect. He turned his back on the two Chinese Resistance fighters and pointed his .45 Colt automatic at the doorway. "Hurry!"

The two men crouched on either side of the radio and hand-cranked the generator. Martin grabbed the microphone, keeping his eyes on the entrance.

"Come in, Mother. This is Son. Over," he said in English. Static crackled and snapped. "Mother. This is Son. Come in."

Rapid gunfire rattled from the street amid the mounting shouts and screams.

"Mother. This is Son. Come in." He cut a glance at the two Chinese silently cranking the radio. They must be feeling as frantic as he, taking a big risk hiding him, helping him as the Japanese Army ran from the Russians. Stalin had declared war on Japan a week ago and hadn't stopped his invasion of China, even though Japan's Emperor Hirohito had ordered an unconditional surrender yesterday. The Russians were killing anyone Oriental, Imperial Japanese Army and Chinese civilians alike.

"Come in, Son. This is Mother, over," the radio crackled.

"Mother. Your presence required my house now. Twenty-two hundred hours. Over."

"Roger, Son. Over and out."

"Over and out." Martin clicked off the microphone.

The men stopped cranking and stowed the radio for travel. He would be leaving it with them once they delivered him to the pick-up point. He'd like to give them more, but he couldn't. He wasn't sure he'd helped anyone. This OSS covert mission was meant to gather information for the Allies, not directly aid the locals. If anything, he'd endangered them further because they helped him. If the Russians caught him, he'd become an American prisoner of war. And his Chinese friends would join their ancestors.

They crept to the temple doors and waited in the shadows, watching frightened refugees scramble for safety in the street beyond the courtyard. A small figure in a peasant coolie hat and baggy leaf-green quilted pajamas escaped the smoke and staggered to the gate. Martin watched him lean on the hewn gatepost and glance behind him. Clutching his left side, he struggled across the courtyard toward their hiding place.

He fell into the temple doorway facedown at Martin's feet.

Martin grabbed a handful of the rough cotton jacket and pulled the body deeper into the shadows. As he turned the man over, the hat fell back unleashing a cascade of shining black hair.

9

"Japanese woman!" growled one of the men and drew a long knife from under his jacket.

"Put that away!" Martin caught the man's arm in midair, pushed him off and knelt over the woman.

Her dark eyes fluttered open and focused on Martin. Slowly, a smile edged the pain on her flawless pale face. "I find you again," she whispered in halting English.

Martin gently cradled her small form in his arms. Her expression crumpled and he saw the deep red stain blossoming on her side. Something hard pressed against his arm through the back of her jacket.

"You've found *me?*" Martin asked, intrigued.

She shuddered with her next breath. "You are Everly, yes?" Though he didn't answer, she continued, "I Baroness Tsuji. The Guardian. I must give to you before—" She swallowed the choking cough bubbling in her throat. "Before I die."

Martin put his canteen to her lips, but she weakly waved it away.

"They come. I must give to you." She raised her small hand to her neck. "Please. Take from my back. I give to you."

Martin hesitated. The woman could be booby-trapped and blow them all to hell. Her imploring expression urged him to trust her. He reached into the back of her jacket and withdrew a Japanese samurai sword dangling from a red silk cord around her neck.

The two Chinese fell back with a collective hiss as Martin turned the beautiful weapon in his hands. The spiraling carved design of the black lacquer wooden scabbard hungrily absorbed the meager light. Even in the dimness he saw that the sword was very old. He was about to slide the scabbard off when she stopped him.

"No! It is not for you. You keep secret. For her. She know what do . . ."

He leaned closer to her lips. "Who am I supposed to keep the sword for?"

"Guardian. Your granddaughter. Help us, Everly. Teach her courage . . . no more killing. Break cycle. She save us all." Baroness Tsuji's haunted eyes lost focus, the last breath escaping in a rattling sigh. Her body stilled as death claimed her, yet her beautiful, tormented face refused the smoothing hand of peace.

"We must go," urged one of his men.

Martin Everly hid the sword in the back of his shirt and pulled its red cord over his head and shoulder. A peculiar oppressiveness spread into his chest. As he led the men outside, he wondered at the heavy cadence of destiny that pulsed through his body and an unfamiliar voice within awakened. Memories flooded his consciousness, reminding him that his fate was joined to the dead woman in the temple and to the sword riding against his back. This lifetime and before.

Chapter One

The sixty-day layoff warning hadn't worried Dorel Everly. Boeing wouldn't lay her off because she was a good engineer, her rapport too vital with the difficult but important customer. TransAsia Airlines wouldn't allow Boeing management to replace her. Dorel had the highest totem rating an employee could receive. She'd believed she was safe until two days after her grandfather's memorial service when Security escorted her out of her Customer Engineering cubical at the Everett, Washington factory.

It had to be a mistake, her manager assured her as she carried a single cardboard file box filled with framed certificates and excellence awards, a chipped 747-300 coffee cup and a two-hundred year old bonsai willow in a shallow raku dish that was last year's Christmas gift from TransAsia. A month before she might have indulged in some pride about her accomplishments during her five years with the company, but today the meager contents of the box just made her want to cry.

Merging onto I-5 South, she discovered that the only benefit to leaving work early was that most of the traffic flowed in the opposite direction. Forty-two minutes later Dorel walked into the condo overlooking Elliot Bay just as the answering machine beeped and hung up.

She ignored it and went directly to her bedroom, eased the box down on a waist-high stack of others on the floor and carefully removed the bonsai.

"Well, don't you look wholly unaffected and perfect as usual," she commented to the miniature tree and placed it on the dresser where it should get sufficient light from the glass door that opened to the wraparound terrace.

Maybe the bonsai would like being outside in the sunshine for awhile, she thought. I know I would if I'd been stuck under florescent office lights for months, and since I have, we'll just get some sun together. Dorel slid the door open and carried the bonsai out to the wrought iron table, placing it in the shade of the large beige market umbrella.

"I'll grab a glass of wine and be right back," she called over her shoulder as she stepped inside and through the antiques and fine art-furnished condominium to the stainless steel kitchen.

Toying with the idea of cracking open something old and expensive from the well-stocked wine cellar, she instead opened the Sub-Zero refrigerator, pulled out a nearly empty bottle of cheap Australian chardonnay and tipped it into the crystal wine glass she'd used last night.

Passing back through the living room that was definitely not to her minimalist tastes, she noticed the answering machine's slow blink. One message. Probably the one that came in when she got home. Dorel stood next to the machine, watching the hypnotic winking, and took a swallow of wine.

She had a hate-hate relationship with the phone these days. It only brought bad news or expressions of condolence that probably made the callers feel better than she did. The calls made her feel guilty for not being able to care for him herself, for not having spent every hour with her granddad. Even though she'd sat by his bedside each evening after work until the end of visiting hours, he hadn't even known she was there.

13

Martin had decided that the VA hospital in Tacoma was where he would get the care he needed at the price he could afford since his costly medical treatments for the last three years had taken everything he had, as well as Dorel's savings.

Taking care of him was the least the government could do. Despite what the military claimed, she was convinced Martin's top secret work on the Bikini Atoll atomic testing project back in the 1950s had given him leukemia.

Everyone who seemed to think they knew Martin Everly better than the granddaughter he had raised said he would have wanted Dorel to forget the past and get on with her life without him.

If that were so, why did she feel like her grandfather was following her around when she was awake and haunting her every night in the same dream where he was a young American Naval officer in some battle in China?

She didn't know much about Martin's wartime service, but was sure his experiences contributed to his fascination with Asian studies. It had been his obsession, not hers. So why would she dream about that?

The doorbell chimed and Dorel cringed. She tiptoed through the foyer and placed her eye to the viewer to see a small Asian man in orange-yellow robes. How did he get past the doorman? She turned her back and leaned on the door as dread wormed in her stomach. Who was this monk? Some old cronie from Martin's Buddhist days?

The bell sounded again and her hand was on the knob, opening the door before she could stop herself.

"Miss Everly?" asked the monk. His placid, aged face was wrinkled like the robes he wore and his shaven head was as smooth as the shoulder left uncovered by the saffron folds swathing his compact stature to his white socks and boat shoes.

"Yes?"

"I am Roshi from your grandfather's former Sangha."

She stared at the meter-long, rectangular black suitcase he held by the handle with both hands. What was in it? she wondered, unusually curious. She swallowed hard.

The monk smiled kindly. "Your grandfather left strict instructions that you were to have this upon his death. May I come in?"

Dorel stood aside and motioned him in. He remained in the foyer as she closed the door, then followed her into the sunny living room.

"Please have a seat, Mr. Roshi." She indicated the sofa and perched herself on the edge of the love seat opposite him. He eased down into a tea rose and lily hued nest of designer pillows and rested the black case on his knees. They sat staring at each other, Dorel willing herself silent and to look at the monk rather than at the black case. It was becoming more difficult by the second to keep her eyes on his. She laced her fingers together in her lap and squeezed.

"Miss Everly, I was a professor of law at Stanford." He reached into his robe and pulled out a folded blue paper. "After I withdrew from public life and entered the Sangha, I acted as an attorney for your grandfather, Martin Everly, in one instance while he was with us. This Eternal Trust document empowered me to hold the item in this case until such time as your grandfather expired. By the terms of the trust, I now release this to you, his granddaughter." He laid the paper on top of the case and held it out to her on his open palms.

Dorel snatched it from his hands. The blue paper slipped into her lap as she set the case on her thighs. Immediately heaviness descended upon her shoulders, flowed down her body, pushing through the floor and into the earth ten stories below. The dizziness in her head and roaring in her ears nearly knocked her off her seat.

"Miss Everly, are you well?" she heard Roshi ask from what seemed far above her.

Her strange symptoms lifted instantly except for the burden of the black case on her lap. Apparently, it was heavier than it looked. "I-I'm fine," she managed.

Roshi nodded, rose fluidly and moved to the door.

"Wait, Mr. Roshi," she called. "What's in this? When did my grandfather give it to you?"

Roshi opened the door, but turned and stared balefully at her. "I do not know the contents of the case. You will note it is sealed with wax. I have not violated Martin Everly's confidence. Ever. He entrusted the case to me when he was a novice at the Sangha, our Buddhist community in Sequim."

She set the case and paper on the Oriental rug and stepped quickly to him. "When was that?"

"He came to us after his wife was killed."

"Three years before I was born," she murmured. Her heart thudded and thoughts whirled until an odd stillness settled over her mind. "Thank you for coming, Mr. Roshi."

"Roshi is not my name, but what I am. It means old teacher, a Japanese Zen master," he said with a slight bow and departed, leaving the door open behind him.

Dorel slammed it, scooped the case and paper off the floor, hurried to her bedroom and laid the case on the pané velvet coverlet. She inspected the green wax sealing each of the two brass snap fasteners on the side of the black leather-covered case no thicker than the span of her hand. The wax looked old and brittle. She picked at the blob on the left fastener and it chipped off easily. In less than ninety seconds both fasteners were clean and she pushed their buttons at the same time.

Pop. Pop.

Her heart pounding, Dorel started to lift when the phone rang. She reached for the cordless, one hand still on the closed case lid. "Premselar residence," she answered.

"Dorel, Candace Premselar here. I tried to get you at work, but they said you'd been laid off. The timing couldn't be worse. Oh, well, did you get my message?"

"Can I call you back?" Dorel asked, impatient to open her prize.

"No, wait. I'm not in London. We're at Kennedy on our way to Seattle."

Dorel grabbed the phone with both hands. "You're coming home?"

Candace gave a tinkling laugh. "Yes, it's the usual thing. Happened in a matter of forty-eight hours. We've been reassigned to Renton for the next year. David has to be onsite Friday. I called you the moment I found out. This is such short notice, I know, but think how we feel. Ordinarily you could stay on until you found another place, but our Dutch *au pair* is with us. The children can't be without her. And she just loves them. We were so lucky to find her . . ."

Dorel listened to her life go into an inverted flat spin as Candace enthused about the Dutch teenager who would literally be taking her bed. She glanced at the stacked boxes containing her papers and keepsakes that she'd moved from one housesitting job to the next during the past three years.

Time to move again. Where would she take her boxes now?

"I'm sorry about this, but I guess you're used to this, right?" Candace asked, sounding hopeful.

What could she say? "Oh, sure. When does your plane get in? Do you want me to pick you up?"

"No, please, don't bother. It will be late, so we'll just grab a cab. The doorman will let us in. Thanks so much for all you've done. You stop by next week. I've brought you something that will look fabulous with that gorgeous skin and red mane of yours."

Dorel hung up and began mechanically pulling her clothes out of the closet and throwing them on the bed. It wasn't until she remembered her bonsai sitting on the terrace that she thought of the Buddhist monk and the case he'd brought her. Somehow, it didn't seem so important now that she had to find another place to stay.

Folding her clothes and neatly layering them into the molded luggage set Martin had given her when he'd sent her off to boarding school so long ago, she decided that she'd have to leave the city to find affordable lodging. The one credit card she possessed was maxed out, so she'd have to pay cash. There wasn't much of that left from her last paycheck and no more coming until she was called back to work. If she were called back. Though once she got a place to stay, she'd apply for unemployment—and would have to start looking for work in a glutted job market already overcrowded with laid-off engineers from downsized high techs as well as those from Boeing's previous layoffs.

Dorel's gaze fell on the black case. Maybe there was money inside. Or something she could sell. Her spirits rose at the prospect and she decided to save opening it as a treat when she got settled in at a decent motel.

The following Friday Dorel was first in line as the convention center doors opened. She wrapped both arms around the black case and held it close to her body as the burgeoning groundswell of gun show fans propelled her forward. The masculine tide carried her past rows of dealers' tables displaying every kind of dangerous-looking weapon for sale.

When she reached the far side of the main hall, Dorel laid

the rectangular case on a table oddly empty of wares and devoid of interested spectators. Clenching her hands together in a tight fist on the lid, she blurted to the man behind the table, "You buy old swords?"

He set aside the double-edged sword he was polishing and wiped his hands on the cloth, looking first at the case then at her. A sly smile pushed up one side of his mouth. "Depends on the piece. Think you have something I'd be interested in?"

"I'm not sure." The urge to grab the case and bolt jabbed her, but she fended off the sensation, forcing herself to unsnap the fasteners and lift the lid.

A Japanese samurai sword lay nestled in white silk. A carved half-inch-wide spiral design snaked up the black lacquered wood scabbard. A twisted red silk cord ran through the small rectangular hole in the iron hilt.

"Ahhh," the dealer breathed, reaching for the sword. His hand stopped short of touching it. "You want to sell *this?*"

Dorel couldn't take her eyes off the sword. When she'd opened the case the first time, she had hoped for money or something that she could turn into cash immediately. There had been no note, no explanation about the sword that was beguiling and dangerous like a black dragon, an image that had superimposed itself in her mind the moment she'd touched the lacquered scabbard. Wondering about the sword, its past and connection with Martin consumed her thoughts and dreams to the point that if she were working, had money coming in or even another house-sitting job, she wouldn't think of selling her grandfather's only remaining legacy of value.

Dorel met the dealer's gaze. "Yes, I want to sell it." The sword abruptly prodded her thoughts again. Maybe she shouldn't give up the last of her meager inheritance.

"Is it yours?" He squinted at her. "Got a bill of sale?

19

An appraisal or something?"

Dorel reached into her purse and handed him the trust papers.

"Says here the sword is 'the sole property of an Eternal Trust.' " He read further. "Some description . . . ah, yeah, here it is. 'To be conveyed upon the death of Martin Everly to his only grandchild, Dorel Everly.' " He glanced at her. "That you?"

"Yes." She handed over her driver's license.

He returned her license and papers, then took a breath and smiled. "Well, Miss Everly, I'm definitely interested in your sword. While it has familiar characteristics, I haven't seen a samurai sword quite like this before."

"What do you think it's worth?" she asked, forcing herself to get down to business.

He picked up the sword and slid it out of the scabbard. "Mind if I take off the handle?"

A shiver of unease shimmied down her back. "Do you have to?" she asked, amazed that his touching her sword bothered her.

"I can't tell much if I don't. I can't tell who made it or how old it is."

"All right. If you must." She leaned protectively across the case, the table's hard edge pressing into her thighs.

"See this peg here?" He pointed to a round spot of light wood in the straw-colored cord wrapping the handle just below the hilt. "Push out and hit the butt with your palm." The shining blade clanked loose in the handle, the sound rattling Dorel from her ankles to her teeth.

The dealer pulled the handle off the blade and removed the iron hilt. "There are some kind of markings here on the hilt. Hmm, don't know what they mean. Maybe the tang will have more," he said, studying the tapered six-inch long metal piece on the handle end of the sword.

"Are those markings the same type?" She pointed to the Oriental-looking symbols etched on the flat tang resting in his hand.

"Um," he agreed, squinting in concentration. "Could be Tadatsuna." He looked up. "That's the armorer, or sword maker. But the temper marks on the blade are different. This piece is old, more than three hundred years at least." He pointed to the gleaming edge. "Been well used, too."

"Does that mean it's worth less?"

He tried to control a patronizing smile. "No, Miss Everly. I was just making an observation. Your sword's an unusual piece. Look at the goddess on the butt of the handle here. It's really unusual, too."

Dorel touched the inch-long golden figurine inset on the oval bottom of the handle. "What is it?"

"Should be a Chinese goddess. But this one . . ." He ran his hand the length of the ten-inch handle. "I recognize these." He showed her a figure on each side wrapped in the cording. "These are the usual dragon goddesses. They're positioned so that when a samurai slides the weapon out of the scabbard, he can feel where his hand is without looking."

"Are you interested in buying it?"

The dealer laid down the handle and rubbed his forehead. "Well, I'm really not sure of the value. You see, I don't know exactly when to date it or who the maker was. The sword could be worth anywhere from twelve to thirty-five hundred. I know a guy, a collector, who could tell us more about your sword. He comes to the arms collectors show every month. If you'll leave the piece with me, I'll have him take a look."

"No. I'd prefer not to. I'd like to sell it now."

"Okay." The dealer ran his thumb across his caramel-colored moustache, thinking. "Well, I can give you twelve hundred right now." He sounded almost apologetic.

"You're low-balling the lady," a gravel voice said from behind Dorel.

She stared at the round-faced bald man now crowding her left elbow. Despite the dense heat of the packed convention hall, he wore a Seattle Mariners blue and gray nylon jacket zipped to his chin. He was only a couple of inches taller than her own five feet eight, but out-weighed her by a good hundred pounds. She edged sideways as he and the dealer locked gazes.

"You know that sword is worth a hell of a lot more than twelve hundred." He turned to Dorel. "I'll give you two thousand right now on the spot."

Before she could reply, the dealer intervened. "Hey, now, wait a minute. She offered me the sword first." He hesitated and looked suspiciously from Dorel to the man. "Okay, lady. You working with this guy?"

Dorel mentally shook herself and moved farther away from the bald man. "Working with him? No! I've never seen him before."

"Then sell it to me now," the indignant dealer said. "I can scrape up twenty-five hundred, if you can wait a few minutes."

"May I see that?" another voice inquired from Dorel's right. She turned uneasily to a wiry man with closely clipped dark hair that waved off his forehead. His butter yellow polo shirt and khaki pants fit his tall frame with casual elegance.

The man's ordinary pleasant face was a stranger's, yet there was something familiar about his eyes, a shadowy recollection, as if surfacing from cellular memory.

Her breathing fell shallow. Could I possibly know him? she questioned as peculiar emotions roiled inside. She tried to search her memory, but conflicting compulsions to rush into his arms or run far away from him confused her.

"Hey, Mike," the dealer acknowledged, looking relieved. "Dorel Everly, meet the guy I was telling you about. This is Mike Gabrielli, one of the foremost collectors in the region. If anyone knows about ancient weapons and their value," he said, looking meaningfully at the bald man, "it's Mike here." Starting to hand the sword to Gabrielli, he asked Dorel, "Okay with you if he takes a look?"

"Listen," the sweating bald man rumbled uncomfortably close to her ear, pressuring her. "They're the ones running a scam here. Working together to cheat you. Sell me the sword. I'll give you what it's worth."

Gabrielli chuckled as he lounged against the table and crossed one tasseled loafer over the other. "You must know something I don't to be so sure of the piece's value. Share with us. We'd like to learn."

The rich timbre of his voice resonated within her, producing bewildering flashes of dreamlike images—long supple fingers stroking bare golden skin, a cascade of raven-black hair brushing a muscular chest.

Dorel swallowed and blinked, struggling to disassociate the dream images from this self-assured stranger who seemed so knowledgeable and trustworthy, like someone's successful doctor-husband. "I-I want Mr. Gabrielli to look at the sword first."

She'd never reacted like this to anyone before. Judging from the intense sensations rippling through her, she must have been saving it up for a lifetime. This was getting completely out of hand.

Gabrielli took hold of the sword's metal tang and ran his other hand lightly up the smooth curving steel. As if he were delicately stroking her own ultra-sensitive skin, Dorel held her breath as his finger traced the odd geometric design etched on the blade back down to the tang. His expression radiated wonder as he examined the engraved characters.

"These look familiar, but at the same time, like nothing I've ever encountered before. I don't believe the sword is from the Tadatsuna armory." His fingertips lingered on the symbols.

As Dorel stared, the etched symbols blurred then sharpened as if in raised block letters, English letters. A deeper and foreign-accented version of Gabrielli's own voice echoed through her mind:

> *When I behold thy embodiment*
> *I will awaken to thy hand*
> *Eternally do we battle evil*

As if she were one with him, she felt Gabrielli's breath hang in his chest and his heart recoil. The scene before her eyes ebbed and flowed into a vast grayness. In an instant it rippled and colored like a neon tapestry stretching seamless in all directions. The sum of human experience, past and future, teemed in its threads.

Tracing a braided strand that glowed brighter than the others, she saw Michael Gabrielli, always a warrior and of many races, wielding the sword he now held with her ever at his side. Myriad incarnations flashed before her frame by frame. Suddenly, Dorel's lungs burned as the scene shifted and smoke swirled around a petite Japanese woman kneeling, weeping over someone lying dead upon the ground. As Dorel struggled to see whom the woman grieved for, the smoke thickened, twisting into a shimmering braid that expanded to a blue-white glow around Gabrielli. Time stood still. Like a pulsing electrical field the brilliance reached toward her, drawing her to his side again.

"What do you think, Mike?" The dealer's question seeped into her stunned brain.

The vision evaporated, stranding her in a mutually shocked, uncomprehending stare with Gabrielli. She turned numbly to the dealer. "Put it back together."

"But Mike hasn't told us—"

"I've heard more than enough." Dorel glanced at Gabrielli's now bland expression. What was happening? What had he done? All she could understand was that he gripped her sword as if it were his own and didn't look as if he would give it up. Ever.

The foreign voice whispered from deep in her consciousness. *The sword is his, a part of him. As are you.*

She gritted her teeth, wanting to clap her hands over her ears.

Gabrielli handed the sword to the dealer who quickly reassembled it and slid the blade into the scabbard. Reluctantly, he returned the sword to Dorel.

Filled with jumbled emotions, she reclaimed her property and immediately felt relief. As she started to open the case, the strange protective wariness resurfaced, prompting her to watch the men peripherally.

The bald man peeled off hundred dollar bills from a fat fold of green. "Here you go. Nineteen, two thousand like I said." He slapped the bills down on top of the case and reached for the sword in her hands.

Dorel clenched the sword closer to herself. "No!" She stepped back against Gabrielli's hard chest, whirling away as he grabbed at her.

"Hey, you said you'd sell it to me," the dealer yelled as he hustled around the table.

Flee!

Her throat constricting with panic, Dorel acted on the silent order. She ran, blindly jostling and bumping from body to body through the packed convention hall, and crashed out the exit doors. Dashing to her car in the Union Street parking lot, she sensed she was being hunted.

A cannonball blow slammed between her shoulder blades. Her arms flew out as she fell forward beside her car, the sword clattering to the pavement. Her forehead smacked the door and a roaring ink-black vacuum sucked her in.

She fought darkness and pulled herself to her knees, nearly overwhelmed with nausea and pain. Gingerly touching the raw lump on her forehead, she tried to focus her tunnel-like field of vision on the man standing just a few feet in front of her and recognized Gabrielli.

He gripped her unsheathed sword with both hands, his handsome profile contorted with ferocious intention. Bellowing "Michael Gabrielli," he swung her sword in a mighty arc, but Dorel couldn't see at what. A piercing, agonized scream shredded the muggy air then quickly faded.

With trance-like slowness, Gabrielli raised her sword toward the sun in an exaggerated salute, then swept it from side to side in a figure eight. Murmuring, he withdrew a long white silk scarf from his pocket and stiffly wiped the red-stained blade. Up. Down. Three times. Holding the scabbard in one hand and the sword in the other, he drew them together on a precise horizontal line with a resounding snap, and then bowed deeply.

"What are you doing?" Dorel yelled as she wobbled to her feet.

Gabrielli turned his fierce gaze on her and strode deliberately toward her. She pushed off the side of her old Jeep Cherokee and moved to claim her sword. "Stop right there!"

His brows drew together, glacier blue eyes shadowed and narrowing. "I just saved you."

"Give me my sword," she demanded then took a short step back.

Still gripping her sword like a club, he moved dangerously closer, near enough that the scented heat from his muscular body warmed her skin. He held her gaze, his lips forcing a gaunt smirk. Turning the sheathed sword toward her and resting it on top of his left arm, he offered the weapon to her, hilt first.

Dorel grabbed it. The sudden movement jolted pain across her forehead. Confused, she gestured vaguely with the sword. "I don't understand. You assault me, but now I don't know whether to scream my head off or just give it to you—"

"Listen, that bullet-headed buyer attacked you, I didn't. He intended to kill you. I stopped him and recovered the sword."

"Just how did you stop him? I heard a terrible scream." She eased back toward her car, praying he wouldn't continue to advance on her.

He glanced over his shoulder. "We should leave."

She followed his gaze. Three cars down, the bald man slumped over the hood of a Lincoln Town Car, arms squeezed across his chest. A smear of crimson trailed him down the shining white metal as he slid to the pavement and fell on his side.

Bile rose in her throat. Panicked, she bolted for the street, the sword clutched to her breast. She looked around wildly, then darted to a taxi waiting at the signal. Jerking open the door, she jumped in beside the startled driver. As the cab leaped forward at the green light, Dorel glanced out the side window, locking gazes with Gabrielli. As he stepped back up on the curb away from her door and the on-coming traffic, the strong urge to stay with him nearly pulled her from the vehicle. But the more powerful demand to escape kept her in the cab until Pioneer Square.

She couldn't afford to go back to the motel she'd checked out of this morning. The sword's sale should have brought her more than enough to cover expenses and then some until unemployment kicked in. But that didn't happen. She still had the sword, apparently worth more than anyone was willing to pay, and which someone had already tried to steal. And they—no, *he* won't give up, she worried, deciding she had to get away, disappear for a while.

Where can I go? Dorel wondered as she paid off the cabby. She had to conserve her cash and retrieve her car. Walking to the bus stop, she considered her lack of options. Depression huddled on her shoulders as she slumped to the bench to wait for a bus to nowhere.

A bag lady edged across the bench toward her. "Gimme that," the woman croaked, poking a finger at the sword Dorel rested on her knees.

She stood up, nearly upsetting the woman's junk-filled shopping cart. Junk! The thought tagged another, producing a destination: Uncle Abie in Auburn! She hadn't seen him since her granddad's funeral. He'd offered his help at the time, and now she really needed it. Uncle Abie had a tow truck and could recover her car. Then she'd hide out at his house behind his junkyard until she decided her next move.

Dorel checked the schedule; the bus for Auburn left in an hour. More people were staring at her sword. She edged away, cursing herself for leaving the case behind. Across the street at an outfitter's shop, she spent forty dollars of her remaining sixty-five on a long duffel bag to protect the sword. She stowed it and waited nervously inside the shop until the bus appeared.

An hour later, Dorel phoned Uncle Abie from an Auburn convenience store. She couldn't bring herself to mention the sword or Gabrielli, although she could hardly think of anything else.

"The Cherokee's starter is acting up, Uncle Abie. Can you get my car from the convention center before it's impounded?" She didn't want to try to get it herself, afraid that Gabrielli would be waiting for her. A notion crept from some murky recess in her mind—she should welcome him. The appalling thought was immediately countered by the conviction she must stay far away from him. But would could she?

"The old heap finally died on you, huh?" Uncle Abie's friendly voice promised safety, but his next words mutated her apprehension to terror. "I'll bring the truck. We can go right away and get it."

"No! I mean, I'm not feeling very well. I've got quite a headache. It's this car thing and Granddad—I really miss him, Uncle Abie . . ." She let her voice trail off, nervously massaging the swollen lump on her forehead, then quickly finger-combed her bangs over it.

"I understand, honey. Don't worry. You just relax. We'll pick you up in ten minutes, then I'll go get your car. Your aunt will be tickled to have you to fuss over while you stay with us."

"Thank you." She hung up, hoping Aunt Verna would be happy. They'd always enjoyed each other, but she'd never lived with her aunt and uncle either. And since they weren't blood relatives, just old friends of her grandfather's, tolerance wasn't guaranteed.

I have to make this work, Dorel thought wearily. She tried to stroke away the worry throbbing between her eyebrows with her fingertips, then conjured a smile for Uncle Abie and Aunt Verna when they pulled up in their new gold-colored Lexus.

Chapter Two

Later that evening when her uncle, Abie Prefontaine, returned with her car he seemed uneasy. "I don't want to upset you, but it's a good thing you left when you did. Just a few feet from where you parked a man was found dead."

Dorel nearly dropped the cup of chamomile tea Aunt Verna had made for her. "Accident?" She lowered the trembling cup to the saucer.

"Nope. Murder. The cops were finishing up when I got to the lot. Talked to one of the guys I know in the department. He said there must have been a fight, a robbery attempt maybe. The dead guy had a gun, but he was sure no quick draw, sliced up like that. They didn't catch the killer, but they've got a lead. Some kind of scarf left at the scene." He dropped the keys in her lap and looked appraisingly at her.

Dorel fidgeted with the keys, then tucked a strand of hair behind her ear and clasped her hands together on the table. Gabrielli had actually killed that man. With her sword. And he was coming for her, she could feel it.

Abie's brown eyes narrowed slightly. "Honey, is there something more you ought to tell me? The police may want to talk to you. When they asked why I was picking up your car I told them it wasn't running and you wanted me to tow it. But you know, it started right up when I got it back to the yard."

She swallowed, trying to clear her tightening throat. "It does that. These intermittent starter problems are driving me crazy."

"Not a problem. Tomorrow you can run the inventory on the computer and see if you can find a replacement starter."

He sat down across from her at the Hepplewhite dining table and lifted a delicate gold-rimmed cup to his lips. "Why'd you go to the arms collectors show, anyway?"

"To meet friends, but no one ever showed up. Then some man seemed to kind of follow me around." She took a sip, almost gasping as the steaming tea punished her lying tongue.

"Oh, yeah? What'd he look like?"

"A real strange Army fatigues-buzz cut type. So, instead of calling you when I couldn't start my car, I guess I overreacted and caught the bus to Auburn." I shouldn't lie to him, she rebuked herself.

"Sounds like you did just right. I don't like the thought of you out like that on your own." He patted her hands. "You'll be safe here with us, and don't worry about the cops. They probably won't want to talk to you, because you didn't see anything, right? You left the lot way before the guy was killed. Yeah, I just hope that guy you said was following you wasn't the one—" He grinned. "Of course he wasn't, and we don't need to give anyone any ideas, right? We'll put you to work here in the office. Hey, you can ride with me in the big wrecker like you used to when you were little and you can watch *Jeopardy* with Verna." He winked, nodding toward the family room where her aunt shouted question-answers at the big screen TV.

Dorel grasped his work-callused, though neatly manicured hand. "Uncle Abie, thank you."

"You don't have to thank family, honey. Helping each other is what it's all about." He gave her hands a quick squeeze and pulled out of her grasp, rising from the table. "I'm sorry that all this has happened. Time to go forward and put together a new life. Your granddad would want you to."

Dorel lay awake well past midnight in the dark guestroom, trying to clear her mind of the day's frightening events, having given up trying to make sense of them. There was no logic to what was happening to her. She was a sensible aeronautical engineer. Pragmatic. Self-sufficient. Honest. Dorel Everly wasn't some homeless stalking victim possessed by voices and haunting dreams so troubling she was afraid to close her eyes.

Exhausted, and escaping roller coaster emotional stress, she didn't have the strength to battle sleep. Her turbulent thoughts barely slowing, Dorel surrendered to the vibrant colors, foreign sounds and erotic sensations of her dreams.

Waiting among the shadows, Michael Gabrielli viewed the sleeping figure tossing restlessly on the canopy bed.

It had to be her. And she still had the sword in her possession. He'd located it easily tonight after having actually held it in his own hands at the gun show, strengthening the already powerful psychic connection between them after having dreamed about the weapon all his life.

But Dorel Everly had never appeared in his visions—until a few days ago. The tall, striking redhead now bearing the sword was a one-eighty out from the diminutive Japanese woman he'd also dreamed about for as long as he could remember.

The sword drew Michael to her bedside. He crouched down and felt for its black duffel on the carpet under the bed, his face just inches from hers.

She moaned and restlessly threw the sheet off her lean body that was barely covered by a sea green lace teddy. Her sensual, floral scent invaded his nostrils and immediately invoked devastating memories of loving so tender, so consuming that his trembling hand reached for her, lightly cupping her soft cheek. Her eyelids shot open and her startled gaze locked on his. Absolute terror marked her face and she screamed.

"Dorel! Dorel, you okay?" yelled a man's voice outside the bedroom door. The knob rattled, followed by a staccato of knocking. "Dorel? It's Uncle Abie. Unlock the door."

In a blinding flash, Michael withdrew.

He lay on his own bed, rejoined with his rigid body. This had happened only once before. A remote viewing target had actually seen him. He'd focused on the sword, followed its essence on the astral plane—and found *her* as if the sword had led him to her on purpose! And whose memories did he experience? Hers? Then why did they feel so personal and real? The incredible intensity of the memories was dissipating with each breath, though centering a painful sense of loss over his heart that vaguely worried him.

Michael wondered if he'd done something wrong, gotten emotionally involved or opened his own energy field to influence. Stupid. He would have to be more careful, perhaps even resort to once again following the protocols as he'd been trained to do as a psychic spy for the military.

There had been one or two on the remote viewing spy teams who'd admitted emotional attachment or feeling that a target had somehow been aware of the viewer's astral body. And several remote viewers joked, claiming to have had out of body sex. But in Michael's experience there had never been any time for personal romps on the astral plane. His team had been over-burdened with rigorous training for employing what skeptics would term nonexistent extrasensory perception to discover hidden intelligence targets.

Remote viewing wasn't phony fortuneteller or psychic hotline stuff. Like the Soviets in the late 1960s, the U.S. military services each established their own special units to experiment with and develop the new technology of projecting the mind's mysterious power to "view" or perceive information that wasn't perceptually available to the viewer's present time and space. The process protocols were scientifically established at a west coast university's research institute funded from deep within government black projects.

As a trained psychic spy, Michael had been assigned to a military base office complex where he and others were given only coordinates or a series of numbers assigned to a "blind" or undisclosed target. After quieting the mind's chatter, impressions associated with the coordinates were observed and recorded. Colors, sensations, sounds, pictures, odors and even tastes could be perceived to psychically trace the chain of custody or energy trail of a target. Secret weapons installations were uncovered as well as enemy locations and clandestine activities.

Not much could be hidden from a highly trained, disciplined remote viewer as long as he could refrain from "information overlay" or projecting his own beliefs and expectations on the incoming perceptual information. To those innately gifted like Michael, using remote viewing was like having a God's eye view of anything, at any time, anywhere in the world.

Once, he'd focused and projected his intent with such force that his astral energy body had a full sensory experience with a target, interacting with and moving objects. The target had even felt his presence, at first as a sensation of coldness, then as a fully formed apparition. That's when Michael was reassigned to an experimental remote assassin program to psychically attack a target to cause severe psychological or physical harm, even death. He knew he didn't have the cold detachment that murder required. Defending his country was one thing, but he hadn't taken a commission in the Navy to be a hired gun for covert alphabet agencies gone rogue.

He resigned his commission and embraced the deprogramming designed to obliterate everything he knew about being a prime operative in Navy Intelligence's remote viewing program. De-programming hadn't worked. He still remembered every remote viewing protocol, every assignment and grisly detail, but told the curious only about his tour flying F-14s—true, and more fun and acceptable than sitting on his ass playing mind games for the spooks.

Michael pulled his thoughts out of the past before his astral body spontaneously followed them, and sucked in a deep breath, flexing his extremities as the revitalizing oxygen circulated through his tissues. When he felt himself safely integrate with his physical body, he sat up and turned on the halogen lamp on the bedside table.

His head was groggy and his reactions sluggish, the physical aftereffects of the hybrid out of body travel that his remote viewing process had become. Like remote viewing, and depending on the viewing target, the emotional trauma and damage to the astral body of the viewer could linger like radioactive half-lives. Even though he'd long ago stopped following the protocols, he'd learned to monitor his thoughts constantly, stringently controlling his emotions to keep from undergoing spontaneous out of body experiences, and had trained himself to function on only five to six hours of sleep.

Each night for his entire life his recurring dream had opened with the Japanese woman extending the sword to him on open palms, then some scene from her past that seemed his own would play out. The dream didn't have an ending that he could remember, but the sword was real, though he had never remote viewed the sword's past or future. It was almost as if the ancient weapon wouldn't allow it. He had long ago stopped wondering at his lack of desire to confirm the existence of the sword. It was real, of that he was certain, and it would become his. It was his destiny, and, no doubt, his past.

A week ago, the mainstay of his dream life for thirty-two years abruptly changed. The Japanese woman vanished, replaced by a modern, young redheaded woman. Michael had immediately awakened with the knowledge that now the sword was coming to him and felt directed to remote view its present location. He'd seen that the same redhead from the dream had the sword in Seattle.

Now the sword lay just a few miles away, waiting for him in a junkyard in Auburn. He'd failed miserably earlier today, returning the one thing he lived for to her when he could have just walked away with it.

The others had failed, too.

But no matter what they tried, they weren't going to get it. The sword belonged to him and he had to secure it before others found it, and her, the same way he had.

Michael got out of bed and headed for a shower followed by a double shot of espresso. There was no time to retrieve the sword now. At 04:30, he was scheduled to take Flight 426 across the Pacific to Narita International at Tokyo. He'd have to maintain surveillance by remote viewing on his twenty-four hour layover. If someone else specific-targeted Dorel Everly and the sword before he landed at SeaTac airport, he would learn very quickly if he could handle TransAsia's new 747-400 and protect them by remote at the same time.

"I was having a—nightmare," Dorel said, standing breathless in the doorway. "I'm sorry I woke you."

The hall light cast a tepid yellow glow on their worried expressions. Uncle Abie and Aunt Verna peered into the dark bedroom behind her.

"Are you sure you're okay, Dorel? Maybe I should plug in

the night light for you, you know, like I used to," Aunt Verna suggested with an anxious smile. "That seemed to chase away the—well, you know, those old night scaries that bother little girls."

"Oh, Auntie Vern." Dorel gave the short, plump woman a quick hug. "That was such a long time ago. I haven't dreamed about Mom and Dad's funeral or slept with a night light for, oh, fifteen years, I guess. But thank you for the thought. I'm okay, really."

"You can count on us, honey." Uncle Abie scowled at her. "For anything you need, like maybe a robe."

She felt a blush pulse up her neck. "Oh, I have one, it's in one of my bags in the car. I didn't have a chance to unpack everything. I just checked out of the Cloud Motel in Renton this morning."

"Dorel, were you living there? Why didn't you come to us before? I had no idea you were in this kind of shape. We'd have been glad to give anything you need." Uncle Abie held up his hand at the refusing shake of her head. "No, now listen. I owe it to Martin. In fact, I promised him I'd watch out for you. He was like a father to me, you know, giving me my start and all. Helping you is the least I can do."

"You listen to your uncle, Dorel. You've stayed away from us too long with this silly stuff about you taking care of yourself. Well, maybe so. We don't want to run your life or anything, just help you like we promised, starting with a robe." Aunt Verna toddled across the hall to her bedroom. Dorel pulled the deep V of the teddy closed with one hand and tried to stretch the lace down her hip with the other.

Uncle Abie shrugged and grinned. "You know better than to argue with her. You're a stubborn kid, but you aren't stupid. Just relax and forget about owing or paying back. Let us do this for you."

37

Tears stung Dorel's eyes and she swallowed thickly. "Oh, stop or I'll blubber all over the place."

"Here we go," Verna said, holding up a blue-green checked flannel bathrobe for Dorel to wear. "Oh my, it's going to go around you three times, but at least it will be warmer."

Dorel shrugged into the robe. "Thanks, Auntie."

They said good night and Dorel closed the door, turning to face the dark. With her back to the wall, she eased around to the large, square window and opened the miniblinds. Grey florescence spilled in from the tall yard light next to the house.

Now that's a night light, she thought with satisfaction, and carefully studied the bleached shadows of the large, furniture-jammed bedroom Verna had decorated in neo-Sleeping Beauty years ago for Dorel's infrequent visits from boarding school.

She pulled the robe's belt tighter around her waist. He won't see anything more than . . . he who? She stopped herself with a shuddering glance around the room.

Michael Gabrielli.

Could she actually have dreamed of him? She clapped her damp hand over her mouth, whimpering. No, no! It wasn't possible. All those dreams, every night since she'd received the sword, driving her crazy with a sex life far better than she'd ever had in reality. And now the man in her dreams had a face, and a name.

Tonight's dream was intense. Extremely real. Too real, as if he'd actually been right here at her bed. She rubbed the goose bumps dancing up her arms, shivered and dashed for the bed. Dorel pulled the yellow eyelet comforter up to her chin, wanting to cover her head, and clenched her teeth. The flannel robe clung to her sweaty skin in the gathering heat under the covers. She threw off the comforter and sat up, her agitated thoughts churning wildly.

It was insane, but she still felt his touch on her sensitized skin, smelled his lemony spice fragrance. Dorel touched her fingertips to her cheek in wonder. Was she dreaming? Or perhaps she hadn't awakened from the nightmare.

"Did you find a starter?" Uncle Abie asked her three days later when he returned from lunch with the Rotary Club.

Dorel shook her head and enabled the screen saver on the computer monitor. After the steady hectic business this morning, the lunch lull allowed her to Web browse for local news about the killing at the gun show last Saturday. She'd also tried the People Finder to see if Gabrielli was online. His address had just scrolled up on the screen.

"I didn't bother. The Cherokee is running fine. So I'll just wait until it quits completely then worry about a new starter."

"Don't be silly," he said, moving to her side and reaching for the keyboard. "I'll find you one right now and we'll get it changed out."

She leaned over the keyboard, blocking his access. "No, darn it. We've got customers and I'm running the counter," she said, nodding toward the two men entering the office. Police badges hung from the pockets of their sports coats. A chill shinnied up her back and she straightened, forcing a weak smile. "Can I help you?"

Abie chuckled and held out his hand to the shorter, younger man. "Hell, Menlow, what are you doing here? I already got my tickets for the game, though I don't know why I bother going. Kent P.D. is going to kick your ass as usual."

"We're here to talk to Dorel Everly." Menlow looked at Dorel and jerked a thumb toward the tall, hollow-cheeked man beside him. "This is Detective Rhett from the Seattle Police."

Dorel's insides went icy and she sucked in a breath. Abie stepped around, partially shielding her and directed his handshake at the Abe Lincoln-looking cop. "I'm Dorel's uncle." He looked at Menlow. "What's this about, Roger?"

The younger man deferred to the gaunt policeman who asked in a gravelly voice, "Are you Dorel Everly?" and stared dead-eyed at her forehead.

"Yes." Her fingers pulled at her bangs, covering the lump she hoped wasn't showing.

"Were you in the Union Street parking lot on Saturday morning about nine-thirty?"

"No."

He stepped closer to the counter. His unblinking shark's eyes locked on her. "We have reason to believe you were."

Dorel stood taller, steeling herself for the lie. "It wasn't nine-thirty. I was already headed for Auburn by then. My car wouldn't start and I caught a cab to the bus stop at Pioneer Square at about eight-forty five, I think."

"I picked it up for her just before noon, then ran some parts and other errands. Towed it home and got here about, oh, six or so . . ." Abie's voice trailed off at the withering look Rhett gave him.

"Did you meet or talk with anyone at the gun show?" Rhett asked, still staring at Uncle Abie.

"No, no I didn't."

"Do you know a—" Rhett flipped open a small notebook, "Peter Osterman or Jonathan Spencer? Michael Gabrielli?"

"No," she said, trying not to blink.

"Isn't Osterman the name of the dead guy?" Abie asked Sergeant Menlow. He nodded but didn't speak, glancing at Rhett as if in warning to Abie who ignored him and continued, "What happened anyway? Are those other guys on a short list?"

"As I said, Miss Everly, we can place you at the murder scene," Rhett said, ignoring Abie.

"I went to the gun show. I was in the parking lot. I didn't see anything or anybody memorable that registered with me." Instead of adding to her fear of him and his questions, the man's badgering was beginning to tick her off.

He pulled a photo from his jacket pocket and jammed it under her nose. "Do you remember seeing this man?"

The bald man lay on his side, a dark red stain covering his jacket front, blending with a small glistening pool on the pavement in front of his body.

Her empty stomach flip-flopped and her throat slickened. She was going to be sick and wrapped her arms around herself to control the shakes vibrating through her body. "N—no," she whispered, unable to draw more breath.

"Get that damn thing out of here." Abie pushed the detective's hand away and put his arm around protectively Dorel's shoulders. "What the hell are you trying to do? I told your guys everything I knew at the parking lot, and Dorel's told you she doesn't know anything, just like I said. Menlow, your friend's way off base coming in here with this crap."

"I think we're through here for now." Menlow put his hand on the detective's arm, drawing him away from the counter. "Sorry, Abie. Miss Everly," he said when Rhett walked out the door before him. "He's a good guy, just real focused. This case kinda has him wigged out. Personal reason or something I guess. See ya."

A sob of relief fought its way out, but she swallowed it back and clasped her trembling hands together after the two officers left the office.

"Sonofabitch!" Abie slammed his big fist on the counter. "I thought something real special was up when I was there. I just didn't want it to be because you were involved."

"I'm not involved, Uncle Abie. I don't know anything but I'm sorry about bringing the police virtually to your door." She moved away from him, avoiding the eye contact that would surely reveal she was lying.

"And they didn't tell us a damned thing. I want to know what the hell is going on." He moved sideways to the keyboard and cleared the saver before Dorel could stop him. Abie stared at the words on the screen, then shifted his gaze to her and asked, "So, do you wanna tell me about it?"

Long ago, catching her in a white lie she readily admitted to, her grandfather had told her, "No matter what, never, ever convict yourself with your own testimony." It had seemed so important to him that she had tried to adopt the advice as a sort of gospel to live by, though lying never came easily no matter how she rationalized it.

"There's nothing to tell," Dorel claimed and headed down the hall beside the counter toward the back door.

By the time she walked into the house, guilt balled hard in her stomach and her appetite was gone. She picked at her lunch while Verna chatted, and barely touched the delicious chicken salad sandwich her aunt had made for her. Dorel delayed as long as she dared before going back to face Abie. When she dragged herself in an hour and a half later, her uncle was busy with a counter full of customers. She took over cashiering as Abie directed parts runners and customers around his twenty acre wrecking yard.

After closing time, as she shut down the computer, Abie sauntered out of his office down the short hall beside the parts counter. He tossed a manila folder on the keyboard. "I guess this is what you were looking for. You go on to the house. I'll lock up after I'm finished with the dailies."

Dorel stared at the folder as Abie ambled back down the hall. She flipped it open to the first page, a credit report. The name at the top was Michael Gabrielli.

Chapter Three

Slamming the folder closed, Dorel scooped it up and hurried out the office's front door. She walked rapidly down the main driveway past the stacks of crushed automobiles and the piles of rusting car parts to the island of green in the back corner of the junkyard.

A large, red brick single story house sprawled behind a five-foot black wrought iron fence. A lush pond of emerald grass edged by rhododendrons and azaleas surrounded the well-kept house. Rather than entering through the double carport as usual, she pushed open the ornate filigree gate and stepped along the round, concrete pavers to the porch.

Aunt Verna opened the front door with a bright smile. "You have a visitor, and such a handsome one, too!" She pushed Dorel through the foyer to the living room.

Michael Gabrielli rose from one of the peach velvet French Provincial chairs. He looked perfect and mild-mannered in his pressed jeans and white button-down oxford cloth shirt with the cuffs turned under half way up his forearms. He took a step toward her and Dorel's ears began to ring. Blackness crept into the periphery of her vision. She started to retreat, stumbling into Aunt Verna directly behind her. With a barely coherent apology, she turned to leave.

"Please, Dorel, we have to talk. I'm sorry about our little misunderstanding. As I've told your aunt, I'm here to make it up to you," Gabrielli said, concern and sincerity flowing through his voice like sweet, warm syrup.

Aunt Verna slipped her arm around her. "You just sit down right here, dear. I'll leave you two alone to talk," she said, guiding Dorel to an ecru loveseat.

Dorel closed her eyes for a moment and swallowed. When she opened them, Gabrielli was crouching at her knees with his fingertips barely touching the edge of the folder in her lap. His ice blue eyes locked on hers, waiting, expectant.

"How did you find me?" Trying to put more distance between them so she could think clearly, she pressed herself into the back of the loveseat until she could feel the frame.

"You look pale. Are you all right?"

"You tell me. How long am I going to live?" Dorel replied.

He shook his head and stood up with a smirk. "Longer than all of us, no doubt. You shouldn't be afraid of me. I'm the good guy, remember? I wouldn't try to kill you for your sword."

"Shhhhh! My aunt might hear you. We can't talk about this here." Dorel got to her feet. "In fact, we can't talk about this at all. I don't know you. That's what I told the police."

"Who? Seattle or Auburn?" he asked in a calm tone, his expression almost bored.

"Both. The man's name was Osterman, did you know that?" she hissed. "Or don't you even care?"

His expression changed to a combination of regret and anger. "Lieutenant Rhett was happy enough to tell me the name when he showed me the picture of the guy who attacked you." He moved close enough that she felt his warm breath on her cheeks as he looked into her eyes. "I protected you, Dorel. You have to believe that."

"Okay, let's say I believe you, but why did you kill Osterman?" she wailed, then remembered Aunt Verna in the kitchen. "Come on, we can't talk here. Let's go outside." He followed her out into the junkyard. She watched him warily as they walked side by side toward the office. "My uncle said they found your scarf. Shouldn't you be on the lam or something?"

"On the *lam?* There's a word you don't hear that often these days. Yes, they traced the flying scarf to me through the vendor I bought it from. Told them I dropped the thing somewhere inside the hall and someone must have picked it up. They've got nothing else. It was stupid to drop—"

"The really incredibly stupid part was when you actually screamed out your name before you killed him, like you wanted everyone to know it was you. That wasn't just stupid, it was insane."

He stopped and gazed down at her. "When someone pulls a gun on me, I defend myself the best way I can."

Abie said the bald man had a gun, she thought with a kind of belief beginning to take shape in her mind. "But why yell out your name? And do that arcane blade-wiping thing? I don't understand that. It was like you were in some kind of trance."

"Look, I'll explain it all, but not now. I came here because you're in danger and I can help you. In fact, I'm the only one who can and, honestly, the only one who wants to."

She stopped outside the front door of the office. "I'm not stupid, Gabrielli. What you want is my sword, not to help me. I'm not ready to turn loose of it quite yet, not until I think all this through and decide what's best for me."

"You haven't told anyone about it, have you?"

"Told them what? Why?" She hesitated to open the office door.

"Because deep in your heart you know you can't let it go. You're waiting, holding onto it—for me."

No! It couldn't be true. Yet, his softly spoken, persuasive words resonated with a growing belief in her, giving voice to the feelings she'd steadily pushed to the back of her mind.

Could the vision at the gun show somehow be true? Were he and she some sort of team?

A time warrior and a—what? A groupie? A camp follower?

Immediately, the sensations of last night's dream exploded in the pit of her stomach and raged hotly through her body. She jerked her gaze from his and pushed open the door to escape.

"Wait, you're not crazy. Or dreaming or imagining anything. It was me in your room last night," Gabrielli said, his voice husky and barely audible. "I'm sorry."

She froze. This was impossible. They couldn't be having the same dreams or hallucinations, could they? "So, you can read minds and invade people's dreams, too. Can you tell the future? What are the winning lottery numbers going to be on Wednesday? I could really use the cash."

"It doesn't work that way. Most times what I see is like hell on earth."

The aching emotion in his quietly spoken words impacted painfully and she tried to deny the strange empathy she felt for him. "You must be joking. I don't believe in that sort of thing. It's all nonsense."

"And the vision we had together at the gun show?"

There he goes again, she thought with a tremor of apprehension. "I don't know what you're talking about."

He grasped her elbow. "Yes, you do. We've been together before last night. In the past. The future, too. I haven't worked it all out yet. I'm beginning to believe that the sword belongs to both of us," he said, glancing into the office behind her. "We better go in."

She pulled away and backed inside, holding her palm up, whispering, "You can't. My uncle knows about you."

"I'm sure he does." Gabrielli pushed past her, walked to the end of the parts counter and looked down the hall. "Sounds like someone's back there."

Abie's voice boomed "hello" from his office and Dorel

47

cringed. When he continued to talk, she realized he was on the phone and motioned for Gabrielli to leave. He ignored her and sidled to within a couple of feet from Abie's ajar door, listening.

"Hell, yes, I can get it!" roared Abie's gravelly voice in frustration.

Grimacing with each tiptoed step, Dorel reached Gabrielli and tried to pull him back.

"She keeps it in a black duffel bag. Yeah. I took a look while she was in the shower. Yeah. Black lacquer scabbard." Abie's voice paused. "Look, I told you I'd get it tonight. Stop worrying. No. No. We won't have to resort to that. No one is to touch her! She's my niece, for chrissakes. Call off your boys, I've got it under control. Oh, Inada, no excuses. If I can't get the half million from you . . . okay, done."

Dorel couldn't believe the conversation. Her uncle had betrayed her. All he wanted was the damn sword. She whirled and charged out of the hall to the front door. As she jerked it open, Gabrielli grabbed her wrist and dragged her outside. Stunned by what she'd overheard, she let him pull her to a silver Land Cruiser sitting behind the Dumpster next to the building.

He tried to push her in the passenger seat, but she fought him. She'd heard wrong. Had to go back. Talk to Abie. Her uncle couldn't mean what he'd said on the phone. It had to be a mistake.

"Listen to me," Gabrielli growled in her face as she fought him out of the car. "He's the danger I was warning you about. He's one of them, Dorel. I've seen him—"

"No, damn you. There's been a mistake. He was talking about someone else. He wouldn't do this to me. He . . . loves me." She stared through her tears at Gabrielli's anxious scowl and dropped onto the seat in devastated silence.

She felt flat, squashed by circumstances far beyond any sort of human control she might be able to muster. Self-protective numbness easing up her spine, Dorel dully stared out the passenger window as they drove past the office. She met Uncle Abie's startled brown eyes gaping at her between parted miniblinds. Saw him mouth her name, but she turned away, refusing to look back.

Now she was completely alone.

"You're coming home with me. He'll never find you there." Michael scowled at the rearview mirror as he gunned the Land Cruiser out of the junkyard.

"We've got to go back. I have to get my sword," Dorel exclaimed as the stark realization jump-started her denial-deadened emotions. Gabrielli stared silently ahead, his face a mask of cool concentration as he turned onto the Auburn-Enumclaw highway.

"Did you hear me? The sword is at the house. We have to go back," she yelled over the howling engine and wind noise as Gabrielli drove like a mad man on the two-lane rolling east across the patchwork farming country.

He shook his head and drove faster.

"I'm not leaving my sword with *him* even if I have to jump out of this thing." She put her hand on the door handle and heard the electric door locks engage with a muffled *ca-chunk*.

Approaching a line of commuter traffic, Gabrielli slowed down and glanced at her. "Look in the backseat."

"What?" She frowned in confusion. Her world was falling apart. Everything was wrong.

He reached his right hand behind the console between the front bucket seats, grabbed at something on the floor and brought it forward. The sword's duffel bag plopped into her lap, sliding to her feet. The dull clunk when it hit the carpet mat testified the sword was still inside.

Her mouth formed an O as she gazed from the bag to his stone-faced profile. "How did you get this?"

"It doesn't matter."

Anger overwhelmed the sense of loss she'd wrapped around herself. "Tell me!" she demanded.

"While I was waiting for you, your aunt left me alone while she went to answer the phone. I slipped into your room, took it from under the bed and stashed it in the Land Cruiser. Simple."

"All that bull about wanting to protect me—you're just a self-serving thief who will do anything, and anyone, to get what you want."

"Yup, sure seems that way."

"I'm not in danger from anyone but you!" Dorel pushed the duffle bag at him. "Just take it and let me out. I won't tell anyone about any of this. That would make me an accessory to murder."

"Where would you go? Back to Abie? That's not a good idea, considering what we just heard. You've got no one but me. And I am serious about protecting you no matter what you think. You're listening to your fear talking right now. You've got to learn to control that. You have to cooperate if you want to live. Start by listening to me so when they come for us, you can help me instead of running away from everything that threatens you."

Dorel gritted her teeth to keep from cursing him with every filthy oath she'd learned from the boys in the engineering pools. Help this egotistical bastard? Never! He wasn't to be trusted. Except why had he run off with her when he had what he wanted? Unless he actually meant what he said. Gabrielli was going to have to prove she could trust him, if he let her live that long.

She tossed the bag into the backseat with a thud and

glared out the gray-tinted window beside her. "You don't know me. Why should you care what happens to me when you have what you want?"

"Now there's the question," he rumbled.

Michael checked the rearview mirror then Dorel Everly's rigid expression. Basically, she was right. He didn't know her at all. What was she going to do? he wondered. *Hell, what am I going to do with her?*

It was only two more miles to the turn-in to his compound. Even if anyone has tracked us this far, I'll have no problem losing them on the back roads, he assured himself.

He turned off the two-lane blacktop onto a shady, narrow gravel road that cut through tall firs. Pressing the garage opener button as they rounded the last curve before the house, Michael sped up, the feeling of being followed crowding him. Maybe that Abie character had trailed them. He saw nothing behind them, yet the heightened sense or instinct that had guided him all his life urged him forward. He pressed on the accelerator, his left foot hovering over the brake pedal. The Cruiser screeched to a halt just inches shy of the garage's back wall and Michael jabbed the door button. *Safe,* he silently proclaimed as the door swung closed.

"Is someone following us?" Dorel tried to turn to see behind her, rubbing her neck under the taut restraining belt. "Get me out of this thing. I think the jolt jammed the buckle. The way things have been going, I'm surprised the air bag didn't explode in my face."

"Nice," he muttered and opened her door. "Give me your hand."

Michael almost smiled as a cautious Dorel reluctantly placed her slender fingers in his and stepped down out of the car, her body brushing his. He couldn't blame her for her apprehension. The day so far had given her nothing to trust and everything to fear—except for him, but she would have to be carefully coaxed and handled to believe him. He hoped the effort would be worth it, for both of them.

They stood face to face, barely breathing. Michael couldn't let go of her and she didn't pull away. He watched her face mirror his own confused emotions. She was frightened. And for the first time, so was he. Not about what was happening, that was his destiny, but about the incredible depth of feelings Dorel Everly produced in him. The vulnerability and sorrow he saw in her eyes made him want to shelter and protect her. Save her from her future. But giving into those desires would endanger his ability to remote view objectively.

Michael abruptly released her hand and stepped back. He couldn't afford to touch her in any way until—*she is completely ours again,* a ruthless voice within advised. He didn't understand the strange warning, but he knew he couldn't let Dorel Everly get to him, couldn't allow her to interfere with his plans.

Unlocking the house, he punched in the code on the security pad beside the door to turn off the alarm. "Wait here," he ordered and went searching for his dog. When he returned a couple of minutes later, Dorel still stood in the same spot. "I wish my Airedale were as obedient as you."

A dark look replaced her guarded expression. "And as quiet, maybe?" she said over the thunderous barking.

"That's Katana. I'll introduce you later when he settles down. Come on in."

She gauged him cautiously for a moment, then hitched the duffel bag's strap on her shoulder and followed as if she were being marched off to face a firing squad.

When Michael reached the foyer, he gestured toward the

long hall on his right. "You can take the last room at the end. You're welcome to keep the sword with you, or you can put it in the closet. Whatever makes you comfortable." He made an effort to smile reassuringly and act casual, unconcerned about the sword. It took a supreme effort, because the thing he most wanted in life was now right here in his own home.

"I'll put it away later," she said, glancing around the living room with a cagey but appreciative expression.

Michael went to the kitchen and pulled a local microbrew lager out of the refrigerator. "Want one?" he asked as she stopped in the doorway, the sword bag still slung on her shoulder.

"Can't stand the stuff." She strolled to the French doors off dining room and peered out. "To afford a place like this with acreage and a view must take a lot of thieving."

He clenched his teeth, then purposely relaxed his jaw muscles and forced a chuckle. "I do okay."

She turned away and moved into the living room. "Do you have some sort of latent Asian chromosome lurking in your background? Look at all this," she said with a sweep of her arm toward the built-in display shelves and bookcases lining three sides of the high-ceilinged room. "Leather-bound books. Probably first editions. My experience housesitting compulsive consumers' expensive toys tells me these collectibles are pricey Oriental object d'art. And look, he's an art collector, too—though I don't know much about Chinese, or is it Japanese, art? Could that be a real Ming vase?" She pronounced vase in an affected v-ah-zz.

She moved lithely around the living room despite her clunky, thick-soled sandals. Her white T-shirt tucked into leotard-tight black jeans showed off her lean, athletic figure. With her height she could have easily modeled, especially with the shoulder length red hair that dazzled burnished gold in the sunlight streaming in the wall of glass facing Mt. Rainier.

Michael joined her in front of the fireplace flanked by shelves and centered on the opposite wall. She stared at the large, black-framed First Flight photo above the native stone mantle.

"That's TransAsia's new 747-400," she said with awe. "I was the customer engineer on that bird." She turned to him, frowning. "Why do you have a picture of my airplane?"

"I'm her captain," Michael said. Her shocked expression was again a mirror of his own astonishment. This incredible connection was another verification of his spontaneous vision at the gun show, more evidence of their mutual destiny. Why in all the remote viewing he'd done of the sword in the last week had he not seen any of this? He grasped the beer bottle tightly with both hands to stop their shaking.

"I thought you were a gun collector," Dorel said, turning back to the picture. "And a thief, right?" She shrugged, her face reddening. "As well as a killer. Though why a big money 747 captain would get mixed up in all this . . . ahhh," she breathed, throwing him an accusing stare. "It's more than the money with you, isn't it? My sword is one of a kind. Must be worth, what did Abie say—a half million? I bet you can get double that. No matter what the price is, what you've done just makes you another cheap killer."

Her words stung Michael's stressed out conscience. It wasn't about money, and it wasn't about the man who'd tried to kill her, and him. Everything he'd done had been about possessing the sword, not how much money he could get for it. Michael absolutely knew the weapon was his to use, that the sword had a destiny, a purpose. But for what?

What were the words that the sword seemed to speak the first time he touched it? *I will awaken to thy hand. Eternally shall we battle evil.* She had heard those words too, he was certain, though she would deny it.

Moment by moment, breath by breath, his conviction strengthened. He had to make Dorel understand that they were inescapably tied together by the sword.

In his last session of remote viewing, he'd caught shadowy, unsettling flashes of their destiny that convinced him he had to continue targeting the past. He had to discover the secrets of the sword and, he hoped, its probable power to change their brief and very deadly future together.

Chapter Four

"Before you judge me a cheap killer, consider this: When you see a worthy person, endeavor to emulate him. When you see an unworthy person, then examine your inner self," Gabrielli said.

Dorel stared at him. "You're quoting Confucius now?"

"Yes," he said and headed for the kitchen.

Not about to let him get away with dropping some self-justifying old phrase she'd heard a hundred times and walking away, she hurried behind him, her sandals slapping the hardwood floor. "Oh, I know the quote, all right. You're giving me a Chinese version of *walk a mile in my shoes* used as a neo-modern *let's not assign blame* thing. Listen, Gabrielli, my inner self hardly requires examination. I'm blameless here. You, however, aren't."

He whirled around to level a disgusted gaze on her. "I'm not going to continue to defend my actions. I've apologized for—spying on you, one might say. I'm not going to apologize for saving you. I've explained the bad guys, your uncle Abie and others to be discovered, as well as the good guys, me, and hopefully, you."

"What do you mean *hopefully* me?" She watched as his stern mouth closed in an obstinate smirk. "At the risk of dangerously annoying you, I will repeat that if there's a good guy to be had in this situation, it is I." She punctuated her proclamation with a righteous upward jerk of her chin.

A slow, appealing smile erased his smirk as his indigo eyes lit with humor. "For now we'll agree to consider that sticking point later, okay? Come on, I want to show you something."

He brushed past her into the living room and stopped at a lighted alcove in one of the teak bookcases.

Dorel stared at the perfect bonsai willow in the alcove. That has to be mine!

"I wondered if you'd recognize it," Gabrielli said with a wily grin.

Amazed, Dorel looked from him to the miniature tree.

"TransAsia presented it to me to commemorate the first revenue flight of the 747-400," he said.

Dorel frowned. "I'd have sworn it was mine. They're even potted in the exact same raku dishes."

"Yeah, I know." He shrugged, his grin turning sheepish. "I saw yours in your bedroom when I took the sword." Gabrielli lifted a small brass mister and pumped a light spray onto the glistening green leaves. "TA told me there was only one other bonsai like this, both grafted from the same root stock. I should have known you'd have the other. This one is *Bishamon-ten,* named after one of the seven lucky Japanese gods."

She smiled. "I call mine Sam."

Gabrielli squinted at her. "Was that just natural perverseness on your part or didn't TA tell you *her* name is *Benten.*" He set down the mister can. "In case you didn't know, Benten is the only woman among the seven gods of good fortune. She is the patron of learning, music, art and literature. A perfect gift for a Boeing engineer, right? What was TA thinking?" he teased.

Dorel's ego smarted at not knowing her Sam's real name or anything else about Japanese folklore. That sort of thing had never interested her until now. "So, what's Bishamon-ten the god of, air transport pilots with deity-sized egos?"

Gabrielli snorted good-naturedly. "Close enough. Come on, I'll show you your room."

Dorel followed him to the left off the foyer and down a long hall. He opened the last door. "Here you go. It's a little small, but it should do okay until we get your stuff moved in, then we'll have to work out something else. The futon pulls down into a bed. There are sheets and a pillow in the closet. Go ahead and use the quilt," he said, gesturing at the quilt folded on the black-lacquered arm of the futon frame, "if you need a blanket. The air conditioning can get pretty cold. I can turn it down if you want."

"I'll be fine, thanks," Dorel said, feeling obligated to say so. She glanced around a tiny room the size of Candace Premselar's walk-in closet.

"Good. I'll leave you to get settled. Come out when you're ready and we'll have a drink on the deck." Gabrielli closed the door behind him, and went whistling to another part of the house.

Dorel went to the closet and gently touched the smooth white material in one of the five-inch squares on the teak grid pattern of the door. It looked like a Japanese screen made with a huge sheet of rice paper, maybe? She slid the door open, hoping the paper was stronger than it looked. A chest-high stack of built-in drawers filled one side of the space. Neatly folded sheets and a pillow sat on top. The rest of the closet was empty, smelling of new paint. In fact, the whole room looked as if it had never been used. She stood the sword bag in the corner against the drawers and eased the door closed.

So much for *getting settled.* Dorel turned to the futon. The navy geometric design on the crème cover wasn't even creased and didn't look very inviting. She dared to sweep her hand across the pristine cushion and found a haze of white hair on her palm. Either a shorthaired platinum blonde had been here before her, or Gabrielli had cats.

Dorel's itching nose voted cat. She rubbed her hands together, balling up the fur as she surveyed the quilt's old-fashioned wedding ring pattern of pink and white circled on the yellowed background, an incongruous accessory to this Japanese teahouse of a room.

As Dorel settled onto the wrought iron armchair opposite Gabrielli, he set his wineglass down on the glass-topped patio table.

"Well, no sense putting off the inevitable. You've got to meet each other sooner or later," he said with a sigh and walked in the house.

A few seconds later a huge, slobbering black and tan Brillo pad towed him out of the living room to the deck. A giant Airedale terrier danced on back legs and pawed Dorel's lap, making choking, wheezing noises as Gabrielli did his best to hold him back by the collar.

"Katana, sit!" The dog plopped down on Dorel's feet. "Good boy," Gabrielli praised and released him.

The dog was on her chest in a flash, grinning hideously.

"Help! Get him off," Dorel cried.

"Off, Katana. Sit! Stay!" Gabrielli passed his open hand in front of the dog's face. Again the dog obeyed, but he kept his big black eyes pinned on Dorel like he was starving and she was his next meal.

She rubbed her legs where the beast's long nails had scratched her through her jeans. She wasn't used to animals and as a child had never been allowed any kind of pet, especially not cats because her granddad was allergic. But she didn't compensate with stuffed animals like other girls. Dorel collected model airplanes instead. "Will he bite?"

"Only bad guys. I hope." Gabrielli took a sip of wine. "He can protect you while I'm at work and you can feed him."

"If he doesn't eat me first." Dorel decided to edge her chair back. To her dismay, the dog sneakily inched forward without lifting its rear end.

Just ignore him, she advised herself and gazed out over the backyard. The sun lowered behind the house, dusting Mount Rainier with a pink haze. Mosquitoes arrived about the same time Michael brought out the tray of salmon filets to the gas grill.

Dorel waved a huge mosquito off her arm and drained the glass. Another of these and she wouldn't even feel the blood-suckers when they took her last pint of blood. Her anxious thoughts began to quiet and she relaxed into the cooling per-fection of the sunset. This was a beautiful, tranquil place. Safe.

She turned her attention to watching the barbecue's smoke curl around Gabrielli's stolidly capable face and broad shoulders. Okay, maybe it wasn't so safe.

He set her serving before her and took his seat across the table. She stared at her plate, reluctant to put a fork to the masterful work of culinary art she'd never be able to create herself. The barbecued salmon was perfect pink and deco-rated with a sprig of coriander. A colorful grilled vegetable brochette nestled three parsleyed new potatoes.

This incredible beauty and flawlessness was surreal sensa-tion, a nearly unbearable contrast to the mystifying, bizarre reality she was living through. If she allowed herself to believe life could be this, she feared she could no longer endure what her own dull existence had become.

Dorel cleared her throat, determined to clear her mind, too. "Wow, and you can cook, too." She flaked off a bit of salmon with her fork.

"Just one of my many talents." He winked at her and took a sip of wine.

Her mouth went suddenly dry. "Everything looks just great."

"I agree."

Dorel caught the way his blue eyes twinkled at her. "I meant the food," she explained, then wished she hadn't when his grin broke into the sexiest smile she'd ever seen. And it was all hers. She almost shook her head to dispel the fantasy.

"Well, I didn't."

She couldn't think of a word to say in return. What do you expect when you've turned into a hermit? she griped to herself. You're out of practice, and quickly becoming a very weird single woman.

Beware, an inner voice counseled, *you know what he really wants and what lengths he will go to acquire your sword, if his actions up to now are any clue.*

That thought dampened all her playful fantasies about Michael Gabrielli.

After a quiet dinner she tried to help him with the dishes. His kitchen was laid out alphabetically, left to right, up to down. She watched him turn everything she loaded in the dishwasher the opposite direction.

And everywhere she turned, Katana was right on her heel. The huge dog made her nervous.

So did his unspeaking master.

They had avoided any talk of the strange happenings of the last few days, as if to speak of it would make it real. She'd endured too much of that kind of reality anyway. And besides, some things were best left unsaid.

"I put a couple of TransAsia's first class toiletry kits in the bathroom for you," Michael informed her when she said good night and started for her room. "I'll bring you some pajamas, if I can find any. Mom gives me a pair every Christmas. Katana uses them in his bed. I don't."

"I think I'll pass on the dog jammies." Dorel stopped at the bathroom. What did his little comment mean? she wondered. Did he expect her to *pay* for her room and board? He didn't seem like the type, but Abie had seemed like an uncle until she really needed his help.

"Okay, how about a bathrobe?"

His wry grin didn't encourage her. Rather, it reinforced her anxiety. She didn't want to talk or even think about anything bed or bath related with this man obviously far more experienced in seduction than she.

"No thanks," Dorel said and ducked into the bathroom, closing the door on Gabrielli's suggestive voice. She showered and wrapped herself in the blue French terry bathrobe she found hanging on the back of the door. Hoping Gabrielli had his own bathroom, she draped her rinsed-out underwear over the shower curtain rod, then carried the rest of her wardrobe to the bedroom. She dumped the T-shirt and jeans on the floor.

Moving to snap on the overhead light, Dorel saw two yellow eyes gleaming from the opposite wall. She gave a little yelp and hit the switch. A fluffy silver Persian cat blinked from the top of the futon's cushioned back.

Michael poked his head in the door. "Her name's Benten, too." He scowled at her clothes piled on the floor. "You want to wash those?"

He obviously suffered from some sort of obsessive-compulsive disorder with this lint-picking, picture-straightening thing he had going on. She would hate to have to housesit for him. "Kind of obsessive, aren't you?"

"Glad you think so," Michael replied congenially and sailed off down the hall with her clothes.

Benten slept with her all night. Or was it the other way around? The chubby cat took up more than her share of the small bed and snored most of the night.

Dorel woke stiff and with a stuffy nose the next morning to find herself eye to eye with the grinning Airedale. A post-it note stuck to the top of his shoulder read,

"Taking a flight. Number by the phone if you need me.
Don't open the door to anyone. M."

Katana allowed her to dress in the clean clothes she found neatly folded on the arm of the futon and watched her as she made a cup of coffee in Gabrielli's big copper espresso machine.

Dorel strolled through the house, idly browsing his collections of Oriental sculpture, pottery, textiles and carved ivory and jade. She guessed it would be hours until he returned and he even might be gone for days. Did he expect her to stay here doing nothing while he flew off to wherever?

They needed to have a strategy session, generate a plan and execute it, like somehow get back her car and belongings. She clung to the belief that by taking action, she could regain control of her life before it plunged into total irreversible disaster.

The doorbell rang.

Katana set up a rabid-dog barking that was sure to drive away even the most determined murderer. The doorbell chimed again. The Airedale lunged at the door, hitting it hard with its front paws. The long gouges in the wood showed this wasn't the first time the dog's claws had raked the door as his defensive training exhibited itself.

Dorel peeked out the sheer curtain covering the long slim window beside the door.

Abie! He'd found her.

"Dorel! Open up! Dorel, it's Uncle Abie. We need to talk."

Not daring to answer, Dorel bit down on her fist to make sure she didn't and tripped backward, stumbling into the howling dog.

"Come on, honey, you don't understand. You gotta let me explain."

The doorknob twisted and she heard a scratching sound. The door popped open to the chain.

Abie put his foot inside. Katana alternately barked madly and attacked Abie's steel-toed work boot. "Call off the dog, Dorel, before he gets hurt." Her uncle slammed his shoulder into the door.

The chain held. Dorel backed away, her gaze searching frantically around the foyer for anything to use to defend herself. She spotted an alarm panel on the wall behind the door. Without hesitating, she punched the red EMG button and retreated deeper into the foyer. A shrill alarm shook the house, woofing louder than Katana and hurting Dorel's ears.

Abie's thick arm snaked around the door and pointed a small black rectangle at the touchpad. Immediately the alarm died. The steel chain links broke with a cracking pop. Abie barged in and sprayed Katana's curly face with something that made the dog yelp in agony and crouch on the floor, clawing at its eyes.

Abie stepped over him, pocketing the small canister, and grabbed Dorel roughly by the arm. He shoved her to the living room and threw her down on the black leather sofa.

"You never give anyone a chance, Dorel," he complained, looking disgusted. "I've been trying to help you, but you go and screw everything up. Why didn't you tell me you were involved with this guy, Gabrielli? Now when the cops arrest him, they'll get you as an accessory."

Dorel huddled on the couch, rubbing her arm. She wouldn't answer. Wouldn't tell him a thing. He would not get the sword.

Abie's fury-warped face relaxed a little as he blew out a big, noisy breath. "It doesn't have to be this way, hon. I can still help you. Help Gabrielli, if you want me to. The police don't have to know he killed that guy. How could they prove it if they don't have the sword? I can solve all your problems. All our problems. I don't know what you think you heard yesterday in the shop, but you've got it wrong."

"I—I don't have the sword any more," she stammered.

He sat down beside her with his arm around her shoulders. "Sure you do. But you've got to know that as long as you keep it, we're all in danger. He'll kill us both, Dorel, don't you see. Verna too. This guy is ruthless, a sick son of bitch. All he wants is Martin's sword and he'll stop at nothing to get it."

"Who wants it?"

Abie gave her a fed-up look that showed her question didn't deserve an answer, then glanced around the room. "I know you've got it with you, Dorel. Just give it to me and he'll leave us alone."

When she didn't respond, Abie stood and glowered down at her, then extended his hand. "Come on outside. I've brought your car and stuff for you. You can just climb in it and roll. I brought you some cash, too." He withdrew a fold of bills from the front pocket of his khaki pants. "When I get the money for the sword, I'll send it to you. But for right now, this ought to buy you a new start somewhere safe."

Dorel stared at the clump of green in his outstretched hand and pulled herself to her feet. The temptation to take the money was incredible. She wanted the money, wanted to be ten thousand miles away from him, but neither was going to happen. "I sold it."

Swear words erupted from his glistening lips at the same

instant he backhanded her across the face. Money shot over the back of the couch. The blow sent her crumbling to the floor beside the burl coffee table, her head narrowly missing the sharp edge. He pressed his steel-toe into her ribs.

She tried to squirm away, but he gave her a short, hard kick. "Who'd you sell it to?" Abie grabbed her by the front of the shirt and jerked her to her feet. "To who, Dorel?"

"A pawn shop—by the university."

"Which one."

"Double A," she gasped.

"Give me the ticket."

"I don't have one, Abie. I didn't pawn it. I sold it."

He released her and shoved her backwards where she sprawled on the sofa again. "How much?"

"Two hundred."

"Thousand, I hope." His dung-brown eyes narrowed with avarice.

"Hundred."

He looked ready to kill. "You stupid . . ."

"I can get it back."

Abie grabbed her arm and shook her. "You don't understand what you've done, Dorel. We're dead, do you hear me? Dead. Unless we get that sword back. We've got to go get it now."

"No! Abie, please." She pounded at his fingers as he dragged her kicking and scratching to the foyer.

Abie booted a disabled Katana aside and jerked her over the dog's quivering body to the threshold. She grabbed the doorjamb with her free hand to keep from being pulled out the door, but he rapped her fingers with his big, knobby fist and she let go.

Once outside Dorel heard the wail of sirens in the distance, growing louder and louder.

Abie heard the sirens, too. He stopped and glanced toward the driveway, then cursed and thrust her back into the house.

"You do what you must to get that sword back, Dorel, and bring it to me quick. If he gets it first, we're all dead," Abie growled and ran for his tow truck.

Chapter Five

Michael couldn't drive any further. From the time he'd pulled out of his driveway, discomfort nudged him. He'd tried to tamp the feeling down, disregard it, but the sensation had a strength of its own. The further he drove from home, the uneasiness seemed to grow geometrically, almost to the point of physical pain as he had inched forward stuck in the rush hour traffic.

Finally, unable to ignore the strange feeling any longer, he took the off ramp and cloverleafed back toward home.

His cell phone buzzed. Michael pulled to the side of the road to let an unmarked police car pass flashing its blue light.

"Gabrielli," he barked into the tiny phone and pulled back on the road.

"Mr. Gabrielli, this is Active Alarm Company. We've got a break-in alert at your home. Someone inside hit the panic button, but the system was immediately knocked off line. We've sent law enforcement."

Dorel! Michael stomped on the accelerator. "I'm on my way." He tossed the phone on the passenger seat. As he aimed off the main highway onto his gravel road, the rear wheels of the Land Cruiser lost traction, throwing the car sideways. He expertly turned into the slide. The car straightened and dived through the hanging gray dust, parting it like a billowing curtain as the vehicle hustled down the winding road to the house.

A white police cruiser, two unmarked cars and an old Jeep Cherokee sat in the circular drive. Michael jumped out of the car, looking around for Katana. The front door of the house was wide open. He hoped the dog hadn't gotten out and escaped through the gateless entrance to his fenced twenty acres. He cursed himself for not getting a gate installed.

He hurried into the house. A uniformed patrolman whirled around in the foyer, moving to pull a gun. Michael held up his hands. "I'm Michael Gabrielli. This is my house."

"Take your driver's license out with your left hand," the officer ordered, still poised to draw.

Michael complied, carefully handing the license over and looking beyond the cop into the living room. He couldn't see anyone.

"He's Gabrielli, and this is his place, all right," said a voice behind him. His gut tightened as he met the gaze of Seattle Police Lieutenant Rhett who'd interviewed him the day after the gun show. What was he doing here? Wasn't this a little out of his jurisdiction? Michael wondered, giving the man a curt nod of recognition.

"Where's Dorel?" He pushed by the officer. Rhett followed him closely.

"I'm in here, Michael," called her quavering voice from the kitchen.

Michael strode quickly through the living area, appraising the state of the room. Although nothing was disturbed, it felt different. Violated.

Dorel sat on the steel gray, slate kitchen floor with Katana's head in her lap. She wiped his tan face with a wash cloth. An angry red welt swelled from her cheek to her eye and she appeared to be fighting to control tears, the glistening sheen in her eyes giving her away. A plainclothes officer stood at the bar, writing.

Michael knelt beside her, stroked Katana, then put a hand on hers. "What happened?" he asked gently, yet wanting to yell and strike out at something his rage was so great.

"A man broke in," Dorel told him and added hastily, "I don't know who."

The lieutenant reached for the report the man was writing. "What is Miss Everly to you, Mr. Gabrielli? Housekeeper? Friend?" he suggested, his tone insinuating. "She didn't seem to know you yesterday."

"I know him. You didn't mention him yesterday, that I recall," she retorted, her own tone heavy with exasperation at the SPD lieutenant's incompetence. "I'm staying with Michael for awhile."

Michael raised the dog's big head to examine its eyes. Katana thumped his tail and weakly lifted his lip attempting a smile. "Who's that?" Michael glanced from Rhett to the man at the bar.

"My counterpart, a detective from the King County Sheriff's department, Sergeant Menlow," Rhett answered and Menlow looked up briefly in acknowledgement. "Says here, unknown assailant entered the premises, sprayed the dog with mace or pepper spray, offed the alarm and struck you. Then just *left?*"

"Yes, that's correct." Dorel stood and rinsed out the cloth in the sink. "He heard the sirens and they scared him away."

Michael stroked Katana's rough-coated head, struggling to keep quiet. He had a thousand questions of his own to ask her but now wasn't the time. He didn't believe Dorel's story either, but he vowed to support her if it got rid of the police. "There've been other break-ins in the area. I think whomever it was just didn't expect to find anyone here. Dorel was a surprise to them, so they left."

"Things have been eventful for you lately, haven't they, Mr. Gabrielli?" Rhett handed the report back to the silent County detective. "Someone leaves your flying scarf at a murder scene. Now *someone* breaks into your house and roughs up your friend. Interesting."

Michael stood and unblinkingly stared the man down. "Very interesting, Lieutenant. I'm beginning to wonder about my personal safety. Apparently, I just missed an attack in the convention center parking lot and now here at my home. Too coincidental, wouldn't you say? And now you are here. Speaking of which, why is a Seattle detective answering an alarm outside the city limits?"

Lieutenant Rhett didn't blink either. "Let's just say I have some prior interest, and the Sergeant here is letting me tag along. In my line of work, I've found things don't just happen. There's always a reason. And eventually all the pieces start falling into place. Maybe its something like an innocent piece of nothing dropped at a crime scene. The perp or someone starts doing things, stupid things, that call attention to themselves. It's like they can't help themselves. They just do it."

"Has someone taken a look at Ms. Everly's injuries?" Michael asked, ignoring the lieutenant's comments.

"She refused treatment," the sergeant said.

The police stayed another thirty minutes, nosing around the house and asking questions. Michael was sure this lengthy investigation was extraordinary for a simple break-in, especially since Lieutenant Rhett had shown a determined interest in everything about him and Dorel.

When the last car eased out of the driveway, leaving only his Land Cruiser and the Jeep, Michael closed the door and turned to Dorel. "Tell me," he ordered through gritted teeth.

"It was Abie. I didn't give him the sword." Dorel took a wary step back at the furious look on his face. Is this man like Abie? she speculated nervously. She gingerly touched her swollen eye and backed up further.

He must have seen her fear of him, for his stern expression

softened and he looked almost sympathetic, sorry as if the attack were all his fault. "He must have figured out who I was from your aunt or got my license number as we drove away from the junk yard."

"He already had the file on you," she said half-heartedly and walked to the kitchen.

Katana lay on a natural straw woven mat by the deck door. He'd shaken off the effects of the mace quickly, but had seemed to need her attention while the police were there. He'd tried to protect her. Taking care of him was the least she could do and had kept her from losing it.

"Abie wants the sword, Michael."

"He'd do this to his own niece," he spat, shaking his head. His knuckles turned white as he gripped the tiled island. "What the hell kind of family do you have?"

"The dead kind. I have no family." She poured out the espresso and began to make a fresh cup. Caffeine was her drug of choice at the moment, and she needed a lot of it. Her hand shook as she measured out the coffee into the filter basket. "Abie Prefontaine was a friend of my grandfather. I've always called him uncle because we spent so much time with him and Verna when I was little. Granddad and he might have had business together, I don't know."

"You don't have any living relatives?"

"No, not even a pseudo-uncle, not any more." Despair slumped on her and she turned the handle on the boiler. Steamy espresso dripped into her cup. She added hot water to it, cutting the strength. She couldn't stand to be any more jittery.

"No cousins? No one?" Michael motioned for a cup of coffee. She handed him hers and began to make another for herself.

"Trying to find someone to take me off your hands?" If

she'd felt better, she'd have made sure it sounded like a joke. Instead, the question shouted *need*. Shame and humiliation twisted in her throat.

"It had crossed my mind a time or two." His somber expression lightened a degree.

But Dorel knew he was serious. There was no room for her in his life, not that she wanted that. She had to get away.

"Why did he hit you?" Michael raised his hand to her cheek but didn't touch. She felt the warmth of his hand smelling of lemony aftershave.

"I told him I'd sold the sword. He didn't like that." She took a shaky sip from a tiny TransAsia Air espresso cup.

Michael dropped his hand. "He didn't believe you."

"Evidently he did, because he tried to drag me away to go get the sword."

His mouth fell open and he sputtered, "He tried to kidnap you? What incredible balls that guy has to break into my home and beat you!"

Since it wasn't overtly directed at her, his anger didn't frighten her. Somehow it made her feel better. He could have raged about Abie's macing Katana, instead Michael was furious that she'd been hurt.

She tried to smile but winced at the twinge of pain from her injured eye. "I've got to do something. Abie demanded that I bring the sword to him and made some really dire threats. I could give the sword to him . . ."

Michael's expression darkened. "Do you really think you can simply *give* it to him and he'll be happy? Or that you can even give it up at all?"

She knew she couldn't. With every beat of her heart, the sword was becoming more a part of her. She'd rather die than relinquish the sword. It belonged only to her despite Michael's claim that it belonged to both of them.

"No, I guess not." Dorel dug in her jeans pocket and pulled out the money she'd grabbed off the floor before the police arrived. "He brought me this as well as my car and stuff. Said if I didn't bring him the sword, we would all be dead." She let Abie's threatening words hang and watched Michael carefully. Abie hadn't said exactly *who* was going to kill them.

Michael's shoulders slumped. "We've got to come up with something else. He'll be back, all right. And he won't be as congenial." He glanced at her swollen eye. "You need an ice pack on that."

"No, it's fine. It doesn't hurt now." And it didn't. She felt only a rising anxiousness pervading her senses. "I do need some air, though."

"Sure." He glanced down at the dog. "Katana could probably stand a walk."

They took the graveled trail from the end of the deck through the Japanese garden to a row of rhododendrons. Beyond the garden, the trail was carpeted with mulched leaves and fir needles. Katana seemed to have recovered from his ordeal and trotted happily ahead of them. Strolling among the dense trees and scratching blackberry bushes in the deep shade, Dorel felt her damp skin cool. She breathed easier and her anxiety abated as she concentrated on walking.

Dorel tried to notice everything, to smell the damp, pungent earth, to separate the infinite shades of green, to feel the warm breeze tickle the hairs on her arms, to hear the shrill cry of a red tail hawk circling overhead. Everything confirmed that she was still alive, sharing the earth on this golden August morning.

She'd never before experienced anything like the out-of-control events that had been happening to her. The Dorel Everly she knew was brave. Decisive. Competent. In control.

Upper management at Boeing had even called her confrontational and combative. Yet, here she was desperate to run away from everyone and everything. She wanted to hide. Very un-Dorel Everly.

"I'll call today and get an electric gate installed," Michael said as he walked beside her.

She supposed he had probably been talking all during their walk, but she hadn't heard him.

He touched her arm. "Dorel?"

She flinched and pulled away before stopping herself. "Yes?" she responded brightly, trying to mask her anxiety. The unsettling suspicion that he knew what she was thinking made her wary.

His eyes narrowed as he cocked his head, appraising her. "You okay?"

No! I'm terrified, she screamed silently. "Do you really think an electric gate is going to keep anyone out? You thought Katana could protect me. That didn't happen, even though the poor thing tried. I've got to get away from here. You know what will happen if I stay." She clutched his arm and looked pleadingly into his hard expression.

"I won't let you go." He grasped her hand on his arm. "You'll stay here, with me. I will protect you."

"What about when you go to work?" I will leave then, she decided hastily.

"I'm taking some vacation time. I have weeks I haven't used." He turned back toward the house with Dorel trailing after him, then stopped and looked apologetically at her. "It seems I can't be very far away from you. That's what brought me back to the house. I didn't even make it to SeaTac airport, and then I got stuck in rush hour traffic."

Her stomach clenched. When could she escape? "I appreciate your concern, but you aren't responsible for me. I need to get in my car and drive the hell away from here. Alone," she added.

"I don't think that will work. You may not understand what's happening yet, but the fact is, we can't be separated. The sword won't let us."

"Stop it. It's not true. You can't believe this. We can't. I won't," she raged, feeling out of control.

Michael grabbed her tightly against his hard chest. She struggled in his embrace, fighting for air. "Shhh, Dorel. Please, don't be afraid. We've got to find a way through this. I know we can discover how to deal with everything in the past. I know how to do this." His voice and manner were reasonable and comforting. "And I can teach you how to protect yourself, and me, from them."

A glimmer of hope ignited in her bleak future and she stopped struggling. He sounded rational and not like he would hurt her, though he was obviously trying to keep her and the sword here. She had to be very careful. All this talk about finding answers in the past and teaching her was insane. In fact, he was crazy. Just go along with him until you can get away, she counseled herself and pulled out of his embrace.

"You've got more to worry about than me. If you had seen the look of angry terror on Abie's face when I told him I didn't have the sword, you would be *gear up* at SeaTac right now."

With a poker face, Michael said, "Hey, if Abie feels froggy, let him leap. He can't touch me. I'm a 747-400 driver. Next to God, you know."

She nearly punched him.

He held up his hand. "Okay, okay, bad joke. But I couldn't help myself." A grin dashed across his lips. "You needed cheering up. Hell, we both do. I had to do something. I wanted to see you smile. I'm sure your mouth will do that, won't it?"

She relaxed a bit, allowing a wide clenched-teeth grin to replace her tense frown.

"That's better. Looks like your parents spent a fortune on orthodontia." He headed back down the trail.

"Not a penny. We Everly's are blessed with perfect teeth," she protested, following him.

Michael turned and gave her a wolfish look. "As well as other perfections."

"My, what big teeth you have," she muttered, skirting past him on the trail, and striding rapidly to the house.

Michael felt sorry for Dorel Everly. No, sorry wasn't exactly right. He couldn't really name the emotion, but he knew she was scared to death. He had been, too. At first. With each passing minute his primary fear was changing, becoming something more, something different. Empowered. Especially when she was near with the sword.

Perhaps it was *only* the sword. He gazed at Martin Everly's books and bound notes neatly assembled on the bookshelf opposite his desk. His mind had carefully cataloged every piece of information that pertained to Everly's study of Asian history, warfare and arms. The man had been an accurate and brilliant, if eccentric, military historian and arms expert. And he wasn't opposed to esoteric or arcane topics, either. He'd extensively researched and written about a number of Japanese ancient families as well as legends of dragons and magical weapons, swords in particular.

Now Michael believed Everly had been researching the Tsuji sword. The one he must have obtained sometime at the end of World War II and left to his granddaughter. The sword that was now here in his home. Where it belonged.

Michael's sense of history had always astounded his mother and teachers, but it came naturally to him, as if he had experienced history as a time or life continuum and remembered everything. He leaned back in his leather chair, closed his eyes, took a deep breath and summoned the image of the sword.

Instantly, a vision shimmered before his eyes and his ears roared with noise.

Smoke combined with the acrid smell of gunpowder, clogging his eyes and throat. He couldn't breathe and slumped to his knees, the front of his khaki uniform was soaked red with his own blood. He heard her muffled sobbing gasps as she struggled to drag him across the stony ground.

In the shadow of a tumbled rock wall she knelt over him, her beloved face tear-streaked. "Fusao, give it to me," she demanded against his lips and tore the sword from his hands.

The vision evaporated, but the touch of death still hovered near. Michael rubbed his chest, feeling his rapid heart beat. He opened his eyes to see Dorel at the door to his study, her face pale with shock. "You saw?" he asked.

"Wh—what?" She licked her trembling lips. "What did I see?"

"Us, I think. In our past life. The one before this." Michael prompted, taking a strengthening breath. "I don't know how this is happening, but you are spontaneously experiencing my OBEs when we are together. OBE, out of body travels where the spirit isn't bound by time or space."

"Impossible."

"To say that you'd have to believe that we're limited to a physical body that eventually dies, then we cease to exist, right?"

"I don't know what I believe. I was raised with the traditional beliefs of my parents, though my grandfather had other ideas. When they died, Granddad told me they were still alive, but not seen because they were on a plane of existence that he said was operating at a different vibratory rate from Earth's. What a thing to tell a kid, right? I figured he only said it to make me feel better, but as I grew older I realized he truly believed. Once when he was ill and hallucinating, he raved that I was an incarnation of someone he met in the war."

"Tell me what he said," Michael said casually and crossed to the doorway where she stood with both hands tightly clasped in front of her.

"He called me *Baroness* and clutched at the side of my blouse. I was afraid it was, well, like he was reliving a sexual dream with some woman. I tried to get away, but he held on to me, muttering about blood and dying. It really terrified me."

Michael watched her, his minding racing. "What happened then?"

She shook her head. "Nothing, really. He let go of me and fell asleep, muttering in Chinese. And sometimes he'd say my name. The horrible thing was, when he did he'd sort of sob and roll his head from side to side."

Michael laid his hand on her shoulder. "That must have scared the hell out of you."

She forced a weak smile. "Oh, yes. It made quite an impression on me. From that time on, whenever he tried to talk to me or tell me anything about his study, I changed the subject or instantly had something better to do. It was a mistake, I know. We spent less and less time together after that, even though we really needed each other. It wasn't until he was sick and dying that I had any real time with him to talk, and listen. Then it was too late. Just keeping him alive and as

79

comfortable as possible took everything we both had. Like people do, we avoided talking about the inevitable and settling our old issues in favor of airplanes and Mariners games. Now he's lost to me."

"Maybe not. What if I told you that I don't believe we die? I believe that our spirit lives on because we are much more than a physical body. We also have an energy body made up of electro-magnetic energy that is the counterpart of the physical body. It absorbs life force or *prana,* which is life force or energy, vitality, and distributes it to the physical body. I also know that each of us has an astral body that responds to our emotions and that we can *mind travel* out of the physical body free of time and space. Everyone has out-of-body travel when they sleep, but most don't remember. All that dies is the physical body, then the energy body dissipates and our spirits return to the light and that place between lives." He took a book from the Everly section of the shelf. "Your grandfather isn't lost to you. You've been brought back together, I think. Look." He pointed to the gold letters on the brown cover, "Journal."

Dazed and a little frightened by Michael's weird lecture, Dorel made herself focus on the book and then up. "Is that Granddad's?"

He nodded and opened the book. Inside the cover, written in a spidery scrawl, was the signature of Martin Everly with the words "For Dorel" scribbled beneath. Michael handed her the open book. "Yours now."

She clasped the book to her breast and tears clouded her vision. How could I have sold this? she scolded herself. Her grandfather had wanted her to keep all his things, she now realized. He had believed she would. But he didn't know what a burden he'd left her. Or maybe he did. She turned the page and read the first words there.

"I'm so very sorry, my dear granddaughter."

"Are those all his books?" Dorel asked, nodding toward the tightly packed bookshelf.

"Yes."

"You must have bought his entire collection from Ben Lera Books. He'd helped Granddad add to that collection for years. When I had to sell and Lera eagerly gave me what I thought was a more than fair price, I worried that he was paying me so much because Granddad and he were friends."

She closed the journal with a snap and huffed, "I'm betting good old Lera had been helping you too, right? Gave me that fine price because he knew he could get double from you. The question is, why? Why would you want my grandfather's collection?"

Michael returned to his desk, hooked a hip on the edge and stared at her. "I really am a collector. And yes, Ben Lera has found many specialty books for me over the years. He knew I would be interested in Martin Everly's collection. And I was."

"Why?" Dorel demanded, becoming more suspicious that Michael had somehow been spying on her and Granddad for a long time, just waiting for him to die so that he could have Granddad's books as well as his sword. The idea was absolutely irrational, but not impossible, she warned herself.

"You really don't know much about your grandfather, do you? Because if you did you'd have known he was an internationally respected expert in Asian theatre war and weapons. And something else," he said with a condemning frown as he reached behind him and picked up a trade-size black book off the cluttered desktop. "Yeah, you didn't know the man. You either didn't care or didn't bother to really check out his things, maybe both, you were so hot to sell them for a few bucks. That includes his sword, which is priceless, and the journal he meant for you to keep. As well as this."

Michael opened the black book and held it out to her. Instead of book pages, Dorel realized the object was a presentation case. She was drawn to it, her gaze riveted on the beautiful bronze medal suspended from a blue and orange-gold striped ribbon resting on the case's gold satin. Lying beside it was a bronze heart hung from a purple ribbon.

"It's a single action air medal, a Bronze Star for bravery," Michael said, pointing to the larger medal. "And this is a Purple Heart. Martin was wounded in China."

"I know that," she snapped. There was no way she could defend selling these things. Michael was right. She hadn't sorted through Granddad's collection. If she'd done that, there would have been nothing she could have parted with, and then what? Certainly nothing worse than what had happened so far.

Dorel whipped around and headed out of Michael's den.

"These still aren't important to you, huh?" he called.

"Save your self-righteous judgment for someone who cares," she tossed over her shoulder and escaped to her room with the journal.

Chapter Six

Dorel slipped away to her room. After three years of housesitting luxury apartments and executive homes, she was amazed she could even consider this tiny space a room. She'd been in houses where the bathrooms were twice this size.

She sat on the hard futon, strangely hesitant to open the journal, fearing the memories and feelings its pages could invoke.

The Persian jumped into her lap. Dorel welcomed the interruption forcing her to set aside the book. She leaned back and stroked the flat-faced cat now sprawled across her thighs. Soon she was lulled by the deep hypnotic rhythm of the cat's purring, and drifted into dreamy sleep.

Dorel, try not to be sad, I haven't left you. Don't waste your time in grief. You must apply yourself to the problem, Granddad seemed to say in her dream.

She sighed. "No, Granddaddy, I'm too tired. Too busy. I've got to think of something."

Dorel, you must study my papers and books. You must learn. There isn't much time. You wouldn't let me tell you when I could have. Now, you must. Or else.

She rolled her head from side to side to escape his voice. "No, Granddaddy, don't tell me any more. I don't want to hear."

It's the only way to save yourself. Please, Dorel. Listen. Study my journal. Let him teach you, but be wary, do not be seduced by his power. They're coming. You must be prepared. Only with all the knowledge of the Guardian can you save yourself.

"I'm not the Guardian!" she yelled and bolted awake. Dorel blinked and focused on Michael's frowning stare from the doorway.

They gauged each other for a moment, each willing the other to speak first. She rubbed her eyes and lay back on the pillow.

"You screamed?" Michael leaned against the doorjamb and held his arms out. The cat jumped off her and into his arms, nesting cozily as he stroked its gray fur.

"Did I?" She had heard her grandfather's voice all too clearly, as well as what he said. She didn't want to talk about it. That might mean—no, she didn't care what it might mean. She wasn't going to think about it. Dreams were just dreams, nothing more.

"You must have had a bad dream. Shall I tell you about it?" Michael's expression became bland, almost disinterested.

"Now, how would you know about what I may have dreamed?"

"You talk in your sleep. I heard your end of the conversation."

Talked in her sleep! The thought horrified her, like being caught snoring or, worse, drooling all over the pillow. She remembered everything about the dream, and Michael obviously wanted her to fill in Granddad's side of the chat.

"Then you've been entertained enough," she snapped, dismissing him with a shake of her head. "Go voyeur elsewhere."

He stared at her then set the cat on the floor. "I've always made it a practice to remember and try to understand my dreams. Dreams are more than subconscious reactions to repressed emotions. They're another avenue to access information, discover ourselves, our past and future, move through other planes of existence. Think about it." He turned and walked down the hall.

Dorel didn't want to think about his silly theory. What she did want was to eat a hot fudge sundae large enough to fill a hot tub while mindlessly watching a marathon of fifties sitcoms. Pure escapism and she needed a large dose very badly.

Swinging her feet off the bed, she stood. The journal fell open at her feet. Dorel picked it up, her eyes drawn to the page, she read,

"Baroness Tsuji's sword was no gift. It is a curse, an ancient malicious burden. If I could rid myself, and Dorel, of it, I would. It's impossible. From the moment she gave it to me, the sword has haunted me. I believe it speaks to me. I cannot escape it even though I entrusted it to the Roshi.

No wonder Baroness Tsuji didn't look peaceful when she died, even though she'd finally handed off her burden. She is not at peace. She knew. Every time I see Dorel's sweet, innocent eyes, I know what her life will be, who she will be. How she will look when she takes up the sword in her future.

I can't bear it. There must be something I can do. Some way to break the terrible cycle of the Guardian and the Defender. I cannot leave Dorel such a hopeless, destructive legacy. I will search, spend every moment and cent I have to find the answer.

My dear granddaughter, if you are reading this, and have the sword, try not to be afraid. Even in death I will not give up until I find the answer to save you."

Dorel blinked back stinging tears. Before closing the journal, she turned to the flyleaf and touched her name he had written, and his. Then she saw the tiny sentence written vertically along the seam of the book.

"Look under the sword case lining."

Closing the book, she held it to her heart and bowed her head in grief and joy. It was as if he had been right there talking to her. Like the dream. Only this time, she listened. All those years apart, he'd been trying to help her. If only she'd known, she'd have done so many things differently. Not wasted her time resenting his work and him for not loving her enough.

If only she'd known how much he loved her.

Dorel heard the phone ring several times in another part of the house. She slipped the journal under the futon cushion and walked down the hall toward Michael's office. As she reached his open door, she heard the answering machine pick up the call.

Michael met her gaze and they both waited, staring at the phone.

"Dorel? Gabrielli? I know you're there. Screening your calls, huh? Real smart. I would too if I had your problems." Abie's gravel voice crawled through the speaker and filled the air between them.

"Michael," Dorel interrupted, panicked.

"Listen!" He held his finger to his lips and frowned intently at the phone.

". . . didn't bring the item I wanted," Abie's voice continued. "I've got that buyer who's got to have that item like I told you. I promise I'll give you everything he gives me, but you've got to bring it. Our lives depend on it, Dorel. I can't wait much longer. You know what I mean? The guy . . . just bring the damn thing right away. Please do it, honey. This is real bad and about to get a whole lot worse. Come now. Don't wait!" The phone clattered on the tape and the dial tone hummed before the machine beeped and hung up.

Dorel wrapped her arms around herself and held on tightly. A cold fury whirled inside her skin making her clench her jaw. She sank onto the square cane seat of the oak stool next to the door.

Michael came around the desk and knelt before her. He tenderly lifted her chin with his index finger, looking into her eyes. "Don't let him scare you. He can't touch us and he knows it. He's just being melodramatic."

She jerked her chin away from his touch. "I'm not scared. For the first time since this all started. I am not scared at all. I'm mad as hell. I'm tired of being lied to. And I'm sick to death of being threatened. I can't just hide here waiting for him to come get me. Because he will, melodramatic or not. Your big dog isn't going to stop him. Or your alarm." She stood, forcing him to his feet.

"Time for some reality therapy, Michael. You can't stop Abie. He wants my sword. So do you. You even believe it's yours and used it to kill a man. And then there's the police. I think they're watching you. Us. They didn't believe a word we told them this morning. They suspect you of killing Osterman, don't they? And they think I might be your accomplice. Be honest."

He pulled himself up straight. "Probably. Rhett didn't accuse me, but that's where he's going with it. It wasn't that difficult for him to put it together. I left my scarf there and that was the only thing tying me to the scene except for the sword. And we have that. Keep in mind that they really can't prove anything without the sword."

"Why did you run, Michael? Maybe you could have saved him. Why did you run?"

He stared accusingly at her. "Why did you?"

"Because I thought you were going to kill me."

"You did not! You knew I wouldn't hurt you. I saved you,

for God's sake. I couldn't hurt you. Ever." His broad chest heaved under his white knit shirt and a frown creased his smooth forehead.

Something deep inside urged her to believe him, believe that he would never hurt her. She also remembered that he had easily killed a man and run away. "You shouldn't have run. That makes you look so guilty regardless of the circumstances."

He jerked his shoulders back and snorted. "Hell, I am guilty. I killed him. He was going to kill me!" he vented with a growl. "I had to defend you and myself, and I did. Even though I don't really remember the details of exactly how it happened."

Desire to believe in and protect him surged in her. The sensation was so strong she wanted to touch him, but held back. "Of course it was. But the police won't understand why you left."

"If I told them, if you told them what happened, they'd want the sword as evidence. Do you think it's going to let us do that?" His tone took on a hard edge. "From the moment that sword came into our hands we haven't been free to act as we want, to do what we'd ordinarily do. We don't have a choice."

Michael's harsh words drove any illusions of freedom from her mind, even though she didn't want to believe the sword *made* them do anything. That was absurd. It was his killing Osterman and her keeping silent about it that was controlling them, and was allowing Abie to harass her.

You can't allow that, an inner voice warned her. *You must protect him.*

"I'm done talking about this. Katana needs to go out." Michael stomped out of the office into the hall, calling the dog.

Dorel sat back down on the stool, stunned at the voice's message. Protect Michael? I need protection from him, and apparently every other man in the world. She rubbed her arms to combat the chill dashing over her skin. She got to her feet as her stomach growled its emptiness and hurried down the hall.

Katana charged in the French doors from the deck as Dorel entered the kitchen. She bent and gave him a hug around his thick neck. For a woman who yesterday seemed terrified of the dog, Katana's slobbery kiss seemed to please her immensely. She smiled and crooned in a cute little voice to the big hairball and Michael almost felt jealous.

"Hungry?" he asked as she stood up, dusting her hands together and smiling down at the dog.

"I thought you'd never ask." She tucked a strand of her shining copper hair behind her ear.

"Why didn't you tell me?"

"I didn't think you were in the mood to be *told* anything. I'll be right back. I've got to wash the dog off," she said and held up hands, fingers splayed out like a little kid.

Michael had ham sandwiches and green salad ready by the time she returned. She slipped into the chair across from him. Despite the welt beside her eye, her face was lovely, glowing as if scrubbed with snow. Her green eyes sparkled a lively interest in the food he'd prepared and he was pleased.

Cooking was a skill he'd acquired as a kid when he helped his mother run their bed and breakfast in Port Townsend. Though he enjoyed creating dishes that people liked, occasionally he struggled against a lurking bigoted idea that cooking was lowly woman's work. It was an old-fashioned even chauvinistic notion that he didn't believe but didn't dare share with anyone, especially not with his very self-sufficient dynamo mother or any other woman these days.

Dorel wolfed down her lunch and sat back, staring at him. He asked, "Can I fix you something else?"

"No, thank you. That was great." She watched him eat for a moment, then added, "You chew your food very carefully, don't you?"

He stopped chewing and swallowed. "What do you mean, *carefully?*"

"About fifteen times each bite?" She took a swallow of iced tea. "My mom was a big believer in *properly chewing one's food.* I used to wish she'd just go ahead and chew mine up for me and leave me alone."

Michael wasn't aware that he chewed a specific number of times, only that he savored taste and texture. Sure, he had his routines and procedures, holdovers from his intensive flight and military training that were sometimes a necessary anchor that kept him focused in the present.

He took another bite of ham sandwich, but couldn't eat with her staring at him. "Now you've got me self-conscious. Why don't you take a stroll in the meditation garden? There's a small rake under the stone bench if you'd like to try making patterns in the sand. It's pretty relaxing."

She slid her chair back, giving him a dazzling smile. "Are you sending me out to play in the sandbox? Sounds like fun," she said, stood up and took three graceful steps to the French doors and went outside.

The second Dorel moved out of view, Michael felt a strong need in the center of his chest to go with her as if they were attached to each other through the heart by a steel cable. Unable to control the urge, he got up and looked out across the deck and saw her, sandals in hand, gleefully kicking the previously carefully raked sand up in beige puffs as she danced like an over-grown garden nymph around the largest boulder.

Michael smiled and positioned his chair where he could secretly watch her while he finished his meal.

After more relaxing in the garden than she could stand, Dorel went to Michael's office where he joined her after making a lot of kitchen cleaning noise.

"What are we going to do? If I don't take the sword to Abie, I know he'll be back for it," she said, trying to keep worry out of her voice as she stared at her grandfather's collection on the bookshelf.

"If that's what you believe, then we better get ready for him." Michael sat down at his desk and opened a book.

"Is that your idea of getting ready?" she cried. This was no time for him to revert to a passive, *let 'em come* approach. They needed to take action.

He stopped reading and tented his fingers above the pages. "If we're going to figure this whole thing out, we need more information about the sword and the power it holds."

"Are you crazy?" She marched to his desk, leaned across the cluttered top and poked his solid chest with her finger. "You listen. I'm not about to be hip-deep in the odd bodies you decide to slice holes in. Besides, bullets are somewhat faster than the blade, I believe. Abie has a very extensive gun collection, most of which he's sure to bring here to show you."

Michael caught her finger and held it a moment too long before gently pushing her hand aside. "All right, what do you propose we do?"

She started to speak then closed her mouth and began to pace in front of the desk. "Well, we just can't wait for him to come, and we don't want to meet him. At all." Dorel turned to face him. "I think we should leave. Go somewhere." She was careful to include him in their escape, though she was determined to get away from him at her first opportunity. Her mind ticked through possible refuges. "The coast. Out to Ocean Shores or Long Beach," she suggested. "I've camped there a lot. No one would find us in one of the state campgrounds. They're always packed this time of year."

Michael grunted and leaned back in his chair with his hands behind his head. "Camping with the swarms from the corporate hives? Not me. You'll have to go without me." He quirked his mouth, his chair groaned as he rocked forward. "No, you can't. And I'm not going anywhere when I have everything I want right here. You stay."

He means the *sword* stays with him, but that was a no-go too. Although he spoke with a near-smile, she didn't like that he'd voiced her fear. Regardless, she wasn't going to stay with him. And neither was her sword.

Retrieve the sword case. The unspoken phrase chased all other thoughts from her head. Her eyes widened as she looked at Michael. Incredibly, he'd heard it, too.

"Why, do you think?" Michael's gaze locked on hers. His lips erased themselves to a thin line and his blue eyes darkened as they narrowed.

"There may be something under the lining." Dorel glanced away, not wanting to see the surprise she knew must be dawning on his face. Why had she told him? The note in the journal was probably just something Granddad had written to himself. Besides, hadn't Michael been through all of Granddad's books and papers? Wouldn't he have seen the writing along the edge of the journal's page?

"Why didn't you take whatever it is out of the lining?" He was already getting up, ready to go.

"I didn't know anything was there. I just read about it in the journal."

"We better go get the case." He walked out the door, but

returned when he realized she wasn't following him.

"We don't even know where it is." Dorel had to get out, get away and hurried to the sliding glass door in the living room. She tried to open it, her hand shaking as she fumbled with the locking lever.

"Dorel, if Martin wrote about the case in the journal, he expected you to have it. You don't. We have to get it," Michael called from the foyer behind her with a tone that had a no-nonsense quality that fired her anxiety.

"No. I don't want to. It's not important. I'm sure." She sounded like a petulant child, but she felt forced to make a stand on this issue. They needed to get away, not waste time chasing this.

"Don't be afraid. We can do this. We're a team. Remember?"

It was true, of course. Whether she liked it or not, they were indeed a team. For now. "Okay." She turned, clasping her hands together. "But I still think it would be smarter not to waste time on the case. We need to get away from here."

Michael raised his hand and shrugged. "Let's take one thing at a time. I really feel it's important to get the case now. Nothing happens by coincidence, by chance. Just as your grandfather's collection came to me and my finding you were not coincidence. I believe you found that message when we needed it. It was waiting for us. Both of us."

Each word he spoke was designed to exude trustworthiness, to persuade, and help to convince her to go with him, until bringing the sword case home seemed like the most reasonable thing to do. And she fell for it despite all her reservations. "Would your dealer friend have the sword case I left on the table?"

"He has it. When he called to tell me the police had been by asking questions about me, he said he was holding the case and asked if I wanted it." Michael grinned sardonically. "He assumed I had the sword."

"Why did he think that?"

"I usually get what I want." He stared intently at her.

She shifted uncomfortably under his appraising look. "Does he think you killed Osterman, too?" she zinged back at him. Was Michael intending to *get* her too, assuming, of course, that he wanted *her* as well as the sword?

"He didn't mention it. If he did believe that, he wouldn't tell the police or anyone else. He's an arms dealer and already has enough harassment from the police. Spence isn't going to put himself in the middle of something that could get his license jerked. Besides he's an old friend of mine from way back."

An idea began to take shape in her consciousness. "Would he have a sword that looks like mine? Or close enough that it could fool someone? For a short time anyway?"

"The same thought just occurred to me. I'll call him and let him know we're coming over and what we need." Before she could agree, he was already dialing the phone. She left him talking to the dealer.

Dorel hung the sword bag's strap over her shoulder and left her room. The cat followed her, blinking and mewing softly. She bent and picked her up, cuddling her. Glancing at a round antique brass mirror over a squat three-drawer campaign chest with antique brass trim at the end of the hall, Dorel checked her appearance. She'd always been proud of her athletic perkiness, her healthy skin. Now dark smudges sat beneath her eyes and her shoulder-length red hair straggled lifelessly. Sick of the jeans and stupid T-shirt, she briefly considered getting her bags out of the car. That would be the same as moving in and unpacking. And she wasn't going to be here that long.

"Ready?" Michael watched her from the foyer. She looked beautiful standing there holding Benten. They both looked like royalty, one exotic species complimenting another. He'd never seen anyone like Dorel before. Never spent so much time with a woman who stirred him as she did. She was the culmination of woman to him, as if he'd always known her yet was just discovering her every time he looked at her. She was changing, in a state of becoming. It was as though her essence ebbed and flowed merging with his.

Michael shook his head. Dorel was looking at him with a bemused expression. Did she know what he was thinking? "Ready?" he repeated and set the alarm.

"Sorry, Katana, you have to stay here," Dorel told the dog who looked all set to follow them out the door. The Airedale drooped his ears in disappointment and sat.

She's even accepted by my animals, Michael observed as she set his cat down next to Katana. Both looked at her as if she were their only concern in their fur-bound existence. All our lives are revolving around her, he admitted to himself, taking in the curve of her hip in the long tight jeans she wore so well.

"Michael?"

"Hmm—what?" He tore his eyes away from her bottom and focused on her face.

"We'd better leave before the alarm goes off." She gave him a confused-looking smile and pressed by him to the Land Cruiser. She smelled good. Was it jasmine? he wondered, sliding into the driver's seat.

"Tell me about your friend," she said as they drove through the dappled sunlight to the main highway.

She kept her gaze focused on the road, almost moving as if she were driving. Checking the mirrors, Michael wished she would watch behind them instead, wondering if he should ask her to keep an eye out for cars following them.

No. He could do it. *I am the Defender,* he heard inside his head. Momentary chagrin quickly evolved to the realization *he, the Defender* had done all and at this moment was the culmination of every powerful previous incarnation.

"Michael?"

He tried to clear his mind and concentrate on her voice as he glanced at her. "Yes?"

Her expression was filled with wonder and disbelief. "I saw or heard or thought it, too," she whispered. "Is that what you think you are becoming, or really are?" Her shaking voice echoed his own fleeting thoughts, or was it fears?

"Yes." Michael felt the transformation solidify within himself with his acceptance. He was the Defender. The path was plain, established for him through time, his purpose set.

Michael Gabrielli merged with the power of the sword Dorel held for him on her lap. The battle cry silently formed on his lips: *Eternally do we battle evil.*

Chapter Seven

At a small gun shop in a Kent strip mall, Michael formally introduced Dorel to his gun dealer friend, Jonathan Spencer. The two men talked quietly between themselves, leaving Dorel to idly browse around.

After the bizarre episode in the car, Michael hadn't spoken to her again, and she was just as glad. What was there to say? In front of her own eyes, or mind, she saw him change. Felt it. He accepted it, and he expected her to embrace it as if it were inescapable. As if it were indisputable truth.

Now she understood what Granddad meant in his journal about being careful. Michael was clearly flying one wing low, two units out of trim. And while she might have to ride the second seat with him for now, she had to make sure she wasn't onboard when he crashed in a fiery ball.

Dorel leaned across the glass counter and studied several different swords hanging on the wall behind it. There were narrow fencing foils, a wicked looking curved scimitar, three wide-bladed knight's swords and a half dozen samurai-type, but none that looked quite like hers. She glanced at the men. Maybe Spencer had something put away.

She returned to Michael's side and cleared her throat. Jonathan looked up from the sword case on the counter in front of him and smiled. Michael continued to talk, ignoring her. Finally, she interrupted. "Mr. Spencer, do you have a sword that would look near enough like mine to—"

Michael cut her off with a withering look. "Spence doesn't have anything like that."

"I might, Mike," Spence said with a conspiratorial wink at

Dorel. He disappeared behind a curtain, leaving her to the disapproving, censuring vibes radiating from Michael.

Why was he so upset anyway? she wondered, refusing to meet his glare. She looked at the closed sword case. Michael's long slender hand rested possessively on top. "Did you look in the lining?" she asked and reached to open the case.

He clamped his hand over hers. "Leave it! We'll get it later," he growled.

She realized he didn't want his *old* friend to see it. Very strange. Michael must not trust him, she decided. Spence returned with a cloth-wrapped parcel and laid it on the counter next to the sword case and peeled back the layers.

"This looks almost like it." She slipped the bag off her shoulder, set it on the counter and started to unzip it.

Michael stopped her. "It's a nice Tadatsuna. Didn't I see that last month?"

"Yeah, you did. I'm surprised you didn't remember how much it looks like her sword."

Michael smiled benignly. "What can I say, the mind goes first." He tapped his temple with his forefinger.

Both men laughed and resumed their conversation.

Dorel huffed away, feeling as if she'd been dismissed like a bothersome little girl. Something outside the large window caught her attention. She walked to the front of the store and peered out the glass door.

Black diesel smoke perked from the big yellow Holmes wrecker's twin exhaust stacks. It lurked in the strip mall's alley between a thrift store and sandwich shop. Inside the tow truck, Abie Prefontaine's gray head was turned toward the gun shop.

Dorel whirled and dashed back to the counter. She immediately switched her sword into the case and stuffed Spence's sword in the bag. While both men stared open-mouthed at her, the whole swap took less than twenty seconds.

"Abie's outside," Dorel breathed, her gaze darting around for another exit.

They turned collectively toward the front of the shop. "Where?" Michael asked, his voice cold steel.

"In the wrecker across the lot."

"Need some help, Mike?" Spence tried to see around them.

Michael turned back to his friend. "I've got to have your sword. I'll pay you later. We're being followed. Don't worry, I can handle this."

"Right. I've got your six. Gimme a call when you get home," Spence said.

Michael grabbed the case and handed her the duffel bag, then pulled her by the hand out the front door.

Dorel got in the Land Cruiser, holding the bag on her lap while Michael opened the back and locked the sword case in the cargo space. He slipped behind the wheel and started the car, positioning the electric side mirror so he could see Abie.

They drove slowly out of the lot. At the light, Michael turned out of the heavy, slower traffic of Kent's Central Avenue onto a rural, tree-lined road that ran beside the Green River. Abie followed several car lengths behind them.

"Why are you taking this road?" Dorel looked worriedly at the winding vacant strip ahead of them.

"No traffic to slow us down." Michael concentrated on the road ahead.

"Oh, Michael. That's just what we need. Abie's diesel is slow to maneuver in traffic. But once he gets going, that truck will run right over us."

"I know how to drive." Michael stepped on the accelerator, passing a slow moving tractor.

"That's not the point. I've seen him drive that truck. He's

like a mad man. Goes right over the top of whatever is foolish enough to get in his way. He's going to catch us."

"Stop worrying," Michael ordered, driving like a mad man himself.

Dorel scrunched down in the seat, put her feet on the dash and held on. She refused to watch him drive her to her death and concentrated on the shades of green whipping by the windows. Thank God August was the hottest month in the Puget Sound area, making the road in front of them bone-dry.

She didn't like the way the top-heavy sport utility vehicle tilted in the corners as if it wanted to roll over. She hoped Michael was as good as he claimed.

He wasn't. Not against Abie. The huge truck nudged their bumper. Dorel knew it was a mere playful kiss on the Land Cruiser's rear end followed by a decided slam that pushed the car sideways out of control.

"Slow down, slow down!" she cried. "You've got better control if you slow down."

"He'll push us off the road," Michael yelled.

"That's what he's trying to do anyway. If you can make him slow down, maybe we can spin around and get away from him."

The next crashing slam made the Land Cruiser shudder, and like a cue ball, it caromed off the wrecker's bumper and slid rear end first into the ditch. It teetered precariously on the steep bank before rolling over on the driver's side and sliding to the bottom.

Dorel's body whipped back and forth like a crash dummy. The seat belt strap scraped and cut into her neck, but it held her tightly in her seat. Her head struck the side window and she briefly lost consciousness until the sound of the still racing engine woke her.

Groggy, she looked down at Michael slumped over the wheel, unmoving. She was on the high side of the car and felt as if she were going to fall onto him. She clawed at the belt holding her until the sound of someone rattling her door open stopped her.

"Dorel, I'm glad you're okay. Hang on, honey, help's coming. You understand I've got to take care of this first," Abie said with a worried frown and leaned in, reaching across her. He pried the sword bag out from between Dorel's seat and the console.

Abie backed out of the car and let the door fall shut. She heard the wrecker go into gear and rev its engine. The beep-beep back up signal diminished as she heard the gears shift. The roar of the engine lessened as the wrecker pulled away.

She waited, holding her breath, praying that Abie would not return and crush them under the huge wrecker. The odor of gasoline sifted in the window on the dust. She struggled against her belt and glanced frantically at Michael. He raised his head and groaned.

"Michael! I can smell fuel. We've got to get out," she yelled and wrenched open the buckle. She fell against him in a scrambling heap.

"Dammit, Dorel, calm down."

She tried to lift herself off of him. It was like pushing a boulder uphill. She put her knee on the console and reached up for the passenger door handle but it was wrenched out of her hand. She stared face to face with a frightened-looking man in a straw cowboy hat. "Help us."

"I will, lady. Don't move, you might be hurt."

"Get us out. I can smell gasoline." He pulled her out and steadied her beside him on the ditch bank facing the dripping underside of the Land Cruiser. "We've got to get Michael out before it blows."

Michael's head appeared in the doorway an instant later and he climbed out on his own power. His whole body was covered with a thin film of chalky dust and his handsome face was marred with a cut above his left eye and reddish bruises were already blooming on his cheek.

Dorel ran her hands over him, checking for broken bones. "Are you okay?" He had to be all right. Had to be.

Michael put his hands on her shoulders, stopping her. "I slowed down, Dorel." He tried to grin despite his split lip.

"And didn't it work great, just as I said?" she returned lamely and tried to laugh. Fire shot up her neck and she grabbed the side of it, grimacing.

"You got whip lash, lady?" asked her rescuer.

"She's fine," Michael answered brusquely for her. "Did you see the accident?"

"I didn't see anybody," the rescuer said. "I came from the other direction. What happened, anyway?"

Dorel started to speak, but Michael was faster. "I slammed on the brakes to avoid hitting a deer." He jerked his thumb toward the Land Cruiser. "The rearend broke loose and we put it in the ditch. We're fine. Can you pull us out of here?"

"I don't think so," the man said. "I've already called the police on my cell phone. They'll be here soon."

The paramedics arrived first, followed by a fire truck and two City of Kent patrol cars. After refusing a ride to the hospital for either of them, Michael answered the officer's questions and filled out a report, a tow truck hooked onto the Land Cruiser and pulled it over on its wheels then up on the hard shoulder. The entire left side of the vehicle was scraped, crushed in and the glass broken out. Before the tow truck driver loaded the car onto his truck, Michael opened the back and removed the sword case.

"Take it to Auburn Toyota," he told the driver as he and Dorel climbed in the tow truck.

Dorel sat stiffly between the two men. She was beginning to hurt all over, especially her neck and shoulders. Michael slipped his arm around her and gently massaged the back of her neck and shoulder. A warm curl started up her spine. It surprised her how strongly her body responded to his touch.

As they were arranging for a rental car at the Toyota dealer, a jarring and familiar voice said, "Well, well, Captain Gabrielli and Miss Everly. We meet again." Lieutenant Rhett clasped his hands in front of his ample belly and rocked on his feet.

"Lieutenant," Michael acknowledged and took the car key from the clerk with a curt thank you.

Rhett scowled at them. "My goodness, you two look terrible. Let me guess, life continues to be eventful for you."

Dorel kept quiet. She wanted to slap the tall, heartless cop. He was persecuting them, following them. Nothing else explained how he had been able to arrive almost at the scene.

"Just a minor car accident. Slid off the road." Michael stuffed the paperwork into his shirt pocket. He put his hand on Dorel's elbow and propelled her toward the door.

"How'd you manage to get the back bumper crunched?" Rhett followed them to the rental car.

"Got hit in the airport parking lot the other day." Michael unlocked the car door. The three of them stood looking at each other.

Rhett leaned against the rental car. "Did you report it?"

"No, I haven't gotten around to it yet. I've been busy."

Rhett stood up and dusted off the back of his pants. "You sure have. Real busy." He stared at the case in Dorel's hands. "Do you own any swords, Mr. Gabrielli?"

"Yes, several." Michael opened the door. Dorel quickly

slid into the seat, trying to obscure the case beside her body.

"I think I'd like to see them." Rhett walked a few steps away and turned back to them.

"Any time, Lieutenant." Michael closed Dorel's door with a thud. She quickly rolled down the window. "Of course, you'll want to bring along a search warrant," he called.

"That won't be a problem." Rhett threw them a jolly wave and got in his car.

"Is he following us?" Dorel asked as they drove toward home.

Michael checked the mirror. "No." His big hands opened and closed on the rental car's small steering wheel.

"I thought he was coming to see the swords."

"He's just trying to put the pressure on," Michael said.

"He said he would get a warrant."

"Not yet, but he's thinking about it. He's watching us to see what we'll do next, I'm sure." His fist slammed the wheel. "Dammit, this is getting out of hand. Who knows how long before Abie will be haunting our door again, looking for the real sword."

"Maybe he won't." Strangely, she felt as if she'd seen the last of him. "The only ones who have seen the sword are you, me, Granddad, Abie briefly, oh, and Spence. Osterman, too, but anyway, maybe Abie's buyer won't know the difference. How could he? Are there any pictures or drawings of the sword that you know about? Does my grandfather have anything in his research?"

"No, but that doesn't mean there aren't any. We have to go through your grandfather's materials. It's more important than ever. Don't you feel that, Dorel?" He glanced earnestly at her.

"Umm, Granddad didn't keep the sword with him," she continued on her line of thinking. "It was held by a Buddhist monk."

"How about the attorney who wrote his will. Would he have seen it?"

"I don't think so. It was delivered to me in the case, and actually had Granddad's seal on it, across the latch."

"Who delivered it and what sort of seal did it have?" Michael turned onto his road.

"A Buddhist monk, a friend of Granddad's. The fastener was wired closed and wax melted over it. He used an old ring with his initials in gold as a seal."

"Well, maybe we'll have a reprieve then before all hell breaks loose again." Michael sighed and punched the garage door opener laying on the dash.

"What if Rhett does come?" Dorel tried to pet an excited Katana and make her way down the hall to the living room. "Should we hide mine or something?"

"We could," Michael threw the keys on the kitchen counter and opened the refrigerator, "but I don't believe he's going to come out here yet. He hasn't grounds, really."

"Still . . ." Dorel clutched the case and looked appraisingly at the vast bank of custom oak kitchen cabinets marching around the kitchen walls. She wondered if he had an aspirin or anything to stop the pain jabbing the side of her neck.

Michael slammed the refrigerator door with disgust. "No, I'm not going to hide it! I need to have the sword available. Ready." A somber shadow of menace crept over his face, darkening his eyes to a startling shade of blue-black.

Her mouth fell open. "Ready, Michael? For what? Are you planning on cutting something important off Lieutenant Rhett?"

"Knock it off, Dorel," he snarled and headed for his den. The door slammed and she was left alone with two hungry animals swirling around her legs. And the sword.

She deposited the sword case in the closet and, followed

by the dog and cat, went back to the kitchen. Michael may be able to go hours without eating, but she was light-headed. She found the pet food and fed the animals.

Sipping a glass of milk and munching soft, melty chocolate chip cookies, she retreated to the bathroom for a good long, mind and body-numbing soak in the tub.

A red and blue bruise flared above her right temple, matching the one Abie gave her. Both were still tender, but nothing like the long ugly diagonal marks on her neck and collarbone made by the car's restraining belt. She finished her inspection with a light fingering of the pale yellow, diminishing lump on her forehead, and turned away from the cruelly beaten woman in the mirror. Dorel inched into the steaming tub, unkinking little by little and relaxed.

She no sooner relaxed than the bathroom doorknob turned, followed by a knock.

"Dorel?"

She sat up and stared at the door. The cooler air raised goose bumps on her wet skin. "Yes?"

"Are you all right?" The knob turned again.

He couldn't actually be coming in. She grabbed for the shower curtain, pulling it across the tub as the door opened a crack. She peered around the curtain's edge. "Michael, I'm in the tub."

He'd already poked his head in the door. "Oh, sorry. You didn't answer. I thought something had happened to you." Instead of withdrawing, he stared at her as if he could see behind the curtain.

"I'm fine. Really." She was acutely aware of his lingering gaze on her, making her self-consciously aroused.

"If you need anything, just yell," he said.

"The line is just whistle," Dorel said.

He gave her a sexy grin and pulled the door shut. She

quickly finished her bath and dressed in his blue robe again, deciding she was going to have to unpack a few things from her car, underwear, at least. She carried her dirty clothes to the utility room. Throwing her muddy sandals in with her clothes, she started the machine and turned, bumping into Michael's broad wall of chest.

He circled his arms around her, stirred by the jasmine scent of her. Her startled expression stimulated him as if this were their first time. His mouth sought hers. Sensation jolted through him making his breath catch. Was it fear or pleasure he felt from her? Either way, she returned his kiss. She raised her hands to his hair and entwined her fingers behind his head. His tongue plunged into her mouth. He lifted her and ran his hands up the silken skin of her legs. His fingers eased around her hips and cupped her bare buttocks. She gasped as he stepped between her legs, relentlessly pulling her closer. He guided her legs around his waist, crushing her against him and kissing her deeply.

"Oh, Michael," she moaned against his lips.

He snapped his eyes open and jerked out of Dorel's arms. What the hell? he wondered, wiping his shaking hand across his jaw.

Dorel opened her eyes, giving him a passion-hazed look that quickly changed to embarrassed confusion. Clutching the robe over her exposed long legs, she slid off the washer.

"Uh, look, uh." Michael rubbed the back of his neck, feeling abashed heat climb his throat. "I'm sorry. I don't know why it happened." He exhaled and shook his head. "I didn't even know it was you."

Dorel let out a rough, strangled breath, her face stony and

flushed. "Well, that certainly makes this little encounter all the more special."

Michael sat at his desk in the dark. A half a cup of cold sake rested on top of the papers in front of him. He wanted to get very drunk, but he hadn't been able to drink any more than a couple of swallows. And they weren't enough. He still thought about her, could see her mouth swollen from his kisses. She wanted him. He knew that, and it was what he wanted.

It wasn't Dorel I was making love to, he admitted to himself. It was someone else. Another time. Another place. Yet, turned on by some vision most likely from their shared past, he was going to have sex with Dorel right there in the utility room.

He thumped the desk with his fist and jostled the sake. It spilled onto his papers and ran off the desk, dripping into his lap. He didn't care. He'd become an animal, anyway. Why not lay in his swill?

Michael pushed away from the desk, strolled to the patio door, stepped out on the deck to watch the moon rise over Mount Rainier. Dorel would love seeing this.

He shoved his hands in his jeans pockets. But he couldn't face her. He'd behaved like some sort of sex-starved action hero. He knew he was changing, his attitudes, everything, but he hated the changes. They were not for the best. Michael Gabrielli was a good guy. A good, competent, well-respected pilot.

It had been a long time since he'd behaved like a macho icon with cast iron balls. But he was beginning to act and think in a way that was both new and old to him. The heavy philosophical Defender burden was crushing his carefully reconstructed life to dust.

Captain Michael Gabrielli, the good guy, didn't have a chance.

He made his way through the darkened house to the living room and flipped on the TV, then went to the kitchen to make a sandwich. Spreading the evening paper on the burl coffee table, he began to eat, dividing his attention between the TV and the paper.

"Long-time Auburn resident and junkyard owner found dead in his tow truck. Details at eleven," announced the voice-over on the news commercial.

Michael's head jerked up from his paper and he stopped chewing. He punched the volume button on the remote, but the news promo was over. He glanced at his watch. An hour before local news started. Flipping to the Northwest news channel, he leaned forward intently.

"Auburn resident, Abie Prefontaine, sixty-four, owner of Abie's Parting Palace was found dead in the King Dome parking lot earlier this evening, the victim of an apparent robbery," the anchorwoman reported with a practiced concerned expression.

The scene switched to a reporter interviewing someone. She stuck the microphone in his face and moved aside for the camera. Lieutenant Rhett scowled out of the TV at Michael. "Mr. Prefontaine was found dead about eight p.m. this evening. We think he was called to tow someone in and they killed him."

"How, Lieutenant?" the woman asked for the grisly details.

"He was repeatedly slashed with some sort of long knife or sword, but no weapon has been found yet," Rhett said, staring accusingly into the camera. Michael felt as if the policeman was staring straight at him.

"Have you discovered the motive? Or was this just random

gang violence? Perhaps a gang initiation?" the newswoman suggested.

"We can't conjecture about that," Rhett said and excused himself from the interview.

Michael listened, completely absorbed as the woman summed up the crime.

"Again, ordinary citizens are being attacked by random violence. Abie Prefontaine was a respected citizen of the valley. He contributed to many local causes and will be missed by all. This is Brandy Garmen for Northwest News."

Michael clicked off the set. A noise behind him made him turn. Dorel stood in the foyer, her heart-shaped face white and drawn.

"Abie is—dead?" she asked, her voice faltering.

"Yes." He walked to her, wanting to hold and comfort her.

She shrank from him and held up her hands. "Don't touch me." Dorel backed away a few steps then stopped. "Did you kill him, Michael?"

"How could I? I've been right here all evening, you know that."

"I don't know anything about you," she said and disappeared into the darkness of the hall.

Chapter Eight

Katana pushed his wet nose into her hand, and Dorel automatically stroked his wiry terrier fur. They'd been sitting on the deck by themselves since sunrise. For several dark hours during the night, she'd loathed Michael with an intense hate that burned from inside out.

This morning's rising sun brought the realization that her rage was misplaced. Michael had been home with her and couldn't have killed Abie. Before the dawn, it had been easier for her to blame Michael for the latest disaster than to condemn Abie for betraying the joyful memories that he and Aunt Verna had given a lonely little girl without parents.

In the light of day, Dorel could forgive his trying to take her sword and running Michael off the road. She could even forgive Abie's hitting her and trying to drag her away, because now she realized that he was afraid, not only for himself but for her. He had spoken the truth when he told her he'd be killed if he didn't deliver the sword. Had the one he'd given the bogus sword to killed him? Abie had done the best he could with who he was, as far as she could tell, and she wasn't going to judge him any more. That wouldn't do either of them any good.

Dorel intended to forgive and forget, reminding herself she wasn't the type to hold grudges. She had trained herself not to care that much. Granddad taught her it was much smarter to let ego boosters and breakers roll off of your back, to not let yourself be controlled by your emotions or held hostage to satisfying a voracious ego. Only then could you be free, or so he claimed. But Dorel understood last night—

111

Martin Everly was never free. And neither was she.

The sound of cabinet doors banging and cups rattling reached her in her little island of introspection. Dorel lifted her legs off the chair and primly smoothed her shorts over her thighs as far as she could stretch the blue cotton material. She bit back a groan and eased her arms to her sides, cushioning her tender ribs. The wreck hadn't done them any good, not to mention her face and forehead. She looked and felt as though she'd gone three rounds with a WWF crusher.

Michael came outside and greeted her with a shy look and a soft, "Good morning." He pulled out a chair from the table, dragged it a few feet away and turned it toward Mount Rainier. He sat, giving his attention to his coffee and the view. His slicked-back dark hair looked shower damp and his freshly shaved face was smooth even on the rugged angles of his chin. He wore a collarless white shantung shirt, long sleeves rolled to his elbows and tail stuffed neatly in aged Levis and moccasins with no socks.

They sat in silence for what seemed hours until Dorel decided she couldn't say what she needed to or apologize because she'd probably burst into frustrated, sad tears. Rather than embarrass both of them, she stepped over Katana and walked to the door.

"I didn't want to bother you or chase you off." Michael got to his feet. "But I do want you to know that I'm sorry for last night. I was insensitive. You've lost someone important to you and I'm sorry. With that said, I'll leave you alone."

The ashamed, vulnerable look on his face disarmed her, urged her to forgive him, deal with him kindly. Dorel looked from him to Katana, their eyes beseeching her almost identically.

"Forget about it," she said, allowing a small, relieved smile. "I know you didn't . . . it's not your fault. None of this is. It's your deck. Stay and enjoy the view. I was just going to get some coffee. Want a refill?"

"Yeah, thanks." He handed her his cup. "Hurry back, we need to talk."

So he wants *to talk*. Dorel entered the kitchen and poured dark, aromatic drip coffee into mugs with gold Navy pilot's wings on the sides. There was certainly plenty to discuss. Enough topics to fill a two-week seminar on weird and unnatural phenomenon.

She heard the phone ring as she started to step outside. Though he'd told her to let the machine pick up the calls, he hustled inside past her and grabbed the kitchen wall phone. She left him to it and continued to her chair on the deck.

Dorel turned her face up to the hazy morning sun and closed her eyes, then heard him say goodbye. She eased back into the house and caught him composing his expression when he saw her.

"More good news?" she asked, though she really didn't want to know who had called or why Michael looked like he'd just failed his flight physical. What if she were to pretend everything was lovely? Beautiful and dandy like Granddad used to say. As if her life weren't falling to pieces with every ring of the phone or dark look from Michael.

"Someone broke into Spence's shop last night."

Dorel went directly to the refrigerator and opened the door, even though she had no appetite. "And?"

"They tore his store apart. He doesn't think anything was taken. They drove through the door. The place is as good as totaled. Pretty bold."

Dorel stared silently into the chilled light of the full refrigerator. What was she supposed to say now? So many tragic things had happened to them in the last few days, that a mere break-in had the emotional impact of a bowl of days-old lemon gelatin.

"Dorel?"

We should go now, she resolved and started pulling things out of the refrigerator. She needed to find something to pack the food in. Did he have ice chests? Back packs? The escape plans whirling in her head were of the irrational, reactionary kind, but she was doing something. She would get them the hell out of here, or else.

Michael gently turned her around to meet his troubled gaze. "I understand how you feel." When she stiffened under his touch, he dropped his hands from her shoulders. "Try not to be afraid. I can handle this."

If only she had his confidence, however unrealistically testosterone-enhanced. "You keep saying that and things keep getting worse. It's like we're an electro-magnet with the power switched on, drawing all sorts of incredible evil to us. Do you really think that's *handling* it?"

"We're not dead," he said.

"Not yet. Is this macho denial a pilot thing?"

"I'm not denying anything. What I should have said was I'm not giving up without a fight." He began shoving the food she'd piled on the counter back into the refrigerator. "Look, we need to get organized. Plan. Find out what's in the case lining, and you should go through the journal."

"For what?" She stood immobile, watching him cancel their escape with each item he put back. What, of value, could Granddad's personal guilt-filled ramblings tell them?

"I've told you before, it's absolutely imperative that we learn as much as possible about how to use the sword. What to expect as we fulfill our roles."

"Oh, hell. Don't start that again. You can get yourself a red cape and tights if you want to, and play superhero whirling my sword over your head. But I'm only interested in getting rid of it." She cocked her hand on her hip. "I'm not 'going without a fight' either, Michael. Except I'm fighting to be free of the sword, not trapped and used by it. I've never been into bondage of any sort, and to me, this whole Guardian-Defender thing is nothing but the worst form of slavery."

"You're wrong. It's a sacred obligation. We're chosen to—"

"Eternally fight evil? Has it occurred to you that *we* didn't win? Can't win? All we do is fight?" She exhaled a tiny, shaky breath. "And die."

"Everyone dies." Michael's blue eyes glittered as he stared beyond her.

"Well, I don't want to!" she countered. "I am really tired of all this dying that's been going on. I mean, sure, someday when I'm too old to separate an Oreo or when I actually consider a toothpick a necessary dental appliance, I might be ready to go in my sleep."

"I'm amazed how you can seem to be so frightened and still have the energy left to be such a smart ass."

"No problem. It's a talent I've cultivated over the years."

"You're an intelligent woman. Why spend all this effort trying to disprove what we both know to be true?"

She put her two fingers over his lips. "No, don't say it," she said, hopelessness seeping into her voice. "Every time we do, it makes it more real."

He held her hand to his lips a moment, then brushed her fingertips with a kiss and gently pushed her hand back to her heart. "It is real. I intend to learn everything I can about the sword. If you'll think clearly for a moment, you'll realize that is what you should do as well. Martin intended you to have the sword and to learn about it. You don't have to face this alone." He stared intently at her. "You have me. We're in this together. Always."

Perhaps that was the most frightening thing of all—being *together* with him. She'd never felt that she needed anyone except for her parents, then her grandfather. Yet, there was always a void, like a piece of her missing, waiting to be fulfilled or added.

Dorel scrutinized the earnest, tremendously handsome and self-possessed man demanding her partnership. Was he the missing half of her being?

Later that morning, Dorel set the black sword case on the old library table in Michael's den and opened the lid. An odd thrill jingled through her as she observed the sheathed sword reposing on the white silk. Beautiful. Deadly.

Michael immediately appeared at her side. He gave her a cursory acknowledging glance, lifted the sword out of the case and reverently laid it on the antique table's worn mahogany top.

Dorel waited while his long, strong fingers inched along the edges of the case's lining, searching for an opening. "You might have to pull it loose," she suggested, her curiosity mounting and patience waning.

He grasped the fabric between two fingers and gave a trial tug. When the lining did not separate from the side of the case, he reached into the front pocket of his jeans and produced a Swiss army knife. Selecting a short blade, he eased the tip along the inside bottom of the case. The slick material parted under the knife. Pulling the fabric back, he reached his hand under to explore the insides.

Michael shook his head and tried the top of the case. This time he was rewarded with a yellowed envelope glued to the fiberboard. He gently inched it off, careful not to tear the fragile paper. Dorel held out her hand for the envelope, but Michael slipped the blade under the flap before handing the opened envelope to her.

She unfolded two legal size pages. Granddad's writing filled both sheets, front and back. The title read: "Partial List of Ownership of the Tsuji Sword." At the top of the list was hand-printed in blue ink, "Baron Fusao Tsuji, Born April 4, 1912—Died August 16, 1945", and a line drawn across to "Baroness Michiko Tsuji, Born July 16, 1917—Died August 16, 1945."

"She was only twenty-eight when she died," Dorel whispered. My age! "How old are you, Michael?"

"Thirty-three," he said, his tone shaded with recognition.

Eight sets of couples, all apparently married or sharing the same surname, scrolled down the pages. Some names were annotated with brief histories of class and family. None had children. All died young, and, apparently, the Tsujis on the same day. The other dates showed only that the remaining couples died within the same year.

Michael reached for the papers and she handed them over willingly.

"Are all those names Japanese?" she questioned, reading with him.

"Japanese, yes, but there are Chinese, Korean and," he turned the last page over, "Turkish, I believe. And there's also one Danish couple."

"How could that be? The sword is Japanese, isn't it?" She pulled out a mahogany side chair with Oriental-looking geometric scrolling carved on the straight back and legs, and sat at the table, her chin on her palm. The names on the sheet intrigued her because they seemed almost like a memory, or maybe it was just that she'd seen or heard names like those before. In any case, now she wanted to know more about them.

"The sword isn't Japanese. I could tell that much the first time I had a good look at it at the gun show. It has the characteristics of a samurai sword, but it isn't. It's more." Michael smiled uncertainly. "I haven't been able to decipher the markings, but I feel really close. I know we'll find their meaning here." He tapped the stack of her granddad's books. "Let's get to work."

He pulled several of her grandfather's books off the bookcase and spread them across the table. "We have to thoroughly study the list and search the journal for additional information."

"What sort of information?" She smoothed the loose papers in front of her that had fallen out of a binder.

"Anything that will tell us the origin and age of the sword and the extent of its power. How was it used? How does it come to the next person? How are they selected? Well, they must be the next incarnation, of course. But how did Baroness Tsuji know to give it to your grandfather?" He ran his fingers through his hair, his demeanor radiating excitement.

"If we can't find that in these," Michael said, pointing to the books with a sweep of his hand, "at least we should find some person or place I can target to establish a chain of custody to the origin of the sword."

Dorel smiled, hoping he was inspired by the history of the sword instead of its power. This side of Michael was very appealing. His enthusiasm and intelligence inspired her trust and affection. She could almost forget the other part of him that seemed to be growing stronger each time he held the sword; the dark, violent soul that both aroused and repelled her. She straightened her spine and reeled in her drifting thoughts. It didn't pay to think too much these days. Maybe she could just lose herself to the work, too.

Michael gave her a happy look. "Since I haven't had a chance to teach you the protocols, I could remote view the past and tell you the information I obtain, but researching together gives us both the opportunity to learn about ourselves at the same time."

"Oh, the reincarnation thing, again. No pun intended." She slumped in her chair and frowned.

"Reincarnation is a reality not a belief, but an experience, Dorel. And if you'll listen to your inner self, you'll admit what I say is true."

"So is that what I've—what we've been hearing? My inner self talking?"

He paused for a moment. "I hadn't considered that. Maybe the voice or the thought is emanating from our higher *selves,* a collective of our past lives surfacing in our consciousness." His eyes took on a detached yet inward viewing cast. "Maybe."

"You certainly get carried away. I say the first thing that comes to me and that sets you off on some sort of new age philosophical tangent," Dorel said.

"I thought you were agreeing with me about reincarnation." He looked affronted.

"No. Well, yes. Maybe. But I treat my current belief system a little more gently than you do. I don't want to just kick it in the teeth and charge away on a quest every time I have a doubt or something else seems plausible to me. Unlike you, I have to think about the problem for at least a minute or two. You're in such a rush to believe this whole ugly business and get involved. I can't do that. Accept without proof."

"I didn't ask to get involved. It sought me out."

"Be honest, Michael. Why don't you just say, *it was destined?*"

"Because I'm not sure. Is that honest enough for you?" He thumped his chest with his fist. "I can't help that I feel in my heart we are destined. Hell, we're the Guardian and the Defender reincarnated! But my logical brain, that organ I've always deferred to in every situation, shouts a resounding NO. Or at least it started that way. Now it's a mere whimper, a quiet little hint that I should at least do what I've been trained to do; gather information, organize it and then make my decisions based on process."

She breathed easier. "So, you still aren't sure. You still feel you have a decision to make whether you are the Defender or not? I'm glad, Michael, that makes me feel a whole lot better to know that you're still thinking, because sometimes, well, sometimes you seem so certain."

"Sometimes I am certain," he replied with a shrug. "I feel strong. Invincible. Destined to fight as though I've always liked the actual combat of martial arts, instead of being satisfied to perfect my *kata,* or form. That's why I couldn't understand when I enjoyed fighting with the sword and actually killed a man with it. That went against everything I've come to believe in. Reincarnation as the Defender, with all those lifetimes as a warrior culminating in me now, bleeding through to this reality, is the only acceptable explanation." Sometimes I just don't know who I am, he admitted silently.

A small tremor vibrated in his hand as he passed it over his distressed expression. "I do know that I feel at one with the sword, and actually like using it. There's a warmth, an energy in the sword that welcomes me, calling me. It's like coming home."

"Well, it's not like that for me. The sword isn't warm, homey fun. It fascinates me, but not in a good way. I wish I'd refused it, then I wouldn't have taken it to the gun show and got all this started."

The corner of his mouth pulled down in a half-hearted frown. "As if you could help it," he murmured then leaned forward. "Tell me, is your life always like this or is this chaos new for you? We really don't know very much about each other to be living together."

Suddenly uncomfortable, Dorel hesitated to speak and traced her finger over the embossed gold letters on the oriental armor book beside her. "A few months ago I thought my life couldn't get much worse. But I was wrong. My grandfather died. He'd gone through all his money and mine in his long battle with cancer. Then we finally had to let the VA take over because the HMO booted us out and wouldn't pay for what they said was experimental treatment. We couldn't pay for it either, so I had to sell his prized collection of oriental memorabilia and everything else to pay the medical expenses. He never told me not to sell his belongings after he died. But as I told you before, we didn't talk about things like that. It was easier on both of us to pretend that he was going to get better instead."

She held up her hand at his concerned expression. "That's over, so let's forget about it. I was just telling you all that in a sort of explanation of how I became the desperate though jolly woman you have so kindly taken in."

Michael leaned back and crossed his ankle over his knee. "You said before you had no other family. How about friends?" He raised his eyebrow in a sly, sexy smile. "Lovers?"

"No. No, and none of your business," she said. "I better go get the journal."

When she returned, Michael was checking the names on the paper against a book. Dorel sat down across from him and glanced at the title, "Ancient Houses of Indochina."

"What about you?" she asked and opened Granddad's journal. "Any family? You mentioned a mother, I remember."

"Hmm?" He didn't look up, but printed precise block letters on a yellow legal pad. "Mom lives in Port Townsend. She runs a bed and breakfast."

She waited expectantly. "And Dad?" she asked finally when he didn't respond.

"I'm the very successful product of a single parent household," Michael said, still absorbed tracing his finger along the lines in the book and printing on the pad.

"Siblings?" She felt like a census taker, dragging information out of the suddenly taciturn pilot.

"None."

"Friends?"

"Legion."

"Lovers?"

"Ditto." He didn't look up, but she thought she detected a tiny smirk.

"I'll just bet you've had a constant procession of women through here," she agreed, and then turned her attention to the journal. Since she hadn't seen any evidence of a live-in in this oriental anteroom of the Smithsonian he called a home, he must conduct his liaisons at their places. She glanced at him, trying to imagine him with a woman in his arms, let alone his house.

Dorel saw herself.

Her breath quickened and she shivered. Snapping the book closed, she headed for the door. "I'm going to take Katana for a walk, okay?"

He barely nodded, his attention glued to the page. "Take Benten, too. She likes walks. Her lead is hanging in the utility room with Katana's." He looked up as she turned away. "Do you need to take the sword?"

"I don't think so. Why?" she asked, determined to leave it behind and be free for a little while.

"No reason." Michael mumbled.

The cat did not like to *walk*. She fought Dorel, planting her four feet like tire chocks and pulled back. Dorel could do nothing but tow her along like a gray dust mop over the garden trail as Katana towed her. They paraded at a snappy pace to the path that took them further and further into the woods.

Well, okay so far. Dorel picked up the filthy, very miffed cat. In minutes they reached the boundary fence and paralleled it for a few yards. Dorel pulled Katana to a stop, set the squirming cat down and leaned against a cedar fence post to catch her breath.

A jolt shot through her as if the barbed wire fence were electrified. Jerking away, she felt a weird urge to return to the house, and to the sword, as if she were on a long, tight lead herself.

The sword. She could almost feel it calling her. She rubbed her neck, accidentally brushing the scrape from the seat belt and cringed. In experiment, she touched the fence again and snapped her hand away at the uncomfortable response jangling through her body.

Do not surrender to the power. You can escape. Be stronger. Resist.

Her grandfather's words whirled in her mind. Yes! There had to be a way to elude the sword, and Michael. There had to be a way, she vowed, grabbing up Benten from where the cat wound around her ankles and rushed back to the house, this time towing Katana. Even if she had to read everything Granddad ever wrote or read himself to find the answer, she would gain her freedom.

Hours later, Dorel looked up from the journal and stretched her arms over her head, yawning. Michael was busy tapping away on the computer. "Cross checking data bases," he'd said. With his dangerous attractiveness, he looked every bit the hotshot pilot. And he didn't look like her jailer either.

She shook that thought off. Michael wasn't holding her here. The sword was. The journal made that much clear.

According to Granddad, from the time the sword was given to him and he smuggled it out of China, he'd felt the influence of the sword's *personality,* as he'd called it and written,

> *"It isn't that it speaks to me, but I feel something. A presence. A need to know about it. A driving compulsion. Not once did I ever think to sell the sword or give it to a museum, even though I knew it to be extremely old and valuable. I saved it for you. I wasn't married when Baroness Tsuji told me to save it for my granddaughter, yet I accepted her words with little doubt. I see now that I should have dropped it into the deepest part of the Pacific, but I know I couldn't. You placed your sword with me for safekeeping knowing that I would be your grandfather, while hoping that somehow the Trust would not continue, that you could rest and not return as the Guardian.*
>
> *Search your consciousness, Dorel. You can find the memories. They've been hidden from you as they are in each incarnation. What can you remember to help yourself break with the Trust that you and he are eternally bound to by the sword?"*

"Reading anything interesting?" Michael's voice pushed her grandfather's silent words from her mind.

"Well . . ." She hesitated, wondering how much she should tell him. "Granddad believes I am the reincarnation of Baroness Tsuji, the woman who gave him the sword." She felt silly even repeating such a notion.

"And?" He looked as though she had just told him what he knew already.

"And . . . that's it. Except he says for me to try to remember knowledge that will help me break an eternal trust of some sort that you and I are supposedly tied up in, with the sword, of course."

"Is there anything yet on the power of the sword? Or more on these names?" He held up one of the yellow sheets from the case lining. "In case you're wondering, I didn't study the journal, Dorel. I never found the time or desire for some reason."

"Ah. I haven't found anything about a supposed power yet, other than he writes that the sword speaks to him and brings us together." She leaned her chin on her laced fingers and blinked innocently. "If I'm supposed to be Baroness Tsuji, then are you the Baron?"

"Yes."

"Is that all you have to say, just yes? Don't you have any thoughts on such a ridiculous idea? Or have you *remembered* our other life together."

"Lives."

She groaned. "Okay. Lives."

"Think, Dorel. I've noticed that you sometimes rub the left side of your abdomen. Does it hurt you?"

She was absently rubbing her left side at that moment. Yes, she had twinges from time to time, a tenderness since childhood that she'd attributed to an occasionally nervous stomach. "Sometimes. What's that got to do with anything?"

"Martin noted here, I think it was his diary during the War, that Baroness Tsuji was mortally wounded on the left side. She'd been stabbed."

"Yes, so?"

"There's an unconventional but very effective alternative therapy for treating patients who complain of paralyzing fears or various physical symptoms. The patient is then regressed hypnotically to past lives when the accident, injury or emotional traumas occurred. When the patient deals with those, releases the negative energy, he's better able to work through his problems in this life and maybe even finds his symptoms and fears disappear. The injury or hurt is left in the past and no longer troubles him in the present."

"You're saying that my hurting stomach is a result of the wound that killed the Baroness, right?" She couldn't believe he actually meant that.

"Possibly, unless you can account for it in your present life." He watched for her response. "Can you?"

Michael's words echoed strangely in her mind and Dorel kept silent as her thoughts began to drift. Her vision blurred and breathing became difficult. She was going to faint.

Suddenly, she was running with crushing pain. Stay on your feet, she told herself. Pressing her jacket into the wound to staunch the flow of blood, she gasped at the incredible burning torture. One foot in front of the other, she pushed through the crowd toward the temple. He had to be there, had to be. The thought drove her forward through the shards of broken tiles that cut her feet through the thin leather slippers as she stumbled across the courtyard. Blackness edged into her field of vision, drawing closer.

She beheld his face and knew she had seen him many times before and would see him again, too soon. She must give the sword to him before it was too late. No, save it for her. She must give it to the Defender.

She was suddenly released, floating easily, feeling an incredible freedom she had never felt in this life. And she never wanted to return to life, to the agony of Earth again.

"Dorel?" Michael's voice drew her back, focused her thoughts.

Dorel covered her mouth with her hands and shook her

head to dispel the odd and painful daydream, dismissing it to her facile imagination. All through childhood and beyond she'd told herself stories, casting herself as a conquering heroine. This daydream felt somewhat the same, but also like some of the nightmares that haunted her. She'd once thought of trying to find out what they meant, but for some unknown reason always kept from doing so.

Maybe she just didn't want to know.

"Dorel?" Michael repeated and gave her a questioning frown. "Where'd you go?"

"Oh, nowhere. I'm just tired, I guess. Almost asleep on my feet."

After giving her a studying look, Michael turned back to his keyboard.

Should she tell him what she'd just experienced? Apparently, he hadn't seen it with her this time. Why was she now seeing visions that he wasn't? Best not to tell him anything, she thought. He might encourage me to do it again and I'd have to remember more terrible pain and desperation.

Remember? she questioned herself. Remember implied that the memories were one's own. She absolutely refused them as hers.

Dorel glanced out the window to the lengthening shadows in the garden. Late afternoon already and she hadn't even put a dent in reading the journal. She wished for something distracting, interesting instead of frightening. She thought about watching TV, but knew Michael would disapprove. He was working hard and the feeling radiated from him that she should be, too.

"Interesting," he grunted, gazing at the monitor's screen.

"What?"

"The list of families. There's one here we've heard before."

"Oh? Which?" She got up and moved to stand beside him at the computer.

"Inada." Michael checked the yellow tablet page. "Yes, it's the same one. The Inada family traces back to the twelfth century. Feudal lord. Shogun. The sword was with the Inada family before the Tsuji family."

"How can you tell? The name looks different to me." She leaned over the desk, her side brushing his shoulder, sending a curious zing through her. "Sorry," she murmured.

"No problem." But his twinkling eyes said otherwise. "They're the same, the spelling varies through the years and with the translators, but it is Inada."

"Where have we heard that name?" Dorel absently rubbed her side with her right hand.

"In Abie's office. He was going to sell it to him, remember?"

"How can you remember that?"

"I remember everything."

The phone rang. Automatically, Michael reached over and picked it up.

"Hello?" He rolled his eyes, the look one implying he wished he hadn't answered the phone. "Yes, this is Michael Gabrielli." He waited a moment then punched the button turning on the speaker and laid the receiver down.

". . . Hiroshi Inada. I am a collector of oriental antiquities." The deep, accented voice paused, waiting. "Mr. Gabrielli?"

"Yes?" Michael finally answered.

Dorel stared at the phone. Her breath turned cold in her throat.

"It has come to my attention that you are in possession of a certain piece of oriental armor. A sword of unique manufacture and history."

"You are mistaken. While it is true that I have a small collection, I don't have any of oriental manufacture." Michael did not raise his eyes from the phone.

"I wish to purchase the piece, Mr. Gabrielli. I am prepared to offer a very satisfactory price."

"Mr. Inada, I told you I have nothing for sale."

Dorel's gaze darted toward Michael. His frown deepened, casting a dark shadow in his eyes and she could see his jaw twitch as he gritted his teeth. "How does he know?" she mouthed silently to him.

Michael raised his hand, impatiently waving her aside.

"I offer five hundred thousand U.S. dollars," the nonplussed voice continued.

Now Dorel remembered. Abie had mentioned that same amount when he was talking on the phone. Had he been trying to sell her sword to this Inada? How did this man know to call Michael?

"You're wasting your time," Michael countered.

"Gabrielli," Inada interrupted sharply, threat edging his smooth voice. "You do not waste *my* time! I have given you a correct offer. Do not make the mistake of the woman's uncle."

A sliver of icy apprehension sliced through Dorel's stomach. She wrapped her arms around herself and raked her teeth over her top lip. Michael's expression hardened and his gunmetal blue eyes flashed. "What?

"What *mistake* would that be, Mr. Inada?"

Inada chuckled. "He knew what I desired and attempted to trick me with a counterfeit. You will not be so unwise."

"I have nothing for you." Michael's whole demeanor seemed to be transforming like the time he'd swung her sword and killed.

"So be it, Mr. Gabrielli. I shall have my sword. It is rightfully mine, as you know. The sword should have come to me as the heir. From *my* family. My heritage."

"It is not for you," growled Michael.

"Ah, I see," dripped the voice through the speaker. "She has given it to you. Unfortunate. It is for me. The Trust is mine. Not yours. She will give it to me."

"Goodbye, Mr. Inada." Michael punched the speaker's button, disconnecting the line.

"Oh, Michael," breathed Dorel, clasping her shaking hands.

He purposefully rose to his feet. "Where is it?"

"What? You mean the sword? It's safe. It's in the closet."

"Bring it to me. Now."

"Michael, I don't—"

"Now!" he demanded, every muscle of his body appearing ready to force her to do his bidding.

She whirled and hurried down the hall to her room. Inside, she slammed the door and leaned against the hard wood. What if she ran right now? Just take it and go? That would be the only way I can leave, she thought rationally.

And he would follow.

That realization made Dorel draw the sword case out of the closet and carry her burden down the hall.

When she stepped into foyer, she caught a glimpse of Michael standing beyond the windows on the deck outside. His shirt and shoes were gone. Bare-chested, he faced her, waiting with his arms extended.

She crossed the living room, slid the door open and walked out to face him. As if by long experience, she slipped the scabbard partially off the blade, gripping it horizontally in her left hand. Her right hand held the handle next to the hilt. She presented the sword to him resting on the scabbard. He accepted and acknowledged the bestowal with a short nod and stepped back.

Turning sideways with a deliberate swing of the sword, Michael began a sensuous dance. Man and sword performed together, serving each other in perfect harmony. They moved as one, oblivious of everything, one an extension of the other. The muscles of his bare arms and chest rippled as he swept the sword repeatedly in an intricate pattern of thrusts, arcs and parries. The setting sun glinted off the blade, throwing flashes of blue-white light around the deck.

Dorel stood transfixed, the rational part of her crying for Michael to stop while another part submitted to the inevitable.

Tears filled her eyes as she realized the sword was winning. Again.

Chapter Nine

Hungry for dinner and refreshed from his shower, Michael pulled on a pair of old, soft jersey running shorts and hurried down the hall toward the kitchen. The prospect of spending some time with Dorel quickened his step. He found her sitting at the counter, the aroma of coffee wafting in the air from the cup she held.

As if he were split in two, his consciousness moved aside as another asserted itself.

He frowned and halted, appraising her. Why hadn't the woman greeted him properly? Had she not prepared the evening meal?

A sharp pain struck between his eyes and Michael rubbed his forehead. What was he thinking? Dorel wasn't the housekeeper or a cook. As the headache diminished, a thought tumbled into his mind—what was she, then? A guest?

For how long?

Those were questions he realized he should be asking or at least thinking about, but it was becoming more and more acceptable to him that she belonged here in his home, at his side.

He stepped onto the cool tile floor of the kitchen with his bare feet, the sensation recalling the liquid-smooth feel of her skin. "Hi."

Dorel jumped like she'd just had an engine cut on rotate. He even thought he caught a suspicious look on her face before she composed herself, and remembered Inada's phone call. She was probably upset about that. "I bet you think I'm trying to starve you, huh?" he asked, trying to get her to smile.

"If I were hungry, I'd eat." She pulled nervously at the legs of her shorts as if trying to stretch them further over her slim thighs. The yellowing bruises and small cut on her face did not diminish her strong good looks. If anything, her unique and appealing features were softened with a cast of attractive vulnerability. His belly hardened as his gaze slid over her body. She was taller than he usually chose, and he didn't prefer redheads, but her exceptional combination of contradictions intrigued him.

"Maybe we could go . . ." He paused. When she didn't acknowledge him, he continued, "Go out. But then it's probably best to stay home, given the recent developments. Right?"

"Oh, I'd say so. What are we going to do? Inada sounded as if he's coming to get the sword."

"Let him." Michael opened the refrigerator door and inventoried the few contents. "How about some dinner?" He wondered what would please her.

"I'm not hungry."

He chose to ignore her tone brimming with irritation. "Oh, sure you are." Michael pulled out a package of chicken breasts and turned to her, trying a disarming grin. "You can't say no."

"Oh, really?" She set her cup down on the countertop with a thud. Her expression was cool and her green eyes glittered warily.

"Ah," he breathed, his gaze centered on her as she crossed her arms below her breasts, molding the T-shirt across them. The sight was exquisite torture to his barely controlled libido, and she didn't even know what she was doing to him. "You're upset because of the phone call, right?"

"Not entirely." She slammed her hand down, bumping the cup and sloshing coffee across the counter. "Why are you ignoring the obvious? We're in danger here. Big time. And you go into some sort of bizarre dance recital with my sword, and won't even try to come up with a viable plan."

"What do you mean *dance recital?* Are you talking about when I practiced my *kata?* I didn't know you were into spying on me," he joked and gave her a wolfish grin.

She grabbed a dishcloth and angrily mopped up the spill. "If you're finished screwing around, tell me what we're going to do. If you can hold it together long enough and not go off to Sword La La land."

A dark lethal seriousness returned, taking hold of him, raising his defenses. What was the matter with her? Couldn't she see? Why didn't she understand her role? He would not suffer an attack from anyone.

"Careful," he warned, pinning her with his stare. His knuckles whitened as he gripped the edge of the counter.

"Or what, Michael? Just what?" She arched the dirty dishcloth into the sink. As it whisked by his head, he jerked to attention, his somber, humorless mood falling away. "You sound as if you're threatening me. Why? Because I asked a question?"

Why does she think I'm threatening her, Michael wondered, confused. "What question? When did I threaten you? If I did, I'm sorry. That isn't what I intended."

"What's happening to you? You warned me to be careful of you. Don't worry, I am. I'm used to taking care of myself. I'm an engineer. If anything, I'm results oriented. And I don't like the results of our partnership so far. I don't have any intention of depending on you and then having you go weird on me. It makes me wonder who the enemy really is."

Michael kept his voice calm and reasonable, hoping it would have that effect on her. "We know who the enemy is."

"Oh really? Apparently, you don't. It's the sword. It's

brought nothing but trouble so far, and I'm going to get very ungrateful and include you in that. Why don't you just admit it? All you want is the sword for your collection. And you just can't figure out how to get rid of me." She jammed her hands on her curvaceous hips, her chest heaving.

"I thought you were realizing the power, the history. And our roles. We can't do otherwise. We have never been able to. We're part of the Trust." Despite his efforts, his patience was about to expire.

"No. I think it's just an excuse so that you can vent your fantasies of being a superhero samurai." She crossed her arms defensively and leaned against the counter. "You dance around half-naked, waving the sword. It's ridiculous, Michael. No, it's weird, creepy."

"What are you talking about?" A scowl formed as his eyes narrowed. He tried to associate her words with an evanescent memory that evaded him.

"Your little performance on the deck an hour ago, as you well know."

He couldn't remember being on the deck, except for this morning. It was as if there was a black hole of time between the phone call from Inada and taking a shower. "I don't remember."

"Oh, please, Michael," she huffed a disgusted laugh. "Stop it. You indulge your proclivities and then do the *I don't remember* thing. It's revolting."

Dorel stood and pulled her chin up. "We haven't talked about Abie. He was apparently a rotten son of a bitch, but he was the only uncle I ever knew. And he was kind to me, and to Granddad. I'm just putting what he did, and didn't do, behind me. I've got to see Verna. She must be paralyzed with grief and won't know why I left or why I haven't come to see her. She'll need my help with the funeral arrangements," she said, her tone matching the desperation on her face.

She's afraid of me, Michael realized with shock. So much so that she wanted to run away from him. But he couldn't let her go. They could not be separated. Not now. Not ever. It was his duty to protect her. He wanted to keep her safe, not harm her. Why didn't she understand this simple thing?

"I'm going to go get my stuff and load the car," Dorel said. "I'll be staying with her."

He stared intently at her as if eye contact alone could make her understand. "It won't work. You know that." Her incredible stubbornness was beginning to irritate him, but he had to be patient with her fear, help her stop this self-destructive fighting with herself, and the truth. It wasn't good for either of them and only helped those who were coming after them.

"You demanded the sword for your little performance and I gave it to you. And now I leave you all my troubles that go with it."

He rested his hands lightly on her shoulders. "Don't be afraid. We're meant to do this together. Always. It's our destiny."

"No!" She backed out of his arms, waving her own wildly. "I don't want to ever hear that word again. Especially not from you. I'm leaving now."

Damn! He forced himself away from her and turned back to the chicken, occupying his hands with balling up the package's plastic wrap. To argue would not solve the problem.

"Go for it, then. See you when you get back." Evidently, she had to learn the hard way.

"I'm not coming back." She marched down the hall, only to return a moment later with her purse and a tote bag of clothing. "The sword is in the case in the closet. I've left Sam on the plant stand in the bedroom and kept my granddad's journal in exchange for the sword."

"Fine." Since she was bent on leaving, he had to let her try, but there would be no exchange and no escape. She would not leave him. The sword and the Trust wouldn't allow it.

It was starting to rain when Dorel semi-trotted outside to her Cherokee parked beside the garage, threw her things inside and climbed in. As she drove down the gravel lane toward the main road, she felt a small unpleasant sensation accompanied by a tiny ringing in her ears. Her feet were tender on the gas pedal and brake, and her left side began to burn. The closer she drove to the road, the louder the static-like noise became until she stopped the car and got out. She looked under the car, then walked completely around it, searching for the source of the din.

The cacophony increased to a roaring in her head. She clapped her hands over her ears and stumbled blindly toward the two lane black top road some twenty feet beyond the gateless posts in front of her. Sharp needle-like pain in her feet hurt so badly, she had to stop again.

The broken tiles, they're cutting my feet.

If she could just reach the temple, all would be well. She had to give it to him. Gun fire and mortar shells exploded all around her. She leaned into her wound and pushed on across the courtyard. And fainted on the temple steps.

"Dorel? Are you all right?" The beloved familiar voice caressed her.

"My lord, Fusao." She tried to smile for him. He must not see her pain; it would hurt him so. Anger him, then he would go meet them again. He could not. He had to rest; he was already so very weak. He thought he could recover. But she knew he would not. "I am fine, husband. It is you who

must be cared for." She caressed his troubled, pale face; incredible timeless love pouring through her fingertips, willing him to mend.

He picked her up and carried her. He should not. She felt so grateful to be off her feet, and at the same time worried at the burden she presented him. It was not to be so. She was the Guardian and must care for him.

"Dorel?" his gentle voice beseeched again, leaden with concern.

She caught his cool hand as he lay it aside her hot cheek, and opened her eyes. His was a different face, but her husband looked out through his strange, round blue eyes, and his touch was the same. "Fusao?" she asked.

He pressed her hand to his face and kissed her fingertips. "Please, don't try to leave me again. I'm afraid of what will happen to you." Michael felt defenseless to help her. The misery marking her lovely, fragile face wounded him. He squeezed his eyes closed against the painful sensation, pressing her hand to his lips. He reeled from the impact of her flesh on his. As if they shared the same skin, the same life, his being flowed with hers, mingling in love and loss.

"Here, beloved. I am here with you. You see, we are together still." He kissed his wife's slender hand, his own pain obscured in the joy of reunion. "Come, there is little time before we are parted, again. Do not leave me until the time, my dearest. I cannot bear it. Nor can you. We must give loving encouragement to each other. For the difficult times. Have courage, for our love never dies, but grows stronger each time. Perhaps the struggle with evil will be won."

Dorel strove to reconcile both voice and the face hovering above and within her with the other that seemed so familiar, so real. "Michael? Oh my God, Michael, is it you?

What happened?" she cried.

His glazed blue-colored eyes lightened and blinked as his tender expression transformed to anxiety. He held her face gently between his palms. "I went to look for you. Found you lying beside your car unconscious and carried you back to the house."

"The noise. My feet." She bolted upright. "It was so real I actually felt it."

"You called me Fusao." Soft wonder filled his voice.

"It was a vision of you. I mean of him and her. I just disappeared." She clutched at his shirt. "Dorel Everly was gone. I felt everything the Baroness did as if I were her. It was so sad. Horrible."

Empathy seemed to fill Michael's gaze. He stroked her cheek. "I know," he said, his voice hushed.

"You couldn't." She drew away, uneasy at his words.

"I experienced the vision as well, but from Fusao's perspective. It was different from how I have been sensing the Defender. All his power was consumed by a deep melancholy that I still feel." A frown formed between his dark brows.

"She loved him." Dorel looked into Michael's solemn eyes. As clearly as she had seen Fusao, she now saw Michael.

"He loves her. He has hope for their future." Michael's lips were so close to hers, his warm moist breath mingled with hers.

To her astonishment, Dorel realized that Michael was as trapped as she, but he was more than accepting. He was willing, and he would destroy them both by his lust for the sword. As he always had.

Dorel gripped his hand. "How could the Baron have had hope for their future? They died horribly. They were driven by the sword. Used by it. And they died because of it. Michael, let's not allow that to happen to us. Let's give up the sword."

He leapt up, all his former gentleness and concern spent as he towered over her. "No!"

"It's the only way," she pleaded. "Then we are both free if we get rid of the sword. I believe it's controlling us, just as you said. Like my grandfather warned. I dream about the sword and the past, day and night. And about people I don't even know who are certainly dead. Let's sell it to Inada. At least we'd profit from all these problems. You may not need the money, but I certainly do. And five hundred thousand would—"

"No," he broke in, his voice steel-tough. "We won't sell it to Inada. It's ours. Our duty. You must understand that we cannot escape our duty." He placed his hand firmly on her shoulder, his embittered expression dimming. "Trust me. Trust what we have to do. What we've always done. You're not dreaming about people you don't know. You're experiencing spontaneous out of body travel to the past."

"Whose past?" she dared to ask, not sure she wanted to learn. His strong touch sent a wave of dazzling warmth through her. If she could just focus on that sensation and let it carry her away.

"Ours."

Instantly the word became reality. And she knew the truth. Before her eyes countless incarnations from the past merged into a confluence becoming herself and Michael at this moment. But they shimmered and dematerialized as two entities seemed to conceal their being.

The Defender and the Guardian.

Dorel identified the Guardian's timeless, unchanging essence as her own, an essence that had always been subordinate to the Defender with the sword.

She groaned and covered her eyes. "This has got to stop."

"You see who you have been. Who you are now. There's no reason to be afraid. You have me. I've proven I can take care of you. Time and again. Don't doubt me."

"You've gotten us killed time and again. Nor do I want to be *taken care of*. Especially this kind of care I can do without." I don't want you to be my master, my jailer or my Defender, she vowed silently.

Michael stared at her, his eyebrow lifting appraisingly. "I'm trying to do as I think best and still give you the freedom you need."

"You don't *give* me freedom. Because you have none to give. We've got to take it, Michael. From the sword."

"I think your grandfather was correct in advising you to search your memories. The more you remember about our lives together, the more you'll understand what we have to do. And it will be with the sword." Michael turned away and walked into the kitchen.

Michael is losing himself to the sword's power minute by minute, she worried. I'll have to save us both.

If I can.

After dinner Michael noticed Dorel could hardly keep her eyes open as they cleared the table.

"I think I'll take a shower and go to bed," she said, closing the dishwasher and turning it on.

He'd let her clear the dishes off the table and load the dishwasher on her own, and she had seemed pleased as if her doing the task was some sort of victory over him.

"Okay. See you tomorrow." Michael watched her leave and waited impatiently, listening for the shower.

Slipping past the bathroom, he eased into Dorel's room and went directly to the closet. Opening the door, he drew out the case and removed the sword. A jolt of recognition shot up his arm and centered in his chest, filling him with power. He replaced the case just as he heard the shower being turned off.

He strode down the hall to his office and stood the sword tip-down against the desk. He sat and brought up the database on the computer screen.

"Inada Heavy Industries, the Post-War Years," appeared at the top of the gray page. Michael scrolled down through lists of subsidiaries and the listing of the board of directors.

"CEO, Yasumasa Inada." Not our boy, reasoned Michael, reading the screen. He continued the search to include immediate family. Ah, here we go. Number one son, Hiroshi. Director, Inada America. Manufacturers of robotics components and processors. U.S.A. home office, Redmond, Washington.

Next, he brought up newspaper archives that described and pictured Inada at one posh gala opening after another. The nouveau philanthropist had a penchant for erotic art, esoteric and obscure philosophies, and American naval history.

And quests.

Inada was a major financier of several failed expeditions to recover the lost riches of Babylon, wisdom and technology from the library at Alexandria and other treasures of the ancient world.

Michael lost himself in the information until he felt Katana's nose bump his elbow. "Just hold on, boy."

Katana waited obediently, but after more than a few minutes became insistent. Michael glanced at the clock. Almost midnight!

He padded to the French doors with Katana following silently. The dog disappeared outside, and Michael stood for a moment but felt tugged back to the office.

Rounding the desk, his hip knocked the sword over. It loosened in the scabbard, sliding half out. Michael lifted the sword free of the scabbard, turning it in the bluish light of the computer screen. The odd radiance of the steel pricked his awareness, recalling the power that filled him whenever he handled the sword. As he carried the weapon down the hall, he shifted it from hand to hand, weighing its perfect balance. It had been crafted especially for him. For the Defender.

Be wary.

A thrill shuddered through him as he grasped both hands around the cord-wrapped handle and stepped into the living room. A huge looming apparition took shape at the door, inside. A figure completely encased in the armor of a seventeenth century Japanese shogun stood in Michael's living room, holding a shining *katana,* a long sword.

Within Michael, The Defender gauged the man's lacquered metal armor against his own flimsy clothing, but only for a moment as the man called Michael was pushed to the background.

He knew this one. From another time when he had refused to serve him.

The Defender served no man.

"I come with the power of a thousand samurai to take back what is rightfully mine," the figure growled in an accented English voice that he instantly recognized.

The Defender assumed a stagger-foot stance, balancing on his toes. His mouth went dry and his spine tingled with a vitalizing charge as the sword warmed in his hand, becoming an extension of his arm. Power hummed within him, pulsating, growing, searching for an outlet.

"The sword is not for you," the Defender rumbled. "Go now, Inada, and take your life with you. Stay and your life will be forfeit."

"You are mistaken, *gai-jin*. The sword is mine. Stolen from my family. It should never have passed to one such as you. I come to take what is mine." He raised his sword and moved lithely despite his armor.

Someone had called her. Called the Guardian.

"Michael!" Dorel screamed from the foyer and clapped her hand over her mouth as the two men swung their swords at each other. Tempered steel clanged and sparks flew in a glittering shower over their shoulders.

The robot-looking figure moved in on Michael, pressing him back, sweeping a sword so close to his chest that Dorel sucked in her stomach. In response, she wanted to find something to attack the man from behind and help Michael. Yet, she was cemented in place, condemned to witness a battle she could not affect in any positive way.

A familiar horrible dread flowed over her. Would this be the time?

The men swirled and clashed in front of her. Once again, she was inundated with sensations and visions of the past. Many battles such as this. Too many. Each one she observed, sidelined to watch in horror as the Defender won, but often not before being terribly wounded.

But he lived to fight again.

Always to fight, as Michael did now, for their lives, until the time he would be killed. Then she must take the sword and flee for her life to save it for the next Guardian.

Dorel wanted to run screaming from this. Refuse to watch the Defender kill or be killed. But she couldn't. She'd already watched him use the sword. She could never forget how he changed, looking dangerously alien and heartless. But that wasn't Michael. Please, don't let me lose Michael, she prayed. Let me save him.

Skirting the sofa, Michael fell back under the aggressive

onslaught of the attacker's flashing sword. He twirled aside, kicking behind him at the shogun's sword arm. Dorel heard the sharp intake of breath as his foot connected with the armored elbow. The man's sword flagged slightly as he staggered back, but he recovered immediately and sliced through the muted light to contact Michael's arm, laying open a thin red line from wrist to elbow.

Michael released a savage grunt and lunged at the shogun with powerful slashing blows. He drove his opponent back to the windows. The man pressed into his chest, holding Michael off sword against sword. A mighty shove pushed Michael back into the room. He tripped backwards over the burl coffee table, putting a hand out to catch himself as he went down. Michael still held the sword out in front of him with his right hand.

The shogun's blade narrowly missed Michael's heart as he twisted to the side and rolled away. The sword skittered across the carpet to the hardwood floor and landed at Dorel's feet. Michael scrambled toward his weapon on hands and knees as the shogun advanced behind him.

She stood frozen. Michael's beseeching gaze tore from the sword escaping him to her. Desperately fighting off the paralysis holding her back, she kicked the sword to him. He grabbed the handle and rolled as the shogun's blade hacked the floor where he had been.

With renewed energy, Michael drove the shogun back toward the open door. But each of his well-placed blows was deflected by the armor.

With a deep growl, Katana charged through the open door and attacked. Ninety pounds of dog hit the shogun squarely in the armored back. The man staggered forward, losing his balance, and fell to his knees. Michael tried for a clear chop at the man, but the Airedale rode him to the floor, biting at the back of the helmet. The dog slid off and grabbed the back of the man's knee, a vulnerable part uncovered by the metal armor.

The shogun roared and staggered to his feet toward the open door with Katana pulling in the opposite direction. He raised his sword and blindly swiped at the dog. Instead, he met Michael's blade. Backhanding the dog with his gloved fist, the shogun barged outside and disappeared into the night.

Michael stood at the door, his chest heaving, the sword poised and ready to continue the battle. Panting Katana flopped down on the deck, his tongue hanging out.

Dorel rushed to Michael's side, needing to touch him, to hold him. Comfort him and be comforted. She wanted to throw herself into his arms, but his wound needed attention. Hysteria clutched at her as she dashed to the kitchen for a towel.

When she returned he was gone.

Looking wildly around, she watched in astonishment while he calmly returned to the living room, a white scarf and the sword's scabbard in hand. She hurried to him, but he held her off with a dark look.

Walking to the middle of the area of combat, Michael ritualistically wiped the blade as she had seen him do in the parking lot. Then he drew the sword and scabbard together and bowed. He turned and presented the sword handle first to Dorel across his bleeding arm.

She tossed the weapon on the couch. Only then did he allow her to wrap his arm in the towel. He silently followed her to the bathroom. Dorel carefully uncovered his wound and stifled a gasp. The cut was long and ugly. She shivered, her teeth chattering, as she dabbed at his arm with the towel.

Finally, she gathered enough air to speak. "Maybe you should have stitches."

"Tape it up," he ordered in a cold, hard voice.

She did as she was told, almost sobbing with relief when she finished. A normal color was returning to his face, but gray still lay beneath the flushed cheeks.

"I need a drink," Michael said and left the bathroom.

She fought nausea while she rinsed out the sink and tossed the blood-soaked towel into the hamper. Suddenly remembering Katana, she rushed blindly out of the bathroom and ran to the deck. The dog wasn't there. Turning to look in the bank of kitchen windows, she saw Katana sitting at Michael's feet at the counter, watching him warily.

Michael lifted a tumbler of amber liquid to his lips and took a long drink. She slid onto the barstool next to him and stared at his profile. His color and demeanor were normalizing, though he stared blindly ahead.

She fought to bring a calm tone to her voice. "We aren't safe here."

He took another swallow.

"Did you hear me?" she asked when he didn't respond.

"I heard you." He gripped the glass with both hands and looked deep into the glass bottom.

"Was that Inada?"

"Yes."

"Are you sure?" The man was covered from head to foot. How could Michael know for sure? she wondered as hopeless despair closed around her.

"Yes, I'm sure."

"He'll be back, won't he?"

"Yes."

Dorel stood and clasped her hands tightly. "Fine. Let him come. We won't be here. Let's go. We can get away together and take the sword." They couldn't leave the sword now. Or maybe ever, but she wouldn't let Michael die without putting up a fight herself.

"No. I'll not be driven from my home. We'll make our stand here."

The finality of his words chilled her heart.

Then we'll die here as well. Her future dawned relentlessly in her mind. "But he'll be back." She had to make him see they might have a chance elsewhere or on the run. Together they could escape.

"Let him come." Michael took another swallow.

"No!" she cried. "If Katana hadn't helped, Inada would have killed you."

He smirked and shook his head. "Such faith. Thanks, Dorel."

He was offended and that surprised her. Surely he knew his own limitations? "You tried very hard, but the man's got armor. He injured you. Weakened you. And now he'll come back to finish the job."

"I have the power." Michael turned to her, his blue eyes nearly black with self-assurance. "Believe that. I do. What's more, Inada now believes. He won't come again by himself. But he will send others."

"Power? You believe the sword gives you power? Like hell! It gives you nothing but trouble. You would have been better off just handing it over to him." She had to take a stand, had to keep fighting the sword's influence.

He turned a scalding look on her. "If I'd willingly given up the power and handed over the sword, something I will never do, then he'd have used it to cut my throat and yours. You should be grateful to the sword."

She gazed at him, nearly sick with impotent frustration and fear. "All I'm grateful for is that you're alive. The sword is nothing to be grateful for. It brings us terrible evil. They'll be back. Yet you refuse to go."

Michael stood, drained his glass, and turned to her with the suggestion of a sardonic grin on his face. "That about sums it up. So don't you think you better get with the program and help me instead of fighting me? Help me find out how to better use the sword."

She stared at him. He was changing again, manifesting a stunning almost palpable, brooding masculinity, a raw power. The Michael she could respect had vanished. The man staring sulkily out of Michael's face now practically ordered her to help him.

There was something more, an unspoken expectation. That she would serve him as was her place. Her destiny.

"All right, Michael," she said, hoping the use of his name would awaken the qualities in him that were being rapidly displaced by an aggressively sinister spirit. "I'll help you on one condition. I'm not going to stand by and watch you get killed again."

He frowned. "Again?"

She blinked and pressed her arm into her side. Had she said that? "I mean fight again. I hate it. It terrifies me. I wanted to help you, but couldn't. I felt helpless."

"Why couldn't you help me?" He moved closer to her, the bourbon on his breath mixing potently with the coarse sensuality radiating from him.

"I don't know. It was as if I were held back. Not allowed to help you in the fight. It took everything I had to kick the sword to you. At least it let me do that."

"It let you?"

"Yes, I felt that the sword was holding me in my place." She stared at her hands clasped in her lap. "I kept thinking about being the Guardian. Wondering if this were the time when you would die and I must take the sword to another."

He lifted her chin with his finger. "Did you care?"

"Yes." Dorel shuddered with the admission. She cared too much.

Michael felt the struggle within himself, a strange sensation as if another vied to possess his soul.

Both of them wanted her.

Her delectable lips trembled alluringly, drawing him to taste them. He lowered his head and touched an exploratory kiss to her warm soft mouth. Commanding desire ranted through him, demanding satisfaction. His tongue obeyed and dived through her lips as he pulled her off the stool, guiding her arms around his neck. Her breasts crushed softly against his bare chest as he swept his hands down her back to her firm bottom. She murmured as he ground his hardness into her stomach. She drew back, but did not leave. Instead, she took nipping bites along her chin to his ear.

"Michael," she whispered. "We could walk out of here right now. Disappear. He'd never find us. We'd be free. We'd be together."

He stopped, passion instantly transmuting into cold rage at her traitorous suggestion, and stepped out of her arms. "I told you, I'll not be driven from my home. I have the power. And I intend to use it."

Chapter Ten

Michael roused early the next morning and stretched in the pool of warm sunlight streaming into the bedroom. He flexed his fingers and the taped wound on his left arm objected with a stab of burning pain.

Can't let it stiffen up. He continued to pump his left hand into a fist despite the discomfort. He took a deep breath and focused inward, increasing the pain by degrees with his mind until he could barely stand it. Then he envisioned the pain decreasing, as if dialing it down to a lower level, and it obediently receded to a vague tenderness that would keep him from over-using it and injuring himself further.

He swung his feet to the floor and headed to the shower. Returning to his bedroom for underwear, he stopped abruptly and looked down at Dorel who lay sleeping curled up on the carpet at the foot of his bed, the sword clutched to her breast. Her sheer, lacy pink nothing nightgown had ridden up exposing long, smooth legs to her rounded hip. The swell of her breasts pushed out of the deep V neckline. She looked sexily accessible, his for the taking.

Lifting her gently, he laid her upon his bed, gazing down at this beautiful woman who was his. She didn't wake as he slipped the sword out of her grasp.

She'd come to him during the night.

His breath quickened. I could make love to her right now.

He glanced at the end of the bed where he'd found her. She'd slept there. Like a servant or a page sleeping at the foot of the master's bed. Realization unfolded within him. She hadn't come because she wanted to. The sword had brought her here. To take her place with him. To fulfill her destiny.

Compelled to stroke her silky hair, he reached a trembling hand toward her, his again.

She shifted and murmured, throwing her arm across the pillows, further revealing the satiny skin of her breast. So perfect. Her lips began to part appealingly.

"No, Granddaddy, I can't hear you," she murmured in a little girl-like voice and tossed her head on the pillow.

Michael snatched his hand back. He rubbed his stubble-rough chin, condemning himself for even thinking of taking her like this. He backed into the bathroom and took a long purifying cold shower. Later, when he peeked into the bedroom, she was gone. On his bed was the sword.

All morning they avoided each other. Michael stayed to his office, not bothering with breakfast. He'd accepted a cup of coffee she'd taken to him with a terse thanks and kept his eyes on the computer screen.

Dorel picked up her journal and papers and retreated to the sun-warmed dining room, trying not to think about awaking in his empty bed. She pushed away questions of how she'd gotten there and what had happened. The question of why she didn't remember nagged at her uncomfortably.

She propped her chin in her hands and stared out the window, savoring the hot clear August weather. Summer was her favorite time, maybe because Seattle weather was so stingy with beautiful days like this. She'd love to sun herself out on the deck, turning herself fiery red, the Pacific Northwest version of a tan.

But there was no time to waste. She had to study her grandfather's fascinating but painfully revealing journal to prepare for whatever horror lay ahead.

And to think I've always wanted excitement, she sighed. Stupid. She'd loved anything active, and wasn't much of a *watcher* or fan, but a bona fide participant. She'd always needed to take charge and take care of herself. Michael was doing all that now. She wondered about his needs, what he was thinking. This was a first for her. Her desire to escape him was waning. If she could persuade him to leave his house, this not very defendable fortress, they still had a chance. They could find freedom together.

She'd had relationships with men before, brief ones, usually ending amicably when the demands became too great on her time and freedom. Her time alone was precious. It was when she felt free and happy. Often, when she guarded her solitude too jealously, her current man or friends complained, but eventually accepted her eccentric ways or they moved on. Right now, she was in a *moved on* period. It didn't bother her. Someone else always turned up if she needed companionship.

Movement in the living room disrupted her thoughts and she saw Michael staring at her. His expression was odd as if he had seen something that disturbed him. An anxious shiver quaked along her spine.

"Do you have it?" he asked in a voice she barely recognized.

"Sorry? Do I have what?" She sat straight, uneasy under his scrutiny.

He approached. She wanted to back up and move away from his intimidating behavior, but she pressed her hands flat on the table and willed herself to remain seated.

"I must have the sword." He stepped forward mechanically and raised his hand in a stiff gesture.

"You know where it is." She'd left it in his bed where she'd found herself.

"Bring it to me." His blue eyes were almost black as he stared unblinking into hers.

"You can damn well get it yourself if you want it."

He stopped and tilted his head slightly as if confused. "Why do you refuse me?"

"Refuse you? You've got two legs. Take yourself there and get it." She pushed back from the table and stood. "Get this straight, Michael. I'm going to find a solution, an escape. For both of us." She picked up the journal. "And this is going to show me how."

He stared at the small leather book in her hands and shook his head as if to clear it. When his eyes met hers again, they were lighter in color, a sky blue. "What were you saying?"

"Go away, Michael," she barked in frustration and sat down, opening the book.

"Why? What's wrong now? If it's about you sleeping by my bed—"

She slammed the book closed. "What is the matter with you? Who are you?" she asked. "Is this Michael or his evil twin, the Defender?"

Confusion clouded his handsome face. "Now, wait a minute. I don't understand."

"Stop the performance. I'm really tired of your mood swings. One moment you act like a brooding macho jerk ordering me around, the next you're Captain Sensitive."

"Hold on," he interrupted, raising his palm. "What do you mean ordering you around? I haven't ordered you to do anything."

"You have, too. Just now. You demanded the sword. Told me to fetch it." She forced her mouth shut, gritting her teeth to stifle a nasty suggestion of what he could really do with the sword.

"When did I say that?" He'd moved close enough to her that she could see the tiny silver flecks in his flashing eyes.

She sucked in a steadying breath, fighting to control her

temper. "When? Just now. You said you wanted the sword and for me to go get it out of your bedroom."

He stared at her for a long moment and turned away, rubbing his jaw. "I don't remember," he said, his tone shadowed with apprehension.

She was prepared for some sort of denial from him, but not for the sincere look of remorseful concern he gave her as he turned away. She wanted to believe him. "What about the other times? When you'd finished exercising?" She flicked her glance away. "That night in the utility room?"

"I remember the utility room, the end of it anyway." He turned and met her gaze solemnly. "I'm very sorry. I don't think I can resist what's happening."

"I'm sorry, too," she said. Perhaps she couldn't resist what was happening to her, either.

She'd apparently done things she couldn't remember. Compassion and empathy for him blossomed in her.

For several charged moments, they stared into each other's eyes before he moved away. Her skin longed for his warmth and she shivered at the loss of his touch. Placing her hand in his, she drew him back to her. "Please don't give in to the sword, Michael. Fight it. We must. I'll help you."

"You can't help." A muscle ticked in his rigid jaw. "You're the problem. I look at you and I want to destroy anyone who comes near you." He ran his hand through his hair in anguish. "I can't believe I said that. I feel pulled in two directions. One part of me wants you to take the sword and run like hell away from me and the other will kill to keep you with me."

"The Defender isn't a part of you. Those aren't your feelings. Michael Gabrielli doesn't want the sword and its power," Dorel countered earnestly. "You wouldn't kill anyone for me. You don't want me like that."

Michael slowly shook his head, his eyes leaden with misery. "You're mistaken. I do want the sword. The power." He captured her free hand within his. "And I want you."

Despair nearly strangled her and she cried, "Not as the Defender, Michael. I don't want him to touch me. Never again."

Michael's arms went around her and she willingly sheltered within his strong embrace. This was Michael. Kind, protective, warm and caring. A man she cared about, wanted to make love with. Could her love compete with the sword's seductive power, supplant his growing desire for the sword? Especially when she had to battle constantly against its growing influence on herself?

She shuddered against him. Who would win? The sword or she?

Michael's mouth nuzzled into her hair, then he held her away from him, looking hungrily at her. "I really want you. But I'll try not to pressure you. You come to me when it's right for you." He dropped his hands to his sides and strolled to his office without a look back.

She slumped onto the chair and stared at the journal lying on the table. The book anchored her, keeping her from being reeled in by him on a taut silken cord of reckless passion. She wanted to make love to Michael, but she couldn't lose herself, and him, to stolen precious moments of pleasure juxtaposed between sword battles and death. If she were going to save them, the journal would show her how. Granddad promised. Dorel opened the book and began to read.

It was hard going. Sometimes Granddad seemed to have been writing directly to her, other times to himself, and generally as if he were giving a lecture. Then there were the passages to Baroness Tsuji, so full of compassion and understanding, they were like love letters. Had her grandfather fallen in love with this dead woman?

"My dear Michiko, I learned more about the Tsuji dynasty today. What an ancient and proud family, though they were terribly corrupt. But then power corrupts, doesn't it? The Baron must have been a man of great personal magnetism and power for you to do what you did. Did you love him? I wonder. Did you even expect to? Arranged marriages seldom are arranged for love.

I believe you had no choice, of course. Just as you had to find me to give me the sword, you had to take the Baron as your husband. It was all arranged, but not by your families as you believed. I wish I could have released you then and saved you. I know now you did not want to pass the sword along, but had no choice. Perhaps you knew this time I would find an answer. This time I will, my dear, I promise. The Trust will be broken."

A tear splashed on the page. The old ink blurred and ran before Dorel quickly dabbed the spot with a tissue. She sniffed and blew her nose.

Has he found the answer? she hoped, not wanting to think about his obviously conflicted feelings for the woman, the woman whose name he'd once called her. It felt perverted, especially since she'd always loved her grandfather so much. But he was the only one left for her to love. Everyone else had gone.

Not everyone, her heart reminded her. You have Michael.

Rain came late in the afternoon, cooling the hot summer day with Seattle drizzle-gray. Dorel and Katana strolled among the dripping trees and bushes, getting soaked but enjoying the freedom of a wet walk unhampered by raincoat or umbrella. When they stepped in the back door, the kitchen phone rang and without thinking, she answered it as she unsnapped the lead off the dog's collar.

"Hello, Ms. Everly," Lieutenant Rhett's voice boomed. "Is Gabrielli around?"

Dorel's stomach rolled and she gripped at the nylon-webbed lead like a lifeline. "Hang on."

"Wait, Ms. Everly. I wanted to extend my sympathies about the death of your uncle . . ." his voice tapered off and he waited silently.

"Thank you, Lieutenant."

"Any date set for the funeral?"

The leash bit into her hand, but she didn't release her hold. Funeral? Good lord, she hadn't called Aunt Verna. "Arrangements are still being made. I haven't talked with Aunt Verna—today."

"Nice lady. Pretty broken up. She told *me* today that she hasn't seen you since, what two-three days ago, before Prefontaine was killed?"

Dorel heard a faint click on the line. In less time than she could think of a reply for Rhett, Michael appeared at the counter. He took the phone from her hand.

"Gabrielli here. Hello, Lieutenant, what can I do for you?" His voice was unemotional and authoritative. A sullen resolve vibrated from him, almost forming an aggressive and threatening aura of dark red around him. "Yes, I'm taking vacation time. Oh?" He paused, listening intently. "Yes, fine. Goodbye."

Michael hung up and met her anxious stare. "Rhett is coming. Soon." He turned abruptly away and walked out of the kitchen. "Abie's funeral is tomorrow at two," he threw curtly over his shoulder.

Dorel's composure quivered and threatened to give way at

what she'd just witnessed. She'd seen the dark metamorphosis seize Michael. The Defender was not at all disturbed by the latest disaster coming their way. He felt nothing, was completely unemotional. If she could make Michael feel, if he experienced emotions as she did, maybe that would bring him to his senses.

"Michael!" she yelled, making herself follow him. "Damn you, Michael!"

He looked up and scowled. "Damn me?"

"You bet, you." She charged into his office and leaned across his desk. Her finger stopped short of stabbing his chest. "Damn you! He knows! He probably thinks you killed Abie, too. He'll get you, Michael, if Inada doesn't first, because you refuse to leave while we still can."

"Rhett has nothing. He's guessing. It simply makes it all the more interesting, for everyone," he said, his manner aloof.

"Interesting?" she shrieked. "We don't want *interesting,* we need a solution, a plan of action, an escape."

"Calm down. Just think a moment. All Rhett knows is that you are related to Abie. So, he's been talking to your aunt. It's natural she'd be wondering where you are, especially at a time like this. Normal, I'd say. We simply made the error of not contacting her when we found out he'd been killed. Now *that* does look suspicious."

"I know. I know," Dorel agreed, warily watching his reactions. She had to challenge Michael, engage his intelligence, get him involved with her and their problem in the present. "It was stupid. I wasn't thinking." She thought a moment, briefly tapping her lip with her tongue. "Could Aunt Verna have known what Abie was doing?"

He shrugged. "You tell me."

"No. I don't think so. But then I can't be sure. I thought

Abie was a wonderful man. I'm not sure what to think now."

He took the bait. "I think you better call her. Try to repair the damage. See what she told Rhett. What he may have said to her. You may have to attend the funeral."

"Me? You mean we. All three of us." She sank into the red leather wingback chair in front of the desk. "Apparently, I can't go off the premises without the sword. And you can't go anywhere without me."

"The sword does pose a problem," he agreed.

Hearing him say that, she rejoiced. Now if she could just get him to give it up somehow. "What about Rhett? We don't want him to find the sword here," she said and stood.

"We can handle this. We'll just wait and play it out. See what develops. Rhett's counting on getting us flustered enough to make a mistake. We've got to keep our heads, that's all. Think! That's the important thing. Be ready. Vigilant."

"If you say *semper fi,* I'll scream. I used to work with an ex-marine pilot. Your little pep talk sounded just like him."

"It should, since I was trained by the Corps. Until I was assigned to special duty with the Teams. Then I lowered my standards to become a SEAL." His face lost its stern edge and his luminous blue eyes held a hint of a twinkle.

Her mouth dropped open. "A Navy SEAL? The ultimate modern warrior?"

"Yup, I was a SEAL," he said, his voice taking on a patina of pride her grandfather's had when he talked about his Naval career.

She didn't want to believe this handsome man she was trying desperately to save was really a highly trained killing machine. Like the Defender.

Dorel clapped her hand on her cheek. "This is worse than I thought. No wonder Rhett is dogging your tracks. He knows you could have done it. Both of the killings." She took a breath, willing herself to be calm. "I asked you once before, Michael. Did you kill Abie? I believe you didn't, but what if you can't remember?"

He looked up sharply, visibly shaken by the thought. "I didn't, I swear. I couldn't have. I'd remember something like that." He glanced away. "You always remember the killing. Can't forget it. I know."

She tried to correlate his pained expression with his being a former SEAL. Until now, she hadn't understood why he so easily accepted the role of the Defender. He was a natural. The culmination of centuries of warrioring. The ultimate warrior wants the ultimate power—the sword.

"Dorel?" Michael's voice broke into her troubled thoughts.

"Yes?" She pushed herself out of the chair, needing some time and distance to think.

"Rhett will be here tomorrow." He stood up and came around the desk, carrying her sword. "This should stay with you, but I can hide it in a spot he'll never find."

"Fine. As long as the sword is here somewhere, I don't have a problem." She started for the door.

"Don't forget to call your aunt."

"I'm not sure what to say to her and I certainly don't want to go to his funeral."

"Tell your aunt you're too shaken up from the car wreck. That's a great excuse for her questions, too. Rhett said we looked terrible." He fingered the nearly healed cut above his eye. "You can stay in bed when he's here." He raised his eyebrows and quirked his mouth. "You really don't look all that good, you know."

She gave his bandaged arm a haughty squint. "You better wear a long-sleeved shirt. And as to my not looking so good, it ain't my fault," she said and hurried out the door.

★ ★ ★ ★ ★

Aunt Verna wept in Dorel's ear for thirty minutes. As it turned out, Dorel's not being with her wasn't a problem because all Verna's relatives had descended upon her.

"I just let them handle everything," Verna hiccuped over the phone. "I wasn't up to it. Abie always took care of things and I just couldn't think. The doctor gave me some Valium. Those little pills help even though things are still really the same, but you just don't give a damn."

"I'm sorry I can't be there with you, Aunt Verna. I've tried to be up and around, but I'm bruised and sore." The half-truth eased over her lips far too easily.

"Get yourself some Valium, honey. You'll still feel the aches and pains, but you just won't give a damn," mumbled Verna. "Come see me sometime, Dorel. Except, not soon. I'm going to my sister's in Portland for a few weeks. I'll call you when I get back. Bye, honey."

The phone buzzed in Dorel's ear.

After talking to Verna, she almost wished she could attend the funeral. It would give her the closure she really needed, because she was sick to death of the open-ended uncertainty of the last few days that showed every indication of continuing, if not getting worse.

He was dying. Shot in the back by a Russian coward while another occupied his sword hand. Her love could not heal him this time. Now she would have to take the sword and run from his killer.

As she always did.

And soon she would join him in death.

About midnight, Michael roused from the dream drenched in sweat that trickled down his back like warm blood. He stood and stretched, trying to release the burning tension knotting his limbs. Exercise would get his mind off the dismal dream or whatever it was. He moved outside to the cool deck. Humid darkness wrapped around him as he began to work slowly, easily into his *kata*. His mind whirled instead of smoothing as it should.

If he could be vigilant, if he could be the best, the culmination of every incarnation, perhaps he could save them. Maybe this time it would be different. They could grow old together. There could be children. A son of his own?

That is not your destiny, the silent words floated on the cool night air.

Michael tried to fend them off, deny them, but they circled his head and body, sealing his fate. He was doomed to repeat the cycle.

And so was Dorel.

Growing up, he was naturally interested in all things. He seemed to have knowledge beyond his years that worried his mother, but she accepted him, helped him, provided everything he needed to become the successful man he was today. Why couldn't Dorel be like her and help instead of fighting him? She was making this so much more difficult. Flying an F-16 or leading a SEAL team into combat was much easier than dealing with Dorel.

When he helped Dorel escape from Abie's junkyard, he'd planned on teaching her the remote viewing protocols so that she could help him discover their past and how to use the sword. That wasn't necessary now. She obviously experienced out of body travel, even pulled right into the astral with him, and she was apparently having spontaneous *visions* that he didn't share with her. That could be a problem.

With a little training, she could be taught control by using the protocols to retrieve information as well as bi-locate at will. But her doing so would ultimately work against him. She'd have freedom that could be dangerous for them both and their mission. Dorel was just going to have to learn that she couldn't run from her duty, and that she couldn't change the past—or the future. They were bound to serve the Trust, and Michael intended to honor that eternal obligation.

He'd left the Navy because he needed freedom from the capricious dictates of others that used him as a tool to accomplish their own objectives. He could have used his remote viewing skills to find things long forgotten, treasures that would make him richer. But he'd spent his life waiting for something to happen.

For someone.

The day he had walked toward Spence's table at the gun show, he knew it was the time. His destiny was at hand.

That Dorel had also seen the time tapestry astonished him. He'd seen the vision of his purpose or perhaps hints of his destiny in this lifetime, or was it another? No matter, it all became clear the instant that he touched the sword. The destiny he'd waited his entire life for was to be shared with her. He was completing the Trust. He was the eternal warrior. Fighting forever.

The feeling of power was incredible, very sexual. It stimulated him. He craved it. As if he could do anything, have anything. All was his for the taking.

Dorel Everly was his by right. Whether or not she believed it, she was his. She would soon surrender to him.

Michael's heated body steamed in the cool night air as he covered his fist with his palm and bowed. He returned to his bed, alone, his body needing her more than ever. He would wait, but not much longer.

The white silk kimono whispered against her bare legs as

she glided to him. She cupped his face with her hand, then reached down, untied her robe and let it fall in a soft puddle at her feet. She heard his breath catch as she took his hand and drew it across her lips and down to her round breast. Her hands went round his neck and entwined in his hair.

He pulled her to him. Her tongue slipped into his mouth and he sucked it gently. He groaned as his groin hardened against her stomach and he lifted her up. He carried her, her legs wrapped around him, and laid her down. He followed on top of her, crushing her tender breasts under his chest. He released her mouth and danced his smooth tongue down her neck to her breast. He took the taut nipple between his lips. She moaned and arched into him, raking his back with her fingers.

Dorel awoke from the dream with a moan in her warm, dark bedroom. It had to have been a dream. There was no other explanation because she lay here alone. She clenched her eyelids shut, trying to block out the images and the feelings of being made love to by Michael. But it was wonderful, so right, as if they'd always made love only with each other. As she drifted dreamily back into the timeless current of consciousness, she realized she'd been making love to another man.

Fusao's name caressed her lips. Her love. Her husband. They always made love after he killed. He needed her as she needed him. They needed the reassurance their love lived still. It might be their last time.

The night before the Russians came. They lay in his quarters warmly entwined in each other's arms, whispering words of love and reassurance of tomorrow. They would live to love another day.

But the Russian officer had mortally wounded Fusao be-

fore he could muster his troops. Stabbed him as they fought sabre to sword. Then another shot Fusao from behind and the officer fled.

She dragged Fusao away to die and to take the sword as she knew she must. There wasn't enough time to hold him or whisper words of comfort in his dying except to tell him they would meet again. Soon.

As she ran from the overrun fort, a Russian soldier caught her, stabbing her with his bayonet, but he too was killed before he could finish her off. She dragged herself toward the temple. The sword must be given to another for safekeeping. It would bring them together again. Eternally.

Dorel shivered and sat up. She had to tell Michael about this strange dream. It may only have been a dream, but now that she'd experienced the wonder of being loved by and loving a man, she wanted that love again. To give it. To take it.

Benten barely stirred as Dorel eased out of bed, sliding the nightgown off her shoulders and down her body. She stood naked in the moonlight streaming in the window, the silvery light dusting her skin and falling on the old wedding ring quilt at the foot of the bed. She wrapped it around herself and opened the door to find Katana lying in the hall on guard. As she stepped over the dog, he stretched to his feet and padded after her.

Wind chimes tinkling from the deck sounded the processional as she crossed the cool hardwood floor of the foyer, the bottom of the old, soft quilt flowing behind her like a train as she glided serenely down the hall to Michael's room.

Love would save them both.

Chapter Eleven

She is yours again!

Michael snapped awake, straining to hear the voice so like his own. He threw off the sheet and started to get out of bed, but stopped as his door slowly swung open. His pulse hammered, but not with alarm.

She stood in the doorway, veiled in glowing moonlight, his grandmother's wedding quilt gowning her slender body. Her sleep-tousled red hair brushed her bare shoulders beguilingly. As Dorel stepped hesitantly inside, Katana lay down in the hall, his back to the bedroom.

Michael held his breath in disbelief and hope. Something held him back, making him wait for her to come to him. She opened her clasped hands, freeing the quilt. As it slid down her erect body, his desire swelled at each curve the hand-sewn material caressed. Her gaze locked on his, she moved to him, radiating essential erotic need that focused fire in his groin. She stopped, her breasts barely grazing his chest.

Lifting her hand to his hair, she wound her fingers into it, gave a slow tug, while her hand trailed down his cheek. He felt her soft skin drag across his new beard as she brought her lingering touch across his mouth. His lips shook and he raised his hand to take control. She gently stopped him, guiding his fingers to her mouth, her velvet tongue skimming the tips.

He longed to delay, to support the round firmness of her breasts with his palm, but she propelled him seductively onward, down her smooth stomach to the heat between her thighs. Her arms went around his neck and he pulled her hips to him and muffled a groan against her uplifted, parted lips.

Lifting her in one fluid motion, he laid her upon the rumpled sheets of his bed.

He fought to manage his body's overwhelming response, to follow where she might lead, but he couldn't. She'd come to him, wanting him. And that was too powerful an aphrodisiac to be controlled. His hands and lips explored her luscious, eager body; a raw, painful craving demanding him to take her hard and fast battled with a tender benevolence that persuaded a loving sharing.

"Michael, please," she murmured into his neck. "You're hurting me."

He fell way from her, panting. She gazed up at him, the small flicker of fear in her eyes searing his soul. Ashamed, he cupped her small face gently in his big hands. "Forgive me. I don't mean to hurt you. But it's been so long and there's not much time until Inada—"

"Shhhh. I came to you tonight for love." She leaned forward and flicked her tongue into his mouth.

Michael let Dorel take control once again, an unspoken surrender on his part. He held his breath as she placed her hand on his chest and pressed him down on the bed.

Straddling him on her knees, she lightly brushed her buttocks across his groin. Her small hands kneaded softly up his sides. The sensation of her touch was heavenly torture. He gasped when she leaned forward and her breasts caressed his chest. A tiny, teasing smile lifted the corners of her mouth as she spread her fingers wide and massaged the muscled plateau.

"I love your chest," she murmured, then dipped to circle one of his nipples with her tongue.

Michael reacted instantly to her stimulation. He stroked her soft breasts slowly, tenderly, her nipples hardening. He lifted his head to her breast and alternately kneaded and licked its tip while he titillated the other with his thumb.

She clutched his shoulders, arched into him, tilted her head back and half-closed her eyes. "Ahhh, Michael . . ."

He raised himself, half-sitting and held both breasts in his hands, bringing them together and rapidly flicked his tongue across their nipples. A soft moan curled up from her throat as she nestled into his ministrations. Her lips went dry from her open-mouthed panting and she rolled her head obliviously from side to side, her hair swirling on her neck and shoulders like wisps of satin.

His hands were gentle, his mouth soft and his tongue wildly darting over her skin, making her warm and wild at the same time. She began to move against him, leaning to his chest, rubbing her cheek in his tickling mat of dark hair, and nipping his skin up his neck to his chin.

She sensed his powerful strength was held in check while he firmly cupped her buttocks and rolled her under him, pulling her tightly against him. She moved higher on him and he paused at the threshold.

Her fingers played in his dark hair, silver-dusted by the moonlight. His strong features were muted planes of shadow and light. His hazy turquoise eyes shone luminous with passion. For her. He wanted her as much as she did him. The knowledge thrilled her, making her feel exquisitely powerful and desirable.

"Tell me, Michael," she whispered against his ear and traced its outer fold with her tongue as she lightly grazed her fingernails down his back.

A shudder rippled through his strong body and his hands tightened on her. "You're driving me wild."

"Tell me again." She wrapped her legs around his waist, forcing him in further.

He swallowed and started to speak. She smiled. "No,

show me instead." She sealed his lips with a lingering kiss and teasing foreplay evaporated in the heat of arousal.

Michael held her tightly against him, her body helpless to resist him. He lost himself in the delicate velvet warmth of her. She moaned against his mouth and moved faster on him, rushing them both headlong into the fierce intensity of climaxing need.

He couldn't perceive where his flesh ended and hers began. They were molded together. One in want and fulfillment. Each called the other's name as they fell together into the charged vortex of passionate pleasure. Dorel floated blissfully on the undulating waves of gratification as Michael's butterfly kisses lit on her eyelids, flitted here to her nose, there to her chin and frolicked daintily up and down her neck.

Her Michael. Her beautiful strong Michael lay in her arms, contentment radiating from his touch and his look as he continued to fondle her reverently as if she were one of his rare treasures. Michael raised on elbow and looked toward the door.

"What is it?" Dorel asked, trying to see what he stared at. His hand slipped over her mouth and he shook his head, a frown riding over his darkening gaze.

Katana stood facing down the hall.

Dorel heard no sound, not from the dog nor from Michael. He eased out of bed and noiselessly crossed to the hand-carved oak wardrobe standing in the corner next to the deck door. He stepped into the wardrobe's tall shadow, and for a moment, she thought he'd left the room.

He reappeared, holding the unsheathed sword. The blade glinting sharply in the moonlight.

Michael's naked form glowed in the same light. Powerful. Vigorous. Commanding. Her gaze crept to his eyes. They stared beyond her, dark and deadly.

The Defender swept his savage eyes briefly over her bare body. She moved to cover herself from him.

"There is no time," he hissed. "They are here. Come." He strode to the door, the muscles of his back and buttocks flexing with each purposeful step.

Dorel didn't even think to disobey. She twisted a sheet around herself as he pulled Katana by the collar into the bedroom and shut the Airedale inside. She followed him into the dark, empty hall and sensed a presence in the living room. Fear demanded retreat. A dreaded need forcefully compelled her to follow him.

He stopped in the foyer, facing the room, his left palm out, cautioning her. Without question, she took her place beside him. Both his hands curled around the handle and he stepped forward into a spread leg, bent knee stance, the sword pointed outbound in a forty-five degree angle. He looked like a classical statue, a life-sized David.

Two hooded, masked figures in black separated from the dark corners of the room. Ninja. She'd heard of them, seen them in movies but never believed them real.

Michael stepped to the center of the large living room. Dorel wanted to scream and hold him back, but she knew her place was behind him. To watch. To guard.

As the Guardian always serves the Defender.

The figures circled Michael, staying warily away from the tip of his seeking sword. They darted in and out, waiting for one to engage him so that the other could find an opening.

Kicking and whirling, the ninja attacked with short swords. Michael spun and struck with his feet, elbows and the sword. No words were exchanged. This was a silent battle except for the thuds of violent blows landing on men's bodies and the unguarded grunt or muffled cry.

Dorel's eyes were riveted on Michael. Watching for him.

Trying to protect him from unseen blows. The attackers could not strike him or cause him to falter. He was a master of movement, of coordination and speed. His intent was deadly and the ninja learned quickly when Michael sliced the leg of one and nearly caught his partner on the same deadly sweep.

Michael engaged two swords at the same time in a dance of death that was terrifying and spellbindingly beautiful. His increasing power pulsing through his naked body was a tangible thing. The ninja wavered before it. They were unable to lay blade or hand on him. Rather than lose strength, he drew from them.

With a deft parry and sideways slice, Michael's sword impaled one of his attackers. For a moment the man hung on the sword, then he slumped to the floor.

The remaining ninja tried to fade back. Michael turned on him, his face a rigid mask of calculating intent.

"You will remove this," he ordered, jabbing a curt gesture at the body on the floor between them.

The man scrambled to his fallen cohort, grabbed up his sword and body, and dragged him out the open door to the deck to disappear into the shadows of the moonlit garden.

Michael and Dorel stood motionless staring into the night after them. He strode to the dining room, returning with a white linen napkin and began the ritual wiping of the sword.

His chanting shook Dorel out of her stupor. She watched Michael stroke the sword with the cloth, cleaning off the blood. Hearing Katana's scratching and whining, she went to the bedroom and released the dog. Dorel followed him down the hall, arriving to see him sniffing intently, his tan beard whisking a wide dark spot on the area rug.

Michael held the sword up and bowed stiffly toward the windows.

This can't be happening again, she thought in horror.

How could she have stood there and done nothing? Watched a man be murdered? Helped Michael murder a man? But it wasn't murder, the reasonable less desperate part of her mind said. It was self-defense. *They came to kill you both.*

Michael turned and presented the sword to her, handle first. The room spun around her. She wanted to back away, and every cell in her body screamed for her to refuse this time. But she extended her hand and received it. Dorel carried the sword down the hall to his room and laid it on the bed. She turned and found herself face to face with Michael.

They stared silently at each other. Dorel walked to him and slipped her arms around his nude waist, laying her head on his damp chest. He smelled of sweat, hormones and sexual excitement. His hard erection pressed into her stomach. It both stirred and repelled her. His arms went stiffly around her and he pressed his face into her hair. She didn't know how long they stood together bathed in moonlight. Then she remembered this wasn't the Michael she'd made love to mere moments earlier.

Dorel forced herself to move away from him, her gaze downcast. She didn't want to see his face, afraid of what she would see. Who she would see.

A great emptiness filled him. He wanted to keep her close to him, safe, sheltered in his arms forever, but she wanted to go. He knew she belonged here. With him. Why did she fight it? What was wrong with her? He offered everything a woman would want.

He had the power!

Michael went after her. The lamp was switched on as he entered the foyer. He watched her go to Katana and pull the dog away from the stain on the carpet. She made him sit before disappearing into the kitchen. When she returned, she carried a basket of cleaning supplies. She knelt and began cleaning the blood from the carpet. On her cheeks, tears rolled silently down, the only indication of emotion.

Barely contained excitement bolted through Michael, seeking an outlet. What was wrong with her? They should celebrate. He had the power. Let the others come. He would conquer them all. Her place was at his side, to celebrate with him. To rejoice in the use of the power, because now he knew the power grew with use.

She bent to her work, the sheet drawn tight around her. He needed her, wanted her again. She was his. His skin tingled from the cooling sweat on his naked body. His mouth was dry. He shook his hands out and trotted a step or two in place like an athlete cooling down. Still on an adrenaline high and looking at the outline of Dorel's round bottom, he remembered the smooth skin of her long legs as they'd wrapped around him. He touched his tongue to his dry top lip.

Slowly and silently, he drew her to her feet and took the wet cloth out of her hands, dropping it beside them. She refused to meet his gaze. He watched her face as he slowly stroked his hands up her arms to her shoulders, up her long neck, the silky copper hair brushing the backs of his hands. He cupped her face with his hands. She trembled with desire. He focused on her quivering lips, wanting to taste them.

It was then he noticed the look in her eyes when they finally met his. Loathing. Revulsion. The woman he wanted more than anyone in the world, the woman who was only for him, hated his touch. His stomach rolled as if he'd been gut-punched. He dropped his hands and stepped back.

Michael walked past her to his office and closed the door. He chopped out with the blade of his hand, knocking the desk lamp to the floor. He swore and made his way around the broken lamp by the faint moonlight filtering in the shuttered windows. Sliding open the door, he stepped out on the deck into the cool air.

Breathing deeply from the diaphragm, in through his nose and hissing out through his mouth, he pressed his palms together and bowed low from the hip. In slow motion, he began to move in the formal, ritualized movements of his *kata*. Focus and breathing coming regular, centering him, helping him to forget her. To remember his mission. To remember why he lived. And who he was.

He had the power.

Early the next morning, Katana growled and shot to his feet, barking. Dorel opened her door. The dog dashed down the hall to the foyer. She shrugged into the robe and tied it closely around her as she eased down the hall. The bell rang—once, twice, three times.

Where was Michael? she wondered and peered into the foyer. She could see someone trying to look through the sheer window covering. Katana jumped up on the door, barking loudly. The bell rang again. Dorel tried to pull the curtain aside a tiny bit to see out, but the dog blocked her.

She felt a hand on her shoulder and Michael pulled her back, jerking his head toward her room. She hurried away as ordered, but her thoughts remained with him. He'd shaved and changed his clothes. Now a distinct contrast to the naked warrior of last night, he looked like an airline captain again in his pleated taupe slacks and crème-colored polo shirt and Italian tasseled loafers. He might be dressed like Michael, but it was only a costume, the Defender's masquerade.

As she pulled on a short denim skirt and a sleeveless blue and white checked cotton shirt, she heard Michael give the dog a command and the barking quiet. Dorel peeked out the door and seeing no one, she dashed to the bathroom.

Michael and Lieutenant Rhett stood at the bookcase when

Dorel entered the living room. A drawer lay open under the bonsai alcove that now held her miniature tree. The detective was turning a samurai sword in his hands.

"Amazing!" Rhett exclaimed. "I've never heard how they make these things. Two kinds of metal, you say?"

"That's right. One type of hot metal wraps around the other and their different cooling rates give the sword its curve," Michael explained.

King County Police Sergeant Menlow came down the hall from Michael's bedroom and shook his head when Rhett looked up. The police were actually searching the house, realized Dorel, and began to panic. She didn't know what to do or where to go. Michael smiled at her, motioning her to his side.

"Dorel, you should be resting." He took her hand. "Are you feeling better?"

She searched his gunmetal blue eyes for the Michael of their passionate lovemaking. But all she saw was the Defender staring back at her. She started to retreat, but finally took his cue from the unrelenting pressure on her hand. She glanced at Rhett with a weak smile. "Hello, Lieutenant."

"Ms. Everly. He's right. You don't look all that good. Your aunt said you can't make it to the funeral today."

"I wish I could, but I'm not good at funerals anyway, and with the accidents . . ." She slipped her hand out of Michael's.

"Accidents?" Rhett laid the sword back in the drawer next to several others of various sizes and types.

"Uh, yes," she answered. "The car wreck and . . . the break in."

The lieutenant didn't look convinced. "Some guy breaks in here, slaps you around and leaves without taking anything? Yeah, that could be an accident, all right. He accidentally forgot to rape you and steal everything in the house. Especially after he'd taken the trouble to mace the dog and kill the alarm."

"But he heard the sirens," she offered.

He shrugged. "Oh, right. That's right."

"Can I get you some coffee, Dorel?" Michael asked with a kindly smile. His apparent concern for her was probably very convincing to others. "Lieutenant, coffee?"

"Sure, why not." Rhett continued his visual search.

Dorel sat stiffly on the black leather settee and watched Rhett poke around the room. He ran his hand along the shelves of books, peered at the carved ivory and jade figurines, and rearranged the puzzle box collection on the long narrow table behind the sofa.

At this rate, if he wanted to read, touch and see everything in this room alone, he'd be here all day. She leaned back, breathing deeply, trying to relax. Her gaze roamed the room and fell on the latte-colored area rug next to the bookcase. Rhett stood with his back to the dark bloodstain.

Dorel almost gasped. She'd tried so hard to get the blood out. Used everything she could think of, but there was so much. Her mind raced as she watched Rhett, and tried to remember. Where had she put the cloth she'd used?

He backed up and stepped on the spot with his left heel. A scream climbed her throat. Leaping to her feet, she called over her shoulder, "Michael, can I help you?"

Michael touched her elbow, the frigid look in his eyes warned her to get a hold of herself. She needed to tell him about the stain that she hadn't been able to remove, so he could think of something to distract Rhett. She looked at him and moved her eyes to look where Rhett stood, hoping Michael would follow.

Michael handed her a cup and smiled, guiding her back to

the settee. "Lieutenant, do you take sugar or cream?" he asked and returned to the kitchen.

Rhett followed him a few steps to where he could see into the kitchen. "Yeah, both. That'll be breakfast." He took the mug Michael offered. "You have all this stuff inventoried and insured?" He jerked a thumb toward the room, then took a sip of coffee and grimaced. "Hot!"

"I keep an open inventory on disk and the insurance company has one as well. Would you care to see it?" Michael headed across the room toward his office. Rhett ambled after him.

Dorel glanced around for the other officer. Not seeing him, she stole to the spot on the carpet. It was still damp and discolored. She shivered, frantic to cover it, to hide it.

Katana stood outside at the French doors, looking in. She opened the door and he ran in. Grabbing him by the collar, she stopped him from barging into the office and dragged him to the spot. She made him sit and then gave him the command, "Down". The dog lay reluctantly, looking as if he were going to jump up the minute she turned away. She waved her hand in front of his face as she'd seen Michael do.

"Stay, Katana," she ordered in a low, firm voice. The dog relaxed into a resigned posture.

Dorel sat down on the settee as the men re-entered the room. She tried to take a sip of coffee, but her hand shook as she brought the cup to her lips. Katana started to rise. "Down! Stay, Katana," she ordered again. Amazingly, the dog stayed put.

Michael glanced at Katana, a flicker of surprise appearing for an instant on his face. Rhett ignored the dog and went searching for his partner. Michael crouched in front of Dorel, his hands on her knees.

"We're doing fine. This won't take long," he said in his

calm, professional pilot's voice like he was informing passengers they were next in line for takeoff.

"I put the dog on the stain that I tried to clean. I don't remember what I did with the cloths."

"They're being washed," Michael answered as he rose and headed out of the room.

She stared after him. The man was on autopilot. Nothing bothered him. He felt nothing and was obsessed with his own destiny and righteousness.

"You know, Ms. Everly," interrupted Lieutenant Rhett, returning to the living room. "I've never asked you why you were at the gun show?"

"I was supposed to meet Michael there, but he was late. A man followed me around. I got nervous and left."

"Left your car?" Rhett pulled a round ottoman up nearly to her knees, his relentless manner willing her to talk.

"I had to. The starter's been giving me trouble. I had to take a cab."

"To Auburn? That's a long and expensive ride from Seattle."

"Actually, I took the bus and called my uncle from a pay phone."

"Why?"

"Why from a pay phone?"

"No, why did you go to Auburn?"

"So my uncle could get my car." She was painfully aware that Rhett was closing in on her.

"But why didn't you go to your home?"

She looked at him, trying to judge what he knew. "I was house-sitting for some people and they'd returned. I don't have an apartment or house of my own."

"Why didn't you come here? To Gabrielli's house?"

"Because she wasn't staying here then," Michael answered behind him. "She hadn't agreed to move in yet."

"Why didn't you stay on at your uncle's place? Your aunt was expecting you to." Rhett leaned forward.

She sucked in an inadequate breath. "Um, well, I wanted to stay with Michael and I didn't want to tell my aunt yet." Dorel tried to look directly at Rhett and lie convincingly.

"We'd thought about moving in together sooner, but Dorel had to finish up her house-sitting job," Michael said.

"Okay, but why the brief stay with the Prefontaines?" Rhett persisted.

"I had to get some things tied up and I wanted to see them."

"But why so short a time?"

"If I'd stayed longer, I'd have been treated like their little niece again. Abie was pressuring me to work there and—"

"You work for Boeing, right? An engineer?"

"Yes, I'm an engineer, but I'm not working for Boeing right now. I was laid off. They'll call me back, but I don't know when." She willed her hands still in her lap.

"Your aunt said you left her house with Gabrielli and didn't come back. Said that Abie packed all your stuff and towed your car to you, but he didn't tell her where you were. Something happen that made you just take off like that?"

Dorel stared at the policeman. She fought the sting of tears, feeling alone and pinned down. Trapped.

"Dorel tried to explain to her uncle that she wanted to move in here, but he was upset. I took her to see him and he threw her out of the office. I brought her home with me," Michael answered for her.

"Didn't you intend to return for your car and belongings? Explain to your aunt?" Rhett pressed.

"I would have eventually." She felt ambivalent at Michael's quick wit and convincing explanation.

"So, you and your uncle had words?" Rhett pressed.

"He said my grandfather would be as ashamed of me as he was and that I belonged with family who could take care of me."

"Sounds like a guy who cared a lot about you," Rhett's tone chided. "We thought maybe he was on his way to tow someone when he was killed. Did you call him to pull you out of the ditch?" Rhett asked.

She shook her head. "We weren't speaking to each other. So Michael had us towed to his garage."

"Who killed Abie?" Michael asked.

"I'm not at liberty to discuss an open case, but I'll tell you that we think the same guy who killed Osterman also killed Prefontaine with a sword. Bits of old, unusual metal were found in the wounds. In the bone," Rhett answered.

Dorel gulped. If the policeman was trying to frighten her, he was succeeding. She swallowed back down the coffee threatening to come up. From somewhere in the house, she heard the muffled sounds of Sergeant Menlow opening and closing drawers and doors. Where did Michael hide the sword?

"Lieutenant, what are you looking for?" she asked.

"Why, Ms. Everly, the sword, of course."

The words clawed her back and grabbed her around the throat. He knew about the sword? "Pardon?"

"The sword used in both killings. I thought I made that clear."

"Why are you looking here?" She glanced at silent Michael's carefully composed expression.

"It's pretty obvious, I'd think. We find a dead guy and Gabrielli's flying scarf at the crime scene near your car. But you say he never showed to meet you, and that you were followed by some man. Maybe the first victim? Your uncle, who picked up your car, then you had words with, was the second victim. And you just happen to be living with Gabrielli, who collects old swords. Pretty interesting."

"Coincidental and circumstantial," replied Michael calmly and rose. "More coffee?"

"Yeah, thanks," said Rhett congenially. He turned back to Dorel. "What do you think?"

She cleared her tightening throat. "I've always heard about being at the wrong place at the wrong time, and it seems to be the situation with me. Beyond that I can't tell you anything."

Rhett stood up and looked at his watch when Menlow came in. "Thanks for the coffee. We've got some other things to check out. As they say in the movies, 'don't leave town'. We'll be talking to you later."

The two policemen started for the front door and Katana jumped to his feet, barking. Alarmed, Dorel watched Rhett stop and turn to look at the dog. "Christ, he's big. What is he, Airedale?"

"Yes," said Michael. "Oorang, largest of the Airedale breed and bred for hunting."

Rhett walked toward the dog with his hands at his side. "Hey there, boy. Gonna let me pet you?"

Katana wagged his tail and stepped forward. Rhett stopped and scratched the dog's big, blocky head. He paused mid-stroke and squinted at the rug behind the dog. "Whoa. Big dogs, big messes," he grunted and with a final appraising look at the discolored spot, turned away and left the house with his partner.

Chapter Twelve

When Michael returned from seeing the police out, he went directly to his office and closed the door, leaving Dorel gratefully alone with Katana. The dog lay at her feet, his head alertly on his paws in guard mode.

She wanted to let go and lose herself in sleep, but she was afraid. Sleep meant dreaming and her last one of the Tsuji's love and her insane acting upon it had disastrous results.

Think, she ordered herself. I must think, keep control. Yet fatigue sucked at her, bleeding off her energy. She tried to fight it, but sleep was too seductive and she drooped into the settee's soft leather, giving into the narcotic warmth soaking through her.

Dorel! Listen to me. Only to me. You have let the memories become too strong. Fight them. Yes, you are Michiko and all the others, but remember the role of Guardian of the Trust is a soul agreement you and he entered into eons ago. It was supposed to be for your mutual growth. You were both supposed to help each other learn love in Earth's difficult school so you could help others. You chose a symbol that you both would recognize subconsciously that would bring you together, the sword. But he succumbed to wielding personal power and convinced himself and you to give up responsibility for your choices and actions and until you both have come to believe that it holds the power instead of yourselves. Fight that.

After every Earth life, the two of you judge yourselves and know that you failed again. You resolve the next life you will choose love and complete the Trust agreement. You, Dorel, are the incarnation who can break the cycle of failure. He knows that, and despite his agreement before this incarnation, he will fight you to keep the power.

"Who, Grandaddy?" *she asked, distracted by the delightful jasmine-scented breeze playing in the wind chimes.*

The Defender.

"Michael?" *She looked toward the stone garden where the robed figure stood under a lone twisted willow tree. He beckoned to her.*

No! Resist him. That is the Defender.

"He needs me." *She started to move to his side.*

He is not the Michael you can save, Dorel. But if you do not listen and act, Michael will never be free. Nor will you.

"I can't help it. The sword is too strong. It's too difficult, Granddaddy." *She gazed longingly at the princely man in the beautiful garden. He took a step toward her, his arms open. She would go to him. Where she belonged.*

No!

Martin Everly blocked her path. He was handsome in his white Navy dress uniform. Blond wisps escaped from the front of his cap, curling on his forehead. He'd been so proud of his hair. But she'd never seen it like this. He was young.

"Granddaddy?" *she asked, momentarily forgetting about the man behind him in the garden.*

He smiled. "None other. Didn't know I'd ever been a good-looking fella with hair, did you? I wanted to present you with an image you couldn't ignore."

She threw her arms around his neck and hung on. "Oh, Granddaddy, I've missed you so much." *Great sobs clogged her throat and she shuddered in his arms.*

"There, there, Dorel." *He patted her back.* "I'm always here. Never left you."

She pulled back a little and wiped her eyes with her finger-
tips. Gazing into his smiling green eyes, her happiness qua-
vered. "But this is only a dream. You're gone. I'm alone." She
looked past his shoulder. "Except for him."

"This may be a dream as you understand it, but I am real.
Martin Everly didn't cease to exist. Our physical bodies die
and are discarded, but who we are, our essence or soul does not.
We choose a new life, a new body and continue to learn."

"You've reincarnated?" The thought thrilled her. She
couldn't bear to lose him again. She would find him—whom-
ever he was now.

He smiled gently. "No, not quite yet."

Happiness skulked away and her shoulders slumped. "Oh.
I see."

"I don't think you do, Dorel. I've a lot to accomplish before
that happens. We all do. I will help you break free. I can do
that now. And more importantly, you can do it."

The man behind him continued toward her, his movements
beguiling her. "What were you saying, Granddaddy?" she
asked, her attention divided between the two.

"Listen to me! In all the other incarnations you were the
chattel of the Defender. There were times in history, windows
where you had an opportunity to discover your own personal
liberty. It wasn't the location, but the energy of the time, such
as the signing of the Magna Carta or in America in 1776. So
there was an opportunity for development or learning, but no
opening for personal liberty because of the incarnation you
chose. You and he as the Tsujis chose the wrong incarnation,
Wartime Japanese, and did not have the chance for liberty.
But Michiko knew Dorel Everly would."

Dorel's gaze stole again to the robed man. His face was
no longer comely, but fierce in rage. He ordered her to him.
His demand repulsed her and she turned her full attention

back to her grandfather. "How did she know I could be free, and to pass the sword to me?"

He smiled at her renewed attention. "It is an intuitive sense. The next incarnation is revealed in the last hours of your life. You know when death is near and the information comes as a voice within or as lucid dreams."

Fear slid down her throat. "You mean dreams like this?"

His expression softened with sadness. "Perhaps. You are not helpless, Dorel. You are an educated woman who has a keen personal concept of liberty, of independence. In fact, it's the theme of your life. You are now able to break those bonds that have always held you to the Defender. You are able to resist the seduction of personal power that you and he mistakenly believe belongs to the sword."

She shook her head. "Every moment it becomes harder. I do things I don't remember, just like Michael."

"You can resist! Unfortunately, you and he are fused together in this struggle. You help or free yourself only as you help him. You must convince him to give up the power and the only way to do that is to destroy the sword. Then he will realize the sword has no power over him. The struggle is with himself and his exercise of personal power."

It was impossible. "It won't let us. It's too strong," she objected.

He glanced over his shoulder, a brief look of apprehension hazing his eyes. "Yes, the belief in the sword's power is strong. You've both spent millenniums strengthening that belief. It is strong, but so are you. Know that. There are countless assassins, Dorel. He must deal with them. That is what he has chosen, drawn to him. And to you. When he is under attack, you must help him or you will both be killed. But you must not kill or you will not fulfill the Trust. You must also help him to remember himself as Michael."

★ ★ ★ ★ ★

"Dorel!" Michael's voice breached the dream.

She tried to hold onto her grandfather, but the scene faded, leaving her coldly alone in the darkness. She opened her eyes reluctantly.

Dressed completely in black, solemn-faced Michael presented an imposingly macabre figure. "They're going after Spence," he said, his voice low and emotionless.

She licked her lips and ventured, "Why? I don't understand."

"Inada's learned that Spence is important to me." His cobalt eyes had a feral glint that held no affection.

"How do you know they're after him?" She willed Michael to look out from those deadly eyes instead of the Defender.

He held the sword and the case out to her. "I heard."

She stood, accepting the sheathed sword. "How?" His answer didn't matter. Now that she held the weapon, she knew as well.

"It warned me," he answered, not bothering to acknowledge the sword in her hands. Had it somehow communicated with him as before, and was it now compelling her to fall in behind him as he walked to the garage? She shoved the sword into the case, wishing she could remember the dream she was having when Michael awakened her.

She settled in the small rented car beside him, the sword case vertically resting on the bucket seat between her and the door. As the little car bounced over the gravel road toward the main blacktop, she asked, "Where are we going?"

"To take them out before they get to Spence. I know where they are."

The only part of Michael she could hold on to was his concern for his friend Jonathan Spencer. She focused on that to stave off the constrictor of fear tightening around her as Michael's words "I know where they are" echoed in her head.

He said nothing further and she was in no mood to talk. Instead, she tried to remember what Granddad had told her. He'd said she could save them. But had he explained exactly how? she wondered, now that the dream or whatever it was had evaporated leaving her anxious.

They rode quietly into Seattle. Dorel's uneasiness grew as he drove into the International District. The Asian neighborhood. The car idled slowly down crowded streets filled with milling shoppers and tourists. Michael scanned the streets looking for something or someone.

The sword case crowded her leg. She was sweating against the leather and shifted away from its uncomfortable heat. Michael pulled into an alley behind an import shop and turned off the engine. He watched in the rear view mirror in silence for several minutes.

"Come," he ordered and got out of the car.

She was about to refuse his terse command when she saw two Asians step out of the doorway. The over-large and definitely threatening men acted as if they'd been waiting for them. They were dressed in flowing black trousers and loose long sleeved tops like Michael. Their foreheads were tied with red strips of cloth. In a flash they each reached behind their necks and came back with gleaming swords.

Dorel jumped out of the car and set the case on the car's trunk and jerked open the lid. Michael could have reached the sword easily, but he did not. Without taking his eyes off the men, he extended his open hand toward her for the sword. She frantically drew it half out of its scabbard and presented it to him handle first.

Michael swung the weapon in a figure eight as though combining his strength with sword's, then stepped toward the two men who circled him. Dorel stood at the car, unable to move, but yearning to drag her beloved away to anywhere but here.

As one, Michael and the sword engaged the men. The clanging of swords echoed off the dirty brick walls of the alley. Each blow struck terror in Dorel's heart. Fear gnawed at her, and every injury she'd sustained in the last few days began to throb and ache in sympathy with the blows landing on Michael. All the street noise faded away. Only she was witness to the harsh breathing and steel meeting steel.

One black-garbed man drove Michael back toward her. As black joined black in the lengthening shadows, she tried to see which shadowy figure was Michael, which man was winning, as the glow of the sword intensified.

Michael jabbed the sword's sharp point into one man's stomach and jerked it out with a great "Heeeya!" The man staggered, dropping his sword and clutching at his wound. He leaned against the brick wall, sliding down slowly leaving a trail of red in the grime and graffiti behind him.

The remaining man circled round charging Michael from the side, but he was not quick enough. Swords met in a huge strike and Michael knocked the other man's weapon out of his hand. The man quickly kicked and twirled away. Instead of dropping his sword, Michael slashed his attacker's foot as he kicked at his shoulder. The man staggered under the cut, but charged with a knife. Michael drove his sword deep into the man's chest. The man fell to the filthy pavement, dead.

Dorel heard people running and shouting somewhere out on the street. They had to escape. She called to Michael, but he ignored her and withdrew a piece of white silk from inside his shirt. After ritually wiping the blade with torturous slowness, he turned to her, his features hard stone with violence, and extended his hand for the scabbard. She thrust it at him, glancing fearfully over her shoulder.

Michael sheathed the sword and bowed to the bodies lying before him. He presented the weapon to Dorel and walked calmly to the driver's side, while she shoved it into the case as she ran to her side of the car. As Michael started the engine, Dorel checked behind them out the back window. He drove slowly out of the narrowing alley as an excited group from the street charged in the opposite end.

Dorel embraced herself tightly and rocked, sobbing silently. This time evil hadn't come to him. Michael had sought it out. She didn't dare look at his face, afraid of the devil she might find. How could she convince this man to give up a power he clearly wanted and took pleasure from using?

When they arrived home, Katana didn't greet them in his usual exuberant way. Instead, he whined and hung back, then followed Dorel at a distance.

At the foyer, Michael went to his wing of the house and Dorel to hers. In defeat, she kicked the sword case under the futon and sank to her knees, her head on her arms on the quilt.

"Take a shower," Michael ordered from the door and threw a white silk dressing gown on the futon. "Put that on."

A sterile blankness anesthetized her senses as Dorel carried the gown across the dark hall to the bathroom. A small piece of her did not want to obey his command yet she was compelled to step into the shower's hot spray still in her clothes and begin to remove them piece by piece. When she was finally naked, she soaped her body and hair three times. As though the number would purify her. She mechanically towel-dried herself and her hair, combing the tangles with her fingers and welcoming the pain that let her know she still breathed, yet sad to be still capable of feeling.

Wrapping herself in the slick white kimono, she tied the thin belt and walked down the hall as if to her execution.

Michael waited on the sofa in the living room, a dark contrast to the brightness of an afternoon sun washing the shadows from the rest of the room. He wore only a pair of drawstring black pants, and held a crystal tumbler. He did not acknowledge her, but took a swallow from his glass and set the glass on the coffee table, then stood and came to her.

His damp hair was slicked back and droplets of moisture glistened on his broad chest. Muscles bunched under the skin of his arms and corded in his neck. His firm jaw was set and his sensual mouth unsmiling as he stared at her with cold blue-black eyes. Dorel almost shrank before his appraising proprietary gaze, which willed her to stand for his pleasure.

She squared her shoulders, tossed back her wet hair and stepped forward. Looking up at him, she saw confidence gleaming in his eyes. The Defender would have her, as if it were his due, his reward.

Her grandfather's soft voice echoed in her head, *Dorel, do not submit. The power is within you. I know you can do it. Don't let the Defender win.* Her hand snaked out and slapped him sharply across the face.

Surprise claimed his sanguine features for the merest moment. He grabbed her, his fingers digging into her shoulders while he hauled her to his chest, and crushed his mouth on hers. Desire flamed into existence. She fought against the arousal she felt from both of them. She couldn't give herself to a barbarian. A killer. To do so would be to die herself.

Loving him would kill her as it always had. And kill Michael as well. She felt death's cold hand wringing her heart, but she used the emotion, transformed it into strength to reject him, to push him away.

An alien angry melancholy embittered Michael's features and chilled her. His expression silently questioned how could she refuse what they both knew was their future? He lifted her open hand to his cheek, and grazed his lips lightly across her wrist and palm.

"I need you. You know your function. It is not ours to question or reject. Neither of us can fight this. I won't tolerate your opposition much longer," he warned, his voice steel-hard.

"You're wrong. I will fight the Defender with my last breath."

Dorel threw herself on the futon in her room and tried to sleep. She wanted to ask her grandfather to explain again this confusing feeling she had, that she could save herself and Michael, if she could find the power.

She may have slept, but didn't dream as she'd hoped and awoke when a strident whispering carried to her room. Lifting her head, she peered into the dimming evening light. She moved carefully off the bed so as not to disturb Katana and Benten crowded next to her and who seemed to prefer her company over that of Michael. She groped on the floor for her clothes, then remembered they were still in a wet heap on the floor of the tub.

She wrapped the gown securely around her body and eased down the hall, drawn toward the voices. The bathroom door was closed to a crack and the whispering quieted as she pressed her ear to the opening. She pushed and stepped back as the door swung inward.

Michael bent over someone sitting on the edge of the tub. When he turned away to rinse a washcloth in the sink, she saw a battered, bloody face she barely recognized.

"Spence!" she cried, lunging into the bathroom. "What happened?"

Michael moved back to his friend. She grabbed the cloth from him and pushed her way in front of Spence. She didn't know where to start for fear of injuring him further. Spence responded to her hesitation and grunted an attempt at a laugh that clearly pained him.

"Go ahead," Spence mumbled, his torn lips barely moving. "Don't think you could do much more damage."

"I don't know," Michael said blandly. "You've still got some teeth left."

She threw him a scathing look. "I won't hurt him. Unlike you, who are probably responsible for his condition." Her barb hit squarely she saw as Michael's wry grin vanished. His stare commanded an apology, but she refused and glared back at him.

"Hey, guys, we don't have time for any more casualties. Can we get on with this?" Spence gingerly touched a scraped, bloody-knuckled hand to his left eye that was rapidly swelling shut.

"You need to go to the emergency room. You probably need stitches," she said, swabbing his torn lips with the cloth. Spence shook his head. "Michael, go get some ice for his eye," she ordered in the next breath. "Are you stabbed . . . or shot . . . someplace?" she asked, trying to evaluate the extent of his injuries.

Again, Spence tried to laugh. "Funny, you didn't ask if I was in a car wreck. Oow, ow," he groaned. "Should have stuck with those ventriloquist lessons. Easier on the lips."

Her hand hovered over his mouth. "Sorry."

"I didn't mean you. Go ahead. Let's see what I've got left to work with." Spence's good eye twinkled, amazing her.

"You're damned cheerful for someone who's been beaten nearly to death." She continued to clean his face, rinsing the cloth more frequently as the cuts and scrapes reopened under the light wiping.

"I think he has plenty to be *cheerful* about," Michael said behind her. Situating a plastic sandwich bag of ice over Spence's eye, he added, "This will all be gone in a couple of days."

She grimaced and wrinkled her nose. "Michael, his nose is broken."

Michael stepped in front of her, straddling his friend's knees and bent over, close to his face. "Ready?" he asked.

"Uh huh," Spence grunted and closed his less swollen eye.

Michael placed his thumbs on either side of the left leaning nose and gave a sharp push. The pop and crack assaulted her and several black spots merged before her eyes. She fought them off to stay conscious.

"You monster!" she cried.

They laughed at her.

"Take it easy, Dorel," Spence mumbled. "I've done the same for him, only it was a dislocated shoulder. Hurts like hell, but it's gotta be done."

"I'll take you to someone who is qualified to help you instead of making things worse." She glared at Michael.

"Can't do that. No time. I was damned lucky to get away." Spence gently molded his swelling nose like clay. "The boys in black jumped me as I was cleaning up the shop. They'll be here next, I figure." He peered at Michael. "You should leave now, like I told you. I'll take the dog and cat with me in the rental. You lock up her car in the garage and take my Harley. I left it in the woods south of the fence. No one saw me. I made sure."

"I can handle them," Michael said quietly.

"No, you can't, Mike. You're not thinking. This Inada asshole has hundreds of these guys. This is a search and destroy thing, and I don't want to know why." He held up his hands as Michael started to speak. "The thing to do is to get Rhett in on this."

"Are you crazy?" Dorel squawked. "He'll arrest us all for

murder." Then realized she should have held her tongue.

"No, he'll go after Inada." Michael's eyes narrowed as he considered the idea. "He's been back to see you?"

"Several times. In fact, he was in the shop when he got a call this afternoon." Spence said.

Dorel caught the secretive look that passed between the two men.

"Witnesses?" Michael cut skin-toned tape into butterfly pieces.

"Yup, but not one could collaborate the other. All they've got are conflicting stories. Nobody able to agree on what kind of car left the scene. Because the cops got there almost immediately, a body still remained. And a sword."

Dorel numbly watched Michael pinch closed a long tear on Spence's cheek and efficiently apply tape, then she became aware that Spence was talking about the alley where Michael had killed two men that afternoon.

"So, he has a sword now?" Michael smoothly continued his repairs on the man's face. "Do we know what kind?"

Spence grimaced. "Yeah, a Tadatsuna from what I heard. I'm betting it's mine, Mike."

Dorel clutched Spence's arm. "You mean the one Abie stole from me?"

"Yes," Michael answered for him.

"Oh no," she moaned. "Rhett will have our fingerprints. He's got us even without my sword—"

"No," Michael interrupted, "Spence's piece will have been wiped clean. It'll have only the necessary fingerprints on it."

"Oh, of course." She slumped against the towel rack, shaking her head. They couldn't possibly get away with this.

Michael squinted as his hand hovered a gauze pad over Spence's puffy lip. "Can you help Rhett connect Inada with the guys in the alley? And the sword? And Abie?"

Spence frowned. "I think so. They'll be calling in an expert. That means me since you'll be gone, and you're a suspect. Ow, take it easy, Mike. That hurts." He batted Michael's hand away from his maimed face. "I've had enough."

Michael grinned. "Yeah, I think you have. Come on, I'll buy you a drink."

That snapped her to attention and she hurried after the two men. "He needs a doctor, not alcohol."

"Hell, if no booze, then got any real hard drugs?" Spence sniped.

"Better." Michael poured two fingers of Napoleon brandy in a crystal snifter.

Spence lifted the glass. "Here's to better days. And soon, by God." He drained it in a single gulp, then reached stiffly into the pocket of his denim shirt. He drew out a set of keys and tossed them to Michael. "Leave her in the hanger. I'll pick her up later."

Michael nodded to Dorel. "You better get dressed. We've got to leave right away. Have you got a backpack?"

"No."

"I'll get you one," Michael said and left the kitchen.

Dorel caught Spence's worried glance. "I've been trying to get him to leave for days," she said. "He's refused every time. Yet he listens to you. Why?"

Spence carefully rolled each shoulder, then his head from side to side. "It's a long story, one you haven't got time for now. Let him tell you when he's ready. It's enough for you to know that no matter what Mike needs or where he is, he can count on me." He smoothed each ruffled side of his red-stained moustache with a shaking finger. "So can you."

She blinked back tears at the brave offer. Intuitively, she

had no doubt he meant every word and would die trying to fulfill his commitment to them. What had Michael done to inspire such friendship and loyalty? "Thanks, Spence, for including me. I could use a friend."

He gave her a shy look. "You've got the best there is already. They don't come any better than Mike. He's not himself right now. I think you know that. But you can trust him no matter what. I can see how much he cares about you."

She shook her head in denial. "Oh, no—"

Spence rose stiffly to his feet. "Guess you'll just have to take my word for it since I can see by your expression that he hasn't shown you how he feels. Just know you wouldn't be with him if he didn't."

"If I didn't what?" Michael broke in, returning to the kitchen. He was dressed in an olive drab T-shirt and forest-colored camouflage pants stuffed into hiking boots. A large black nylon pack was slung over his shoulder.

Spence cleared his throat and limped toward him. "None of your business. Gimme the car keys, and round up that livestock of yours. I gotta get out of here."

When Michael turned to take the keys out of the basket under the wall phone, she spotted the black rectangular butt of a pistol nestled against the small of his back. For some unfathomable reason she was glad. At least he was thinking enough to not rely solely on the sword. Especially since Inada had "hundreds of men" as Spence said. They would come after them with more than swords.

"Put a change of clothes in here and whatever extra stuff you might need." Michael handed her the backpack and pulled out a pair of gray and purple hiking boots. "If you don't have any boots, wear these with two pairs of socks. They should work okay for you. Wear jeans, a long-sleeved shirt and bring a sweatshirt or a light jacket, too."

Dorel took the boots and backpack and headed for her room. When she returned dressed as ordered and in who-knew-whose boots, the kitchen was empty. She laid the sword case and pack on the counter and went to look for the two men.

She arrived at the garage just in time to see Michael park her Cherokee and Spence back out the rental. Katana crowded next to the door with the cat carrier between him and Spence. The dog hung his head out the window, howling a soulful farewell as the little car disappeared into the dark.

"Come on," Michael said in a hushed voice. "We've got to go. We'll see them again. I promise."

She followed him silently through the house as he turned off lights and locked up. Returning to the kitchen, she picked up the sword case and Michael shouldered the pack. After he set the alarm, they exited the house at the back door. A motion sensor security light blinked on as they crossed the dusk-shadowed deck to the garden.

"Stay close to me," Michael ordered next to her ear. "Do exactly as I do. Try to not to make noise."

As she crept behind him through the dense fir trees and underbrush, she wondered anxiously where they were going. But did the destination really matter? Not in her mind. They were leaving. That was the important thing. The Defender might be leading her into danger, but she vowed to bring Michael home.

At the boundary fence, Michael stepped on the lowest strand of barbed wire and held the next up so she could crawl through. Her pants caught, holding her back. He freed the fabric and slipped between the wire.

"You okay?" His expression was indistinct, but his voice was gentle. The embrace of his concern soothed her and stoked her hope.

She rubbed her stinging leg. "Yes, fine. Let's go."

They found Spence's big chrome and black motorcycle hidden in a grove of blue spruce on the tree farm adjoining Michael's property. He strapped the pack and case on the back rack, and she helped him push the bike clear of the trees. With a cursory look around, he swung his leg over the Harley and turned the ignition key. The motorcycle rumbled to life with a low powerful purr. He motioned her to get on behind him.

The motorcycle bounced fluidly over the rutted dirt road to the main highway. Once out on the blacktop, Michael opened the throttle and they burst through the cool evening toward the last of the sunset.

She'd thought they would head east over the Cascade Mountains to Yakima, but he drove through downtown Auburn. Dorel worried they'd be spotted by Inada or the police at every turn.

When they pulled into the parking lot at the municipal airport, she was sure he'd made a mistake until he inserted a card into a box at the ramp-access automatic gate. Clanking and squeaking, the gate slid open and he drove through, idling past rows of parked airplanes. In front of a tall T-shaped hangar, Michael shut down the engine.

She climbed off the bike, combing her fingers through her wind-wild hair, and carefully scrutinized the surrounding shadows as Michael unlocked a broad, metal hangar door and pushed it up. A light came on when the door hit the top. She gasped and took an excited step forward.

"A float plane!" she exclaimed, drinking in the pearlized white of the amphibian airplane. It looked like a giant dragonfly perched on two mammoth white bananas. A tiny wheel draped over the front tip of each pontoon and a larger black wheel hunched under the middle of each float.

Are we actually going to leave in this? she wondered in dizzying anticipation. Now her hope took wings. "You've got a Dehavilland Beaver on floats," she said with awe.

Michael pushed the Harley inside to the wall behind the plane. "And I can even fly it, too."

She was aware enough to hear the humor in his voice, and it thrilled her as much as the prospect of getting her first ride in a float plane. Until she remembered they weren't going for a pleasure ride.

They were trying to escape.

Chapter Thirteen

They flew to the remote upper Columbia River basin of northeastern Washington, but it wasn't far enough for Dorel. They could have gone far into northern British Columbia with the amount of fuel the Beaver carried, yet Michael was setting up on a final approach and turned on the landing lights. The plane gently slipped down through the crosswind barely rippling the moon-silvered water of the wide Columbia River somewhere between Kettle Falls and the Canadian border.

The Beaver kissed the water with a smooth precision that darted a flutter of admiration through her. Dorel glanced at Michael's strong profile set with tranquil confidence. She loved airplanes and flying, and this pilot. It seemed there was far more to Michael Gabrielli than she'd ever dreamed, or hoped for in a man. Perhaps they were made for each other.

Tall black trees flashed by as Michael high-speed taxied the plane a short distance up the river. Approaching a long tree-studded finger of land jutting out from the east bank, he slowed down. The landing lights glinted off black boulders rising at the water's edge, but Michael eased the Beaver safely by them to enter a tight passage.

Dark evergreens closed in, nearly brushing the wing tips as the Beaver growled over the water. Dorel gripped the edge of her seat, craning her neck to see beyond the lights into the gloom ahead. From countless flights with Granddad in his old wood and fabric Bellanca, she knew better than to distract a pilot with questions. Even though they both wore headsets and could communicate, Michael was obviously very busy keeping the plane in the center of the thin ribbon of black water.

Michael reduced power until the plane was barely making headway. As it rounded a sharp curve, the right wing tip scratched through fir boughs. Dorel cringed and made a mental note to check for damage when they stopped.

Upon entering a small cul-de-sac cove, the propeller gave a final burst of power, shoving the plane forward upon a sliver of beach, and clanked to a stop. Michael removed his headset, hung it on the yoke and toggled off switches except for the landing lights.

He rummaged under his seat, pulled out a coil of yellow nylon rope and pointed out the windshield. "See that iron stake on the beach there? Hook us up."

Dorel pulled off her headset and took the rope. She climbed out on the float, taking a sip of humid pine-spiced air. After shutting the door, she inched forward on the slippery pontoon, holding on to the side of the airplane to the front tip and jumped off onto the jumble of small rounded stones. A cloud of mosquitoes lifted off swarming around her as she hurriedly looped the rope around the stake and ran back to tie the other end around the cleat on the float.

The landing lights blinked off, leaving her swatting the darkness around her. Her eyes adjusted to see Michael pulling on his huge backpack, and stepping off beside her.

Handing her the sword case, he half-whispered, "Let's go."

"Wait, Michael. Go where? Don't you think we ought to have a look at that right wing tip?" She turned toward the plane.

He put his big hand on her arm and pulled her back. "It's okay. Just got cleaned off a little. Always happens."

A mosquito stuck the back of her hand and she wiped her

hand on her jeans leg as others circled her head with a high-pitched whine. "We'll have to catch it on our pre-flight, right?" The bugs didn't seem to bother him, but if she stood here any longer, they would carry her off. "Are we going far?"

"It's about a three or four hour hike. It'll take a little longer in the dark. We should make it just before dawn. Are you up for it?" he asked in a hushed voice.

"I'll do fine." Dorel fought the urge to run from the swarming mosquitoes. "I've done a lot of hiking and camping." Covered with bug repellant, she added silently, scratching a rising lump on her hand.

"Good. I hope the boots won't be a problem for you." He adjusted his pack and glanced back at the airplane, then set off without waiting for her reply.

She called to him, "Have you locked the Beaver?" Then wondered if she should have whispered as he had. Who did he think could hear them?

Michael stopped. "No. If someone wants to get in, I'd rather they opened the door than break a window." He looked at her for a moment. "You need a jacket?"

She shook her head, rubbing her arms to stop shivering. "No, go ahead. I'm okay." She guiltily eyed his bulging pack as she walked behind him, and was grateful he carried most of the gear. So far, what there was of the trail was hard going and would require everything she had to keep up with him. "Where are we going?"

"I've got a hunting camp." He strode easily over the rough ground. "There's a cabin of sorts. No amenities like electricity or an indoor toilet. Or even water inside, except where the roof leaks." The mirth in his voice encouraged her as she trudged behind him.

Since Spence had come to him for his help, Michael was acting less like the Defender. Maybe way out here, with four hundred miles of wilderness between them and the people trying to kill them, she had a chance to persuade Michael to give up the sword. Especially, if he didn't use it. She suddenly remembered more of Granddad's instructions from her dreams. He'd said the Defender's influence grew when the sword was used. And when he killed, if he killed again, Michael and she would be lost. Dorel resolutely picked up her pace and reached for Michael's hand.

He paused and looked down at her. "Do you want me to stop?" The considerate-lover quality of his voice smoldered over her skin, evoking the memory of their lovemaking, and racing an intense flash fire of desire through her.

"No, I just didn't want you to get away from me." She laced her fingers through his. She couldn't see his face clearly in the murky light of the waning moon, but she sensed his deep caring in the gentle, secure pressure of his hand.

It was near dawn when they arrived at the little ramshackle log cabin. Birds were beginning to chirp awake in the dense firs scalloping the edges of the fifty yard-wide clearing. Michael shrugged out of his pack and leaned it on a tree stump in front of the rickety-looking porch. Dorel sagged against a tall Douglas fir. She didn't dare sit yet, or she might not make it back up.

Even though he had stopped often to take compass headings, she knew the real reason was to let her rest. She was dead on her feet, anyway. And those feet ached terribly. They would be covered with hot blisters from the ill-fitting boots. Dorel silently cursed the idiot woman who had maliciously left them behind at Michael's home.

He moved across the cabin's front yard, around to the west side to the back and reappeared at the other side. Looking for what? Dorel wondered wearily. He ducked under the low porch roof and pushed the door. A woeful creak filled the air. Michael shined a flashlight inside, following the beam into the interior.

When he didn't reappear, she rocked forward and limped for the porch. "Michael?" she stage-whispered, straining to see inside the cabin.

"Right here." He suddenly materialized beside her.

She staggered in alarmed surprise. He reached out and steadied her against him. Resisting the urge to collapse into the cradle of his strong arms, she pulled herself away and asked, "Weren't you inside?"

"Just checking things out." He glanced around again. "Come on in. The cabin is currently unoccupied. Sometimes it isn't." A hint of a grin touched his mouth. "There've been skunks, owls, even a bear or two."

"Bears?" She was too tired to waste the effort on being scared.

"Yeah, they really tear the place up. I've learned to keep the supplies locked up."

"What about people? Don't they use this place?" She scanned the brightening clearing surrounding the cabin. It was inviting, a perfect place to rest. No backcountry hiker could resist its beautiful seclusion.

He lifted an eyebrow. "Dorel, no one knows about this place except for Spence. I wouldn't have brought you if they did. We're safe here for as long as we need. Trust me."

She wanted to believe that they were safe, and would just have to trust the changes she saw in Michael as evidence that they were not in immediate danger. He was calm, responsive and his eyes an affable sky blue. And he smiled.

Michael was irresistible.

"Okay," she agreed, relaxing bit by bit into the enticing shelter his bearing and words promised.

"You need some rest." He guided her by the elbow into the cabin.

The odor of ancient smoky fires and moldy dust assailed her. But the cabin was not as bad as it smelled, she saw with relief. It was spartan and clean. A gray fieldstone fireplace served as one wall and apparently as the stove. A blackened metal rack sat between the andirons and a cast iron Dutch oven, frying pan and a smoke-filmed blue enamel coffee pot clustered together on the wide raised hearth.

Michael opened the rough plank shutters on each of the three small windows cut into the thick, stacked logs of the walls. Immediately the crisp morning fragrances replaced the stale air and cheered the one room cabin with light.

"I'll get a fire going." He pulled logs and stick kindling out of the wood storage opening in the rock wall. When he crouched to arrange them in the firebox, she noticed again the pistol resting against the small of his back.

Worry prickled in her stomach. If they were safe here, why was he still wearing a gun? She turned abruptly away. "I'll bring your pack in."

"Stay here. I'll get it." He gave her an appraising look. "It's too heavy for you to wrestle with. Relax. Let me take care of everything."

When he returned he unpacked their gear, laying it out on the handmade table of peeled, split logs in the center of the room. She watched him work, quietly warming herself by the fire, shifting forward by tiny degrees as the heat baked her tired body.

Michael unrolled two foam ground pads, spread them open on the log and rope-strung double bed and covered them with an unzipped sleeping bag. He crooked an index finger at her. "Give it a try. You won't even feel the rope."

She drowsily pulled herself away from the fire. "Probably

not," she murmured as she lay down and closed her eyes. "I'm too tired."

Did he say something? she wondered sleepily, as he removed her boots and pulled a soft cover to her chin. She snuggled down to the comforting sensation of a feather-light kiss on her lips and drifted into dreams of her grandfather.

You are doing well, Dorel. But do not let down your guard.

"*I have to rest, Granddaddy.*" *She tried to turn away from him.* "*My feet hurt.*"

I know they do. It has been difficult for you. I'm sorry. You must be careful still.

"*We're safe here.*"

You are safe nowhere. The wielder of the sword draws evil. Evil seeks and finds him, because he is too confident of his own abilities and uses them gladly. He puts you both in danger because of this flaw.

"*But the Defender—*"

Michael still believes he can take care of you and himself despite the inescapable circumstance with which you are faced. His own individuality and high intelligence as Michael are nearly eclipsed. The Defender's cunning and destiny consume him.

"*You said we could escape. That the Trust could be completed.*" *She wanted to weep in bitter disappointment.*

You can. But not his way. Only with aggressive peace can you escape the cycle you two set in motion. Only by destroying the sword, giving up the pursuit of personal power, can you be free and complete the Trust in this life.

"*The sword won't let us destroy it,*" *she argued.*

If you can't, another can. Give it to one you trust to destroy it. Both of you must agree to this.

"Out here, away from danger, I can get Michael to give it up. I know I can. If I just have a little time."

You do not have it, Dorel. They are coming, have no doubt.

"Michael would know if that were true. He wouldn't have brought us here."

I have told you he will hear only the Defender because the lust for power absorbs him.

"Then why hasn't the Defender told him we aren't safe here? Why do you know?"

Remember, Dorel, Michael is the Defender. He hides this even from himself. You don't realize how he battles himself. He is losing, but it is to his credit that he fights the Defender the best he can. You can help him, but you have to go now.

Dorel jerked awake. "Go where?" she asked, but the room was quiet except for the occasional snapping of the fire. The homey aroma of coffee and beef stew shooed away the sense of anxiety that woke her. She'd had another dream conversation with her grandfather, something about aggressive peace, but the rest was fading with each breath.

Dorel sat up and rubbed her eyes. Noon sunlight poured through the open front door, highlighting the uneven knot-hole-pocked floor. Michael was nowhere to be seen, but she heard the rhythmic cracking thud of someone chopping wood. She stood and immediately regretted it.

Sitting down, she examined her right foot. The heel was one big oozing broken blister as was the ball. Each toe boasted its own glistening bubble, and so did her other foot. She groaned and swore under her breath until she noticed the chipped enamel pan of water sitting next to the foot of the bed. And beside it on a blue hand towel was a package of moleskin bandaging and small scissors poking out of a Swiss Army knife.

Bless him. She scooted down the saggy bed to the pan. Easing her toes in first, she gloried in the soothing warmth of the water, until she submerged her heels.

She yelped.

"I've never seen feet that bad." Michael's large frame blocked the sunlight in the doorway. He carried a bundle of firewood to the storage bin and began to off-load.

"I wish I hadn't." She grimaced and gingerly worked each foot.

He smiled apologetically, turning to her and dusting off his hands. "Sorry about the boots, but I don't think you'd have made the hike in those sandals of yours. You'd have been on your knees within a mile."

"How far did we come?"

He ladled stew out of the Dutch oven with a sierra cup into a blue speckled enamel plate. "Maybe five miles."

"My feet say more like five hundred," she countered, accepting the plate from him. Her mouth watered at the delicious smell of gravy-doused meat and vegetables.

"I'll bet." Michael sat in a crude bent wood chair and began to eat.

"Mmmm, this is so good," she mumbled with her mouth full, glancing opposite her at the ceiling-to-floor open cupboard sparsely decorated with the backpack items. Michael's gun lay on a stack of freeze dried food packets and brown packaged military MREs neatly stacked at the end of the shelf next to a wide closet. She swallowed the last bit of stew. Hoping for more, she cleared her throat and thought about hobbling over to check the pot.

Michael looked up. "More?"

"Yes, please. It's really good."

"You're just hungry." He filled her plate. "Canned stew's never been a favorite with me."

"Oh well, I'm happy to finish it up for you."

"We should be so lucky. Got about a case of it because Spence loves the stuff." His mouth gave a wry twitch as he returned her plate.

She glanced at the cupboard again. There were no canned goods. "You come here together?"

"Usually. We try to get away a couple of times a year, but we haven't had the opportunity lately."

"Speaking of Spence, how is it that he knew what Rhett's call was about? Rhett couldn't have told him, could he?"

Michael grinned. "No, he didn't tell Spence anything. Let's just say that he has his ways of securing information and leave it at that."

She wasn't about to leave it at that. "Does he do what you do? The out of body trips?"

"I don't think we ought to discuss Spence. It's not our business."

"Yes, it is. He was involved from the moment I took the sword to the gun show. And now his store has been wrecked and he's been beaten up because of us. It's definitely our business. So, tell me."

Michael picked up his plate and shoved the stew around with his spoon. "We were both SEALs assigned to a special ops program where we learned a unique method for obtaining information about intelligence targets. The method was called remote viewing. It's a sort of mind power or mind projecting process to perceive information about a given target without occupying the same time or space of the target. But Spence wouldn't have to use remote viewing to hear Rhett's conversation at the shop. He's also an electronic surveillance genius and probably monitored Rhett's cell phone's frequency and recorded the conversation."

She stared at him and swallowed her mouth full of stew in a painful gulp. "You're saying that the government was training people, you and Spence specifically, to spy with some sort of ESP? Come on, that's too X-Files for anyone to believe."

"You can say that after all you've seen and experienced in the last few days?"

"Oh. Yeah. I guess my life has been an X-Files episode lately," she said with a shudder, then scooped the last bite of the stew into her mouth. "So, where's the case of canned stew you said you packed in?"

"In the cellar." He tapped his boot heel on the floor. "I didn't pack in the stew. We bring long term supplies once a year in Spence's Bell Ranger chopper. I only carry the back-pack in case I get delayed hiking. The cabin is well stocked with everything I need."

"Why make that hike to hell if you can simply fly here?" she asked, momentarily annoyed. She could have saved her feet all the torture. Another concern nibbled at her, but she couldn't remember what.

"I'm really sorry about your feet, but we had to walk be-cause I'm not rotor-wing qualified anymore." He took her empty plate and set it in a plastic dishpan on the cupboard. Squatting in front of her, he lifted her right foot out of the water and rested it on his knee. Patting it dry with the towel, he continued, "Besides, the hike is a challenge that keeps me in shape. Or so I like to think."

Michael's raven-black hair curled freely around his ears, stubble covered his chin and the G.I. Joe attire combined in a sexy howl of unrestrained male hormones. "I think you're in great shape," she said impulsively, her husky voice surprising them both.

The towel paused and she was vitally aware of every millimeter of contact between them. Keeping his eyes on his task, he slipped his work-roughened palm up her ankle, easing the pant leg ahead of it. "You too," he said quietly.

She stroked aside the dark curl on his forehead and leaned forward. "Michael—"

"Wait." He caught her hand and frowned, his troubled gaze meeting hers. "I have to ask you something."

She cleared her throat and sat back. "Okay."

He wrapped her feet in the towel and began to open the package of moleskin. "I hate to ask, in fact, I feel pretty stupid about it. But as you pointed out, I'm having trouble remembering."

She waited, almost holding her breath, at the strained look on his face.

"You came to my room last night? Well, the night before, I guess it is." He gave her a guarded glance.

She nodded her head, willing herself silent. He had to talk, work it out for himself. It would help him separate himself from the Defender. She prayed that he would try. Painful emotions crawled across his face as he struggled to speak.

"I can't remember." Michael looked back down and began to cut pieces of skin-colored pad and apply them to her feet. "The images, memories all flow together. I don't know where the past stops and the present begins. When Spence showed up, I almost killed him. I think if I'd had the sword, I would have. And thought nothing about it." Shaking his head in disgust, he added, "He had to knock me on my ass to bring me to my senses.

"Out here, it's better. There's no one within five miles. I don't hear the sword or whoever's talking to me, and I don't see visions." He shrugged. "Not yet. But I can feel something hovering in the background. Just out of range." Rubbing the back of his neck, he sighed. "Feels like I'm losing. Losing myself."

"No, Michael." She cradled his face with her hands. "You're winning. I can see the change. This is you." She swept her gaze around the cabin. "And this is reality. The present. We can't be touched here by anything. We can destroy the sword safely and be free. No one can stop us."

Sadness shadowed his eyes. "I wish you were right. But I can't give up the sword, I know that. The Trust cannot be broken." His voice rose in anger, almost shouting, "I hate it! I'm helpless. Was everything I've ever done in my life for nothing? Everything I've learned for nothing?"

His surrender to fate radiating from him, Michael whispered, "I'm not going to make it, Dorel."

A sob exploded in her throat. The truth he spoke tore her soul, nearly destroying her, but she continued to argue. "Yes, please. Yes, you are. Say it, Michael. Say it," she cried, knowing they were both lost. She couldn't fight the sword and him, too.

He sat on the bed, pulling her into his arms. "Shhh. We'll be all right. Everything will be fine," he crooned and rocked her like a child as she wept.

But she couldn't bear the lies he mouthed for her comfort. He didn't believe them. He'd given up and would kill again. Then die, not as Michael, but as the Defender. There was no stopping it. As he said, the Trust would not be broken. They were as good as dead already, and had been from the day they'd been born. They'd wasted so much time apart in this life. What was the point in going on, of continuing the inescapable suffering? There was no one to help her. Not even the man she loved.

Michael held her away from him and searched her eyes. "Don't give up. I need you. You're what keeps me fighting

213

this, and I am fighting it, Dorel." He watched her shake her head in denial, then her tear-swollen eyes widened as a look of comprehension flared within their green depths.

"I remember now!" Dorel exclaimed and grabbed his arms, pressing her teeth into her lip in tearful concentration, thinking. "Granddad came to me again in a dream this morning. We can break the cycle, complete the Trust. We can do it. He said so. He said he could help us." Her eyes rounded with fear. "Oh, no! Michael, he said someone was coming. We've got to leave now or we won't have a chance to break the cycle," she cried, her voice shrill.

Anticipation undulated up Michael's spine. His sword hand clutched open and closed involuntarily. He ran his tongue over his dry lips. Yes! They were coming. He felt them now.

"Where's the sword?" He glanced out the front door. They were very near. Why hadn't he known they were coming until too late? He tightened his stomach and straightened his shoulders. Was today the day? The last day of this life?

"No! You can't use the sword again. If you kill anyone, we can't stop the cycle," she warned as he set her away from him. "We have to destroy the sword."

"Don't be stupid," he threw over his shoulder and hurried to the sword case under the bed. "You know we can't do that. I need the sword. It's our only chance if we want to survive."

"We're not surviving, Michael. We're just waiting."

The tomb-quiet of her voice jarred him. He opened the case on the end of the bed and ran his hand through his hair. She was right, of course, but he wasn't going to die without a fight. Wasn't that the point of all of this, the battle against fear? Against evil? He won some, then he lost, but he always returned to fight another day. That was his reason for being. He had a mission. A purpose.

"I am the Defender," he vowed under his breath, drawing the sword out of its scabbard. Flashes of sunlight danced on the silver blade as he carried it to the doorway and pushed the heavy door closed, throwing the black iron bolt to lock it. Strolling from window to window, he latched the shutters closed, darkening the interior. She'd said nothing as he made the cabin secure. He turned to find her alertly watching him.

"Michael, what—?"

"They're here." He cocked his head at the faint whop-whop of the approaching helicopter. It had to be about four miles away. He glanced at the fire. Damn! He'd given them a smoke signal right to the cabin.

Michael felt a shift within him as the ancient Defender surrendered to the modern warrior. All of his experience, military training and survival skills united in empowering self-possession. He would fight them on his terms. And defeat them. But not here.

Michael tossed the sword into the case. "Get your boots on. Hurry. We're leaving in ninety seconds."

Joy cavorted across her features only to blank out when she heard the chopper. He was encouraged that in spite of her wounded feet, she dashed to the bed and struggled into her socks. Good, she hadn't given up. This was the woman he'd come to admire and love. Like him, she wanted to live more than anything. Like him, she was a fighter.

Sweeping everything off the cupboard into his pack, he grabbed his .45 Colt semi-automatic and stuffed it in the waistband at the small of his back.

Dorel stood in her boots, wincing for a moment, then jammed the sword into its scabbard and snapped the lid closed. She grabbed up the case by the handle and ran to the door.

"We're not going out that way," Michael cautioned and

215

stepped to the open double closet.

Her gaze darted to the windows. "But there's no other way," she said in a small, anxious voice.

"There's always another way. Especially if you have the will." Pulling her into the closet beside him, he rotated the clothes rack behind him a precise three-quarter turn counter-clockwise. A dull click sounded and the counter-weight ratcheted and dropped the closet into the dank gloom below.

Chapter Fourteen

The cabin over their heads shuddered in the landing helicopter's rotorwash as the dumbwaiter closet settled into the cellar. Michael turned on a small penlight and guided Dorel through the murky cellar as the closet whooshed back up out of sight.

His lips brushed her ear. "There's a tunnel to the tree line." Holding the flashlight in his teeth, he shoved boxes aside. A two foot-diameter hole covered by a rusty metal grate gaped in the root-entwined rocky wall.

She peered into the dark when he rolled the grate away. "How long is it?" Anything could be in the smelly pit. She didn't like the idea of getting in there with dead things that sharp-toothed alive things chewed on.

"About twenty-five yards. It's part of an old hand-dug mine shaft, so it's pretty close in there. I'll have to drag the pack." Michael slipped off the pack, bent to his hands and knees and crawled into the tunnel, pulling the pack behind him.

Dorel watched the darkness swallow him and shivered. She hesitated until a painful message from her tender feet finally got through to her anxiety-absorbed brain. She dropped to her knees, if only to be off her feet, and crept into the dark, straining to see the weak ray of light mostly blocked by Michael's hunched form.

Chalky dust sifted up her nose and into her eyes, but she couldn't rub them. Her whole body was occupied with crawling and pushing the sword case along in front of her and trying not to touch the tunnel walls. She followed Michael,

217

hustling forward like a scuttling beetle. He scrambled up a slight incline and hoisted his torso into the sunlight. He lifted himself out and latched onto Dorel's outstretched hand, heaving her topside.

The sun-cleansed air rattling into her lungs tasted like a lemon drop and almost made her giddy. She started to speak, but Michael covered her mouth with his hand and shook his head. He pulled her down next to him behind a clump of scrub oak and pointed to the clearing in front of them.

An ominous dull black helicopter sat a few yards from the cabin, its rotor still whirling. Dorel's fingers dug into Michael's thigh and she glanced worriedly at his profile. His beard-shaded jaw flexed as he watched two fatigue-dressed men carrying compact olive green assault rifles charge out of the cabin. They split up, circling the clearing in opposite directions. Dorel shrank back and tried to make herself invisible. Michael pressed her down, nearly putting her face in the dirt.

"Stay exactly here. I'm going to take them out." Michael started to move away.

She snatched a handful of olive T-shirt, holding him back. "What do you mean, *take them out?* I beg you, Michael. Don't do this to us. You can't kill them."

He knocked her hand off. "The hell I can't. It's them or us. And I'm making sure it's not us." He carefully jacked his gun's slide so it slid home almost silently, and rolled away.

"Freeze!" A blocky man materialized in front of the cluster of oak. He stood spread-legged and pointing his rifle at Dorel's chest. "Come on out of there."

Dorel slowly stood up, her knees quivering and blood rushing in her ears. The man's ugly mouth smirked as he looked her up and down. He cocked a finger at her and beckoned. She stepped around the bush, leaving the sword case behind on the dusty pine duff.

"Where's—" The man's eyes bulged as he rose on his toes and pitched face first into the dirt at her feet after Michael bashed his head with his gun butt. She stared down at the unmoving body. Michael pulled him by his legs into the bush, then picked up the rifle. He slung it on his shoulder and motioned to her.

She couldn't move.

Michael dragged her along as he ran through the forest. She stumbled and tripped mindlessly along, thinking only of the man. Was he dead? She prayed that he wasn't. Even though Michael wasn't using the sword, he must not kill—with anything.

"Michael, did you kill him?" she asked between gasps for breath.

"It was him or you," he threw over his shoulder. "I chose you."

"Is he dead?" A fir branch slapped her face.

"We better hope." He crouched behind a rock outcropping and glanced around as he tucked her in behind him.

"Where are we going?" She pressed against his side. Heat radiated off of his sweat-damp shirt.

"Back to the plane." He gave her a quick appraising look. "Can you make it?"

"I'll make it." She tried to sound convincing, tell him what he seemed to want to hear. "But how can we get away?" What was the point, she wondered despondently, if he had really killed the man?

"We've got to stay ahead of them." He stood and pulled her up with him. "They'll be hunting us with the chopper, and they've got people on the ground."

The coldness of his voice oppressed her. He'd killed the man, all right. But she pushed on anyway as the will to survive pulsed through her with each reassuring thump of her heart. Maybe there was still hope. To more than survive. Maybe they could still complete the Trust.

The sword case banged against her leg as she jogged behind Michael. What if she just dropped it? Left the weapon behind. Their pursuers would find it and leave them alone.

No! The Guardian is bound by the sword to the Defender of the Eternal Trust. This is your life. It is your inescapable duty to guard it. You cannot do otherwise.

Michael stopped so abruptly she slammed into his pack. "Did you hear that?" He looked around and turned to her. "The sword spoke. It's the first time I've heard it since we've been here. Maybe you better give it to me, so I can have it ready."

"No, I'll carry it." She wouldn't let Michael touch it again. "You heard. It's my duty. You're doing fine without it."

Michael frowned, unzipped a side pocket on his pants leg and withdrew a slim bullet-loaded magazine. Stuffing it in his front pocket, he again flashed his gaze around the area. "Okay, but we can't have that voice any more. We don't know if others can hear it."

He listened intently, holding up his hand, cautioning her. "We've got one on our tail and the chopper, too. Let's move. Stay with me and be quiet," he commanded in low tones. "We can't stop again."

The whopping sound of the helicopter behind them pushed her to her feet and she dashed to catch up with him. Running panicked, every part of her body seemed to work against her. The boots tortured her and the sword case banged against her legs. Suddenly, it occurred to her to discard the case.

Jogging lamely, she cracked open the case and yanked out the sword. She hurled the case as far away through the trees as she could. Michael whirled around at the sound. He gave her a quick approving nod as she slipped the sword into the back of her shirt and draped the silk cord around her neck.

The cool sword next to her skin felt natural and safe. And seemed to fill her with energy and confidence. Her movements smoothed into coordination and her breathing came easier even though her feet and left side hurt.

Automatic rifle fire burst through the forest. A shot thumped into a tree, throwing a chip of bark as she dashed past. It hit her arm and she yelped, jumping sideways. Michael's hand grabbed her shirt, jerking her behind a larger tree.

"Run like hell that way." He pointed south. "I'll take care of this guy." He melted into the shades of green, and she lurched into a terror-fueled sprint.

More rifle bursts rattled, striking the ground around her, sending up puffs of gray dust. Her frantic breathing and the pounding of blood rasped in her ears. She had to make it to the plane. Had to.

Had to find him. He was waiting for her.

Green hues blurred. Acrid smoke sailed up her nose and she clutched her burning side. The pain grew with each pounding step she took.

My feet. The tiles are cutting my feet. I must take it to him. To the temple.

The sword warmed against the curve of her spine, pushing her forward. She couldn't see clearly. Her surroundings washed out in a strange silvery glow like a fog bank. Sweat ran between her breasts and down her back, but she shivered with cold.

She fell face down into the temple.

He turned her over, and she opened her eyes. His gentle, sweet face radiated caring. It comforted her.

"Dorel! Wake up."

You are Everly, yes? She was so relieved to find him.

"Stop, Dorel. That time is past. You don't have to live it again. Listen. You must get up. Run. Run for the plane. Take the sword to Spencer. He will destroy it for you and release you from the cycle. Make Michael promise. He will be bound by it."

No, it is not for you. You must save it, for her. She wondered why he called her that strange name. Why would he not listen? He must take the sword.

"Wake, Dorel. Run. Help Michael. You can."

"Dorel!" Michael fell to his knees beside her. He gently turned her over, his hands sweeping her body for wounds and brushing the dirt off her smooth skin. She couldn't be dead. She couldn't be, he raged silently, furious tears stinging his eyes.

He jerked his head up at the ponderous thrumming of the oncoming chopper. He'd charge back and kill that murdering son of a bitch he'd left gagged and hanging upside down. He'd let him live only because she'd begged him not to kill, because he'd almost believed her, believed that they could break the Trust. Now the Trust was all he had left.

He'd bring that chopper down. Kill them all. Every goddamn one of them. His gaze clouded and he swallowed a cry of anguish at her pale face brutally marked by the short time they'd spent together. He couldn't stand to see her suffer again. To repeat this hell.

The chopper roared nearer and he glanced in its direction, gauging the distance.

"Mi—Michael," he heard her mumble, wrenching his gaze back to her now open eyes.

"Thank God, Dorel. I thought—"

She smiled weakly. "Not yet. And I still can't get very far away from you."

He hugged her to him. "Good. We won't ever do that again. You're staying with me." The sword against her back pressed into his arms and he eased his embrace for fear of hurting her. "Are you hit?"

Her arms went around his neck. "I don't think so. I guess I just passed out," she murmured against his lips.

The feel of her alive and warm against him drove away the blood lust of revenge. He surrendered to gratitude-inspired desire and gently touched her mouth with his. The flesh to flesh communion shattered his control. He couldn't help himself, his tongue plunging between her accepting lips. Her hands caressed his face as she pressed against him, fondling his tongue with her own.

She pulled her intoxicating lips away, her green eyes hazeled with passion. "I love you, Michael. Not anyone or anything else. Only you."

Her declaration exhilarated him. But before he could savor it, the realization overwhelmed him that her love and every feeling between them was scripted and assured by the Trust. It crushed the emotion out of him. "I know you do. That's the way it's supposed to be," he ground out, glancing away. The chopper was practically on top of them. "We've got to go."

Michael stood, bringing her up with him. He didn't have to see her face to know how his harsh words affected her. Confused, angry regret shouted from her silence as she pulled away from him. She was sorry she'd given voice to her feelings.

Michael was sorry, too.

The helicopter had to have long-range fuel tanks to stay in the air so long. Dorel wearily half-jogged every other step. They'd been on the run for nearly two hours now, trying to stay under the cover of trees, but the chopper gave relentless chase. A man in the open door, standing on the skid took shots at them at every opportunity.

What was the point of going to the plane? She focused on Michael's back weaving through the dusty green in front of her. The gunner would have a clear shot the instant they were in clearing. He'd shoot up the Beaver.

Why go there? Why go anywhere?

Thirst choked her. She needed to stop. Needed to rest. She tried to muster more energy to keep going, but it drained away with each hot, pain-jarring step. Michael's pointed rebuff of her admission of love had cost her dearly. Remorse and resentment tormented her. She loved Michael, but her love evoked the Defender. That's what had happened after she'd made love to Michael. The Defender appeared and killed as if he were energized by her love.

Michael scooted under the low branches of a twenty-foot Douglas fir and paused next to its rough brown trunk. He turned to her, holding out his hand.

"Run, zig zag to the plane. I'll cover you. Start the engine right away. Can you do that?" His face was tinged with a gray weariness and his blue eyes somber as his searching gaze stopped briefly on her. He pulled out his .45, swung the rifle off his shoulder and snaked his left arm through the sling, holding the rifle hip high.

She craned her neck to see through the thick branches, surprised to catch a glimpse of the Beaver resting in the late afternoon sun-flooded cove. They'd made it.

"You want me to go to the plane?" Dorel felt terribly exposed as if she'd already been caught.

The black helicopter began to orbit a couple of hundred feet over the cove. The door gunner's machine gun silently waited for her to step into the open.

"You can do this. I'll hold them off. Trust me. With a little luck, I'll bring them down." He charged the rifle, jacked the .45's slide and started to step away from the protective screen of pine boughs.

"Wait, Michael," she cried. "I—I . . . let's run together. I don't want to leave you."

A caring grin livened his haggard face. "No chance." He cocked his head toward the plane. "I'll be right behind you."

A current of electrifying love propelled her to him and she threw her arms around his neck. The rifle butt poked her ribs. "Tell me you love me. Now. Or I'm not going anywhere."

His arm snaked around her waist and he kissed her deeply. He abruptly broke off the kiss that threatened to drown them both in unrequited yearning, and stepped back. She unclasped her hands from behind his head.

"Michael, you love me—Dorel. You love *me!*" she asserted, holding onto his arm, willing him to admit his feelings to her. And to himself.

"More than you know," Michael murmured. He moved away from her and stepped out from under the tree, squinting into the sun, his rifle and pistol both pointed skyward.

She bolted past him and ran, holding her breath across the twenty feet of pebble-strewn beach. The helicopter's rotorwash twisted dirt and spray around her. Her hair lashed her face and stung her eyes. Bullets ricocheted off the ground. She didn't look back or anywhere else, only at the Beaver waiting for her.

Behind her, Michael's guns barked at the helicopter, encouraging her, making her tuck her chin and run faster. They reached the plane at the same time. Michael jammed the pistol in his waistband and ripped the rope loose from the cleat. They pushed frantically on the pontoons, backing the plane into the water. Dorel scrambled onto the float and crabbed to the door, wrenching it open. She dove inside as a bullet hit the float beside her foot.

Taking off the sword, she tossed it into the back and settled into the right seat. She glanced at the gauges on the dash and at Michael on the beach blazing away at the circling chopper now forced to fly higher to avoid his accurate gunfire.

Switching on the engine magneto, she cracked open the throttle and pulled the fuel mixture lever to full rich and pushed the starter button. The propeller slowly started to turn, but the engine coughed a backfire and the propeller stopped. She stifled a horrified, panicked sob, reset the throttle and tried again.

Thump, pong, pong.

Bullets struck the airplane

Dorel prayed they wouldn't hit the fuel tanks. Again, the engine cranked and burst to life with a huge puff of gray smoke.

Michael dashed into the water, grabbed a pontoon, and pulled himself around to the left door, staying clear of the invisible spinning prop. Hauling himself up on the float, he turned and grabbed for his pistol as he raised his rifle at the sky again. The .45 tumbled from his waistband into the deep green water.

Dorel firewalled the throttle. The plane shuddered and bucked, rocking back under the force. She immediately cut power and tried to guide the drifting plane into the middle of the cove, but it was sluggish to respond and continued to coast toward the opposite beach.

The door opened and Michael bailed in. He grabbed the controls and stabbed the rudder pedal as he applied throttle and spun the plane around.

"Shoot, damn it. Shoot," he yelled, shoving the rifle at her as he slapped on his headset and taxied the Beaver to the mouth of the narrow passage.

Dorel scanned the sky, ducking to see up and out of the windshield. Pushing open the door, she pointed the barrel out and pulled the trigger. The burst of gunfire almost ripped the gun from her hands. The helicopter veered away behind them. She couldn't see them now. But the gunner would have a good open shot at them until they made the cover of the tree-lined corridor. She pulled on her headset, muffling the roar of the engine.

Flinching involuntarily with an impact, Michael cried, "We're hit!"

Dorel searched frantically behind her into the backseat as if she could see the damage and pressed the mic to her lips. "Where? Can you feel it?"

"Rudder, I think." Michael mashed the pedals alternately, the plane zigzagging lethargically. "Yeah. But it's still operational. Just."

He pushed the throttle and the Beaver leaped forward into a storm of bullets hailing the water in front of them. "Good thing he's a lousy shot."

Dorel's gaze was riveted on the waterway in front of them being rapidly gobbled up by the staggering Beaver. More than the rudder was damaged, she judged, clenching her teeth until her ears hurt. She sucked a shallow breath and tried to relax, but it would take an ocean of revitalizing oxygen to accomplish that.

The gunfire from the helicopter was becoming sporadic, she realized, trying to see behind them out the side window. Then she saw that the trees that threatened to tear the wings off the Beaver also protected it. The gunner only fired when he could see them.

"How far to the lake?" she yelled into the mic.

His gaze flashed over the gauges and back to the path

ahead. "About a hundred yards. I'm going to take off speed now and lift off as we clear the mouth."

"No! Michael, that's too dangerous." Dorel clamped his thigh with her left hand.

"And this isn't?" he said with a cheerless laugh. "When we get airborne, I'll come around on them and I want you to blow them the hell out of the sky."

"I can't. I can't kill them." Her right hand dropped off the gun heavy in her lap.

"Don't worry. Just aim at the rotorblades or the tail rotor. They'll auto-rotate in and probably survive." Michael shoved on the fully opened throttle, trying to increase the engine's power, but it was already giving him all it had. He gripped the shimmying yoke with both hands. "More important so will we."

That was the important thing. She wanted to live, though the way the Beaver was half-taxiing, half-flying down the skinny alleyway with long, thick tree limbs grabbing at it, there wasn't much promise of living any longer than the next sixty seconds. She prayed that he could continue to muscle the aircraft straight down the middle, despite the plane's attempts to veer to the right bank.

In the slight chop of water of the main channel, the Beaver broke loose of the river, wobbling into the air as the plane cleared the opening. She saw the chopper sweep down out of the sun, flashes from the man's machine gun blinking as it flew by them. Unbelievably, they missed.

Michael banked the climbing airplane and Dorel was afraid it would stall. What the hell, she rationalized in the next moment, a stall or bullets, both would be equally lethal. She hung on as the plane tipped on its right wing and she looked straight down at the blue-green river a mere couple of hundred feet below.

Suddenly, the chopper was ahead and below them. Dorel stared at the black skin of the helicopter they were rapidly overtaking. How had Michael done this?

"Aim low and walk the fire up to the rotor," Michael said in her ears.

She shook her head doubtfully, her hand closing around the rifle's smooth stock.

"You can do it. You have to." He lifted the gun in her hands, urging her to do as he ordered.

Dorel stuck her foot in the door to keep it open and pointed the gun out again, trying to sight on the chopper. She squeezed the trigger and clamped her eyes shut, gritting her teeth. Noise and smoke filled the cockpit and the gun stopped firing.

Empty.

The helicopter banked to the left in a climbing turn and disappeared behind them. Dorel threw the useless gun out the door and closed it. She glanced at Michael's tense profile. "I'm sorry."

"It can't be helped," he grunted, peering around, trying to find the chopper. "Hard to hit anything without bullets."

She obviously couldn't hit anything with bullets, because she hadn't really wanted to. Dorel sat back and stared through the haze of propeller, waiting.

The helicopter didn't appear. There was no sound other than the clamor of the Beaver's engine and the rattling set up by the increasing vibration. Her engineer's mind grappled with the cause. The airplane was heavily damaged, more than just the rudder, she decided, evaluating the sound and feel of the unusual vibration.

Dorel checked the sky out the window, wishing she could see behind the Beaver. Any moment now she expected to be ducking bullets, if not riding the plane in as it crashed in a fiery ball into the rolling carpet of emerald green below.

Maybe I actually hit the helicopter, she thought anxiously when the expected attack didn't come. What happens now?

Placing her hand on Michael's arm she asked, "The helicopter's gone?"

He nodded with a reassuring smile. "Yeah. Let's go home."

Dorel stared at the sun perched above the western horizon, refusing to consider what had really happened to the helicopter. Instead, she wondered what awaited them in Auburn. Rhett? Inada? Or nothing?

If they'd gotten this far alive, maybe the cycle was being broken, the Trust completed, but she remembered her grandfather's words: *Destroy the sword. Take the sword to Spence. Make Michael promise.*

How? How could she convince Michael to give it up? He would have to love her, want her more than he did the sword. Did he? She turned and looked at the weapon lying on the backseat.

Dorel grabbed the sword, pulled it into her seat at the same time she opened her door. She forced the sword out into the violent stream of air. Its red cord whipped her hand, wrapping around her wrist. The buffeting nearly ripped it out of her hand as she opened first one finger then another.

"No!" Michael grabbed across her, but he couldn't reach it.

"I'll drop it, Michael," she yelled over the howling wind. "I drop it unless you promise me."

"You can't do it," he groaned, his face going pale with fear and shock.

"I'll go with it if I have to," she replied. "Promise me."

"Dorel, bring the sword inside and close the door. I'll promise you anything."

"You'll make your promise and keep it. You have to, you

know that." It was true. The Guardian and the Defender were held together on an unbreakable trust with each other. She would use it to destroy the cycle as they should have many lives before.

Sweat broke out on Michael's upper lip and he blotted his white face with his arm as he kept his alarmed gaze fastened on her. "Okay, okay. What do you want me to promise?"

"That we take the sword to Spence and have him destroy it."

"No! I need it," tore from his throat in a tormented howl.

"Not any longer. You protected us without it. Without killing anyone with the sword. It has no power for you or over us." She leaned against the door, pushing it open wider in the pressing wind that battled with her grip on the sword. Michael's hand clamped on her left arm, holding her back.

Tranquil purpose soothed her. She wasn't emotional about the prospect of dropping out the door with the sword; she had nothing to lose. She glanced at his white-knuckled fingers grasping her arm. "You can't stop me, but you can save me, and yourself. You can break the cycle's power. The Defender knows that. You know that. My grandfather told me that we will be free this time. I won't give up, and I won't let you. Make your promise, Michael. This is the life we do it right."

Michael silently wrestled with her truth, his conflicted emotions giving harsh strength to the fingers that dug into her. Finally, he let go and placed both hands back on the yoke.

"I promise," hissed from Michael's clenched teeth as he stared into the sky ahead.

Dorel closed the door and sat back, the sword resting across her lap and glorying in the knowledge that Michael loved her more than the sword. His promise to her broke the

Defender's hold, she could sense it. They were united in a new promise of life.

Michael will feel the wonderful freedom and joy that I do after the sword is destroyed. Dorel smiled out the window at the gorgeous pink clouds building on the horizon to the southwest.

Chapter Fifteen

"No! You can't be serious. I won't do it." Jonathan Spencer turned his back and continued to disassemble the Beaver's rudder, muttering under his breath.

Dorel looked to Michael for support, but he shrugged and rummaged busily through the rollaway toolbox sitting next to a long workbench. Oh, no you don't. You're going to do this. You promised.

"Spence, it has to be destroyed. Michael and I have realized this. As long as the sword is in one piece, Inada or someone else will never stop. They'll keep coming to take it until we're all dead," she explained as he silently worked on the damaged rudder while Michael handed him tools, both men operating like a highly trained surgical team.

Michael had called him the moment they'd touched down in Auburn, and within minutes Spence had screeched up to the hangar in Michael's rented Corolla filled with a grinning, happily barking Katana and yowling Benten. That was the upside. When the words *destroy the sword* had spilled from her mouth as she patted the dog through the car's open window, the two united against her, with Spence doing the talking, the refusing for the pair.

The Defender was not going to use Spence, or Michael, any more, Dorel resolved. She put her hand on Michael's shoulder, pulling him aside. "Michael, you promised," she said in a low voice, gazing intently into his resolute face.

He shifted uneasily and took a deep breath. "They'll keep coming after us. But if I have the sword I can use it against them. It wouldn't fail me."

233

"It always has," she reminded him. "The Defender part of you knows that. You're hiding it from yourself."

In a flash of inspiration, Dorel recalled everything her granddad had told her in her dreams since his death and it all came together now. "The sword has never spoken to us, Michael, or made us do anything. It's been only ourselves doing and speaking. All of ourselves, all that accumulated energy building, seeking an outlet through our present incarnations. The sword doesn't have any of its own. It's only the tool to galvanize our chosen events for ourselves."

It was so strange to hear herself saying this, and was almost as if the words emanated from another source. But this was no barrier to understanding.

Dorel spoke the truth, and she knew it.

"You never needed to research the sword's history to learn about its power," Dorel persisted now that she had Michael's full attention. "You already know all. Conducting research is simply the way your present incarnation approaches problems. My granddad spent his life searching for the key to our freedom from the Trust. But it was not in any book or history or manuscript." She lifted his hand and touched his fingertips to her heart. "The answer is here." Gently moving his hand back to his own chest, she murmured, "And here. We don't need to look any more or run away. Or fight. We are free. We will destroy the sword."

Even Spence appeared moved by her words. He'd stopped working and turned his swollen eyes on her. She released Michael's hand and turned to Spence. "Destroy the sword."

Spence blinked and gave her a thoughtful look. "You and Mike may not want the sword any more, but that doesn't mean that others don't. Don't destroy it. I'll sell it for you. It's too valuable to destroy."

"You don't want it, believe me," Michael said, his penetrating gaze still fixed on Dorel.

Spence swore and shook his head. "Mike, we've been to hell and back together, but this has got to be the worst. I don't understand all this, but I do know it's crazy to give up a one-of-a-kind sword worth millions. If you can't stand the pressure, hell, sell it to someone who can and is willing to protect it. Make everyone happy. You get big bucks and some collector gets an incredible piece." He tossed his screwdriver in the toolbox and wiped his hands on his khaki pants.

"If Inada is the collector you're talking about, he isn't going to buy the sword when he's got the troops to take the damn thing," Michael countered.

"He's gone," Spence said simply and lifted off the fractured rudder. "He disappeared the minute I put the evidence before Rhett yesterday. He had intelligence, bugs everywhere. Must have put his airborne guys on you before he beat it out of country. No one will be coming after you now. Old man Inada is scrambling to salvage what sonny boy has screwed up. The prodigal son's expensive habits have attracted lots of unhealthy interest in Inada America from subterranean levels in D.C. and Langley. It's cost Daddy big and for the last time."

Relief smoothed the muscles across Dorel's shoulders. She walked to the airplane and took the sword off the seat.

"You guys owe me big," Spence added with a grimace as she returned to Michael's side. "Rhett's got my Tadatsuna. Don't know when or if I'll ever get it back. He was glad as hell to talk to me, because I gave him a murder weapon and a suspect," he glanced meaningfully at Michael, "other than you. He put it all together as nice as you please with Inada thrown in to make it really worth his time and promotion.

"Seems that Abie Prefontaine was killed in a fence deal gone bad by the body in the alley—when it was still alive.

Prefontaine had a reputation for merchandizing just about anything and probably offed the guy at the gun show with the sword that was later used to kill him."

"Where do you get all this?" Dorel asked, amazed.

"Let's just say I'm a simple traveler on the information super highway," Spence said cryptically.

"And we're not talking the Internet," Michael mumbled.

Spence focused on her. "The point is, profit from this, Dorel. Don't throw away the opportunity for financial independence. Sell the sword. You're free to do that now."

His persuasive speech snaked into her logic. Yes, why not? She wanted freedom in its entirety. All of it. And that meant having money, which she needed desperately.

There is no liberty unless you give up the desire for that which shackles you.

Dorel didn't know if Spence and Michael heard the words still reverberating in the muggy air of the closed hangar. It didn't matter, she knew what to do. Sliding the sword out of the lacquered scabbard, she held it out to Spence. "Cut it up. We don't want it or need it. Neither does anyone else."

Michael started to prevent her from handing over the sword, but he clamped his hands at his sides, and gritting his teeth, kept his promise to her. He threw Spence a gruff look with a single sharp nod of permission.

"Ah, crap. This is crazy, guys." Spence shook his head morosely. "Absolutely crazy." He lifted an acetylene cutting torch off the welder's rack and held out his hand.

Dorel calmly handed the sword to him, feeling nothing and hearing nothing. She didn't look at Michael, sensing that he was in danger of losing the battle with himself. He still wanted the sword, but he would keep his promise if it killed him.

Spence tightened the sword's handle in the vise squatting

on the end of the workbench. He lit off the torch and hesitantly touched it to the steel. Dark circles swirled and glowed on the blade. It shrieked as the steel heated, constricting, fighting for its life. Three inches from the tip, the blade drooped and fell to the counter with a clank.

Spence shook his head in grief and proceeded with his destruction, cutting the sword into five pieces. He finally stopped, leaving four inches of blade in the handle.

They stood in silence waiting for the pieces to cool. No one had spoken during the cutting and there was nothing left to say after the deed was done.

Michael picked up the heat-distorted pieces, dropped them into the scabbard one at a time and replaced the handle. He'd thought giving up the sword would rip his heart out. Instead, he only felt a sense of absence. Like an amputee, he experienced the phantom pain, but the limb was gone. As he handed the dead sword back to Dorel, she raised on her toes and kissed his cheek.

"Thank you, Michael. You're the bravest man I've ever known. I love you with all my heart," she whispered into his ear, hugging him.

Her reassurance transformed his loss, heartening his purpose and reawakening his strength. The void within began to shrink as freedom dawned in his consciousness. The waiting was over. His life was truly beginning at this moment. Now they could live. Now they had a future.

They drove the rental car home, talking shyly about what to do with the sword. By the time they'd parked in the driveway, they'd decided it was best to treat it like the rest of Michael's collection. The red twisted silk cord and gray iron hilt stuck out of the battered, carved spiral design of the black lacquered scabbard. The sword had a beguiling beauty still.

Dorel opened her door and got out, pulling the passenger seat forward. Katana muscled by her and dashed after Michael to the front door. She pulled the cat carrier out of backseat and watched Michael open the door, holding Katana back by the collar. "Wait there," he said over his shoulder. "We'll check it out first." He released the dog and stepped into the foyer behind him.

Dorel waited calmly by the car with the now quiet cat. Michael wouldn't find anything wrong in the house. It was over.

After a couple of minutes, a cautiously smiling Michael reappeared and took the cat carrier from her. "Everything's okay, but I had to check, you know."

Dorel followed him into the living room where he released the Persian from her box. The cat took off in a furry silver streak down the hall.

"Aw, come on, Bennie, don't hide," Michael called and hustled after her. "It's tuna time."

Dorel returned to the car for the sword and pack, wondering was this the kind of man Michael Gabrielli really was?

A big, handsome, cat-loving . . . what?

Now that they weren't being hunted and running for their lives, what if the only thing they had in common was the terror of the last few hellish days? If they weren't fully engaged in some bizarre struggle to live, would they even feel anything for each other?

Before Michael agreed to give up the sword, the increasing intensity of their passion had almost eclipsed her being. Now, though she loved Michael, the emotion was subtly altering. Becoming more contained, less acute. She still felt connected to him, but not compelled or helplessly bound to him by uncontrollable circumstance like before.

Dorel found Michael in the living room at the bookcases, staring into the open sword drawer with Katana sitting alertly at his feet. He looked up and put his hand out for the sword. The old anxiety threatened to return as she handed him the weapon, and Michael placed the useless sword in the back of the drawer behind the others.

As he slid the drawer shut, she felt her spirit lighten. Dorel wanted to spread her arms and dance in a widening circle. She was free! To go. To stay.

Things are different now, a damper of doubt suggested. She didn't have to remain in his house unless she wanted to. Would he want her to stay? Do I want to? Dorel wondered.

"Come on, let's check my messages." Michael squeezed her hand, pulling her along to his office. "We've got to have some good news for a change."

The answering machine's red light blinked rapidly. Michael gave her a here-goes-nothing look and punched the button.

"Dorel. This is Aunt Verna," the recording said. "Boeing Human Relations has been trying to get you all day. You got your job back, I guess. Don't worry about me. The funeral went fine. I'm going to Portland with my sister. See you, dear." The machine beeped and the next message came on.

Dorel hugged herself gleefully and hoped the next message was more good news.

"Captain Gabrielli, this is TransAsia crew scheduling. Sorry to tell you your leave of absence has been canceled. Please give us a call for your flight scheduling for tomorrow."

"Is that good or bad news?" she asked uncertainly.

Michael slipped his arms around her. His eyes glistened and he glanced away, clearing his throat. "I can't believe we made it, Dorel."

She circled her arms around his waist and melted. "Let's celebrate us, Michael, not pretend nothing's happened or be complacent about what we've come through. I want to know you and for you to know me, who I am . . . in this life. If you—want me?"

"Yes, I want you. And I'm sorry you have to ask." He clasped her hands to his chest and gazed down at her. "We've got to start making a new life for ourselves. Together, if you'll have me. Stay here with me."

Dorel hugged him, nearly crying with happiness. "Oh Michael, I don't want to leave you. Ever."

"Good. Hang on, I'll call in and see when I have to report, then let's finish what you started the other night in my bedroom and get on with that new life together."

Michael lit a candle in each of the pagoda-shaped metal lanterns that sat around the square pool of steaming water. Dorel waited at the door, barefoot on the smooth cedar decking in the smoked glass-enclosed pool gazebo adjacent to Michael's bedroom. He slid open the gazebo's glass door onto the dark garden. Cool honeysuckle-scented air filtered inside, tickling the wind chimes that hung from one of the open beams.

Silently taking her hand, Michael led her to the pool and turned her to face him. He ran his hand behind her neck and gently guided her mouth to his lips. His fingers slid to her shirtfront, unbuttoning it with torturous slowness. She fumbled to help him, but he brushed her hands to her sides. "Let me," he whispered against her lips. "Let me love you."

Dorel surrendered, trembling with desire and anticipation as Michael's languid, sensual undressing of her continued. When the last of her clothing fell to her feet, he quickly stripped out of his, gathered hers and deposited them on a bench against the wall.

Dorel moved to the illuminated pool steps and started to step in.

"Wait," Michael said behind her. "That's not how it's done. We wash first. Come here and sit."

She obeyed and sat on a low stool near the edge of the pool. Michael dipped a small twine-wrapped wooden bucket into the steaming water and returned to her, carrying a loofa sponge. He dropped a bar of greenish soap into the bucket and set it on the deck beside her feet, then swished the sponge in the water. Starting the loofa at her shoulders and neck, his smoky gaze riveted on hers, he squeezed warm water down her body and propelled the soap over her hot skin.

The sponge scoured over her, rubbing and circling, to her back, her sides, around to her breasts, down her stomach to her thighs, stimulating her so much she had to touch him. He shook his head as she reached for him. "Let me," he repeated and continued to bathe her until his hand washing slickly over her threatened to drive her crazy with need.

"Michael, I can't take much more of this," she groaned, pressing her top teeth into her bottom lip.

"Yes, you can," he whispered into her ear. "Wait for me." He dumped the dregs of soapy water out and dipped into the pool for more. A cascade of sensation flowed over her body with the rinse Michael poured slowly over the back of his hand. "Now, go relax in the pool while I clean up."

Dorel wobbled to her feet and made her way into the pool. She waded into the breast-high water, feeling weightless and glowing, as if she'd lost herself completely to the consuming sensations Michael created in her. She floated in the soothing, heated water and watched Michael wash the sponge over his strong, solid legs, up his torso and then dump the bucket's remains over his head. He shook the water out of his glistening black hair and turned to her with a smile.

"Are you waiting for me?" he asked, easing into the pool.

"Always," Dorel said and moved into his embrace.

She wound her fingers into his hair, watching him. His stubble-rough cheeks were blushed with excitement and his mouth was slightly open as he regarded her with half-closed eyes. She ran the tip of her tongue over his top lip then nipped at his bottom lip.

As they made love to each other, a flush swirled up her neck, heating her face. Her ears tingled and her mouth went dry as she hung on the edge, knowing he waited for her. Her ragged breathing caught and held as the sensational frenzy exploded and pulsed from him into her, thrusting them over the brink. They fell, clinging to each other, from the stark heights of driving passion into the opulent arms of love.

She gradually stilled against him and he folded his arms around her, shielding her hot, wet body from the cooling breeze drifting over them. He brushed his cheek against her hair, smiling at the intriguing fragrance of green tea soap and her own special smell mingling in the silky strands. He kissed her forehead resting against his chin and stroked his hand down her broad back.

"My Michael," she whispered. "I do love you."

It was a mistake, the HR weenie told Dorel the next morning. Her promotion paperwork had gotten into the layoff pile by some sort of weird computer error no one could figure out.

"Why didn't you know that when I got the layoff warning and called over here? You couldn't find any paperwork then either, but that didn't stop you from having me escorted off the property."

"We apologize for that, but this promotion should more than make it up to you, don't you think?" the eager woman who looked all of twenty enthused. "Think of this last week and a half as a much-deserved vacation—at your new salary, of course."

Dorel stood, picking up her briefcase. "It's been no vacation, no matter how much you pay me," she told the woman and left to report to Customer Engineering.

Everyone greeted her like a long lost friend as she waited outside her manager's office. She was glad to be back. Like all jobs, this one had been grisly at times, but now that she knew what the alternatives were, working here was a precious gift.

Life was great. That it could go from abysmal to perfect astounded her. She felt terrifically alive and found herself wanting to share the feeling with the world.

"It seems so sudden," she told the manager as he ushered her to a chair. "I didn't know I was being considered for promotion."

"Nice surprise, huh," he replied. "We need you. Always have, and we'll make this layoff thing up to you. In fact, I want you to be the management engineer on the Worldwide Air account. They've ordered fifteen triple sevens, with options for fifteen more. I was going to put you there when I got the word you were cut. Now I'd like for you to take it. There'll be a nice raise that I hope makes up a little for what you've gone through."

This was like a dream. A very good dream. "Thanks, Jerry. I'd be glad to take the account."

The rest of the day went even better. Michael called later in the afternoon. "Hi." His warm voice flooded over her and toasted her toes.

"Hi yourself. What do you mean by calling here and distracting me? I'm terribly busy with my new job." She leaned back in the chair and twisted the phone cord around her finger.

"New job?"

"Oh, Michael, it's so great," she exclaimed. "Everything is wonderful. I've been promoted to management. Hey, where are you? Did you take the flight to Singapore?"

"Nope, Honolulu. They reassigned me at the last minute and had me fill in for a guy that crunched his Beamer coming to work on I-405. I'll be home in the early a.m."

"How about you? Are you okay?" Dorel wondered if he suffered from losing the power of the sword. It had become such a part of him.

"Sure. I'm tired and trying to take advantage of crew rest instead of hanging out with the crew like usual. In fact, I'm just looking forward to seeing you."

"Me too." Dorel felt his sexy smile through the phone and blushed, thinking of last night. Neither one of them had gotten much sleep between the love making and revealing secrets about their pasts.

"Anyway," he continued, "TA's board is sponsoring a fund-raising charity event for literacy or some damn thing at the Seattle Aquarium tomorrow evening. I've been commanded to appear in a tux and I think you should have to suffer, too. You wouldn't be into that sort of thing, would you?" Though he'd said it in an off-handed manner, it sounded important to him.

"You mean, am I into suffering?"

"Naw, that's been established. I mean do you want to go to a black tie affair with your favorite captain?"

"I don't have a black tie, neither does my favorite captain. Can I borrow one of yours?" Dorel grinned into the phone.

"If that's all you'll wear," Michael's voice caressed her and her body responded readily.

"Hmm, do we have to leave the house?"

"No. I'll keep you as my love slave in black tie."

He said it jokingly, she was sure, but his words jangled her nerves anyway. She'd felt so free, that when she was reminded that she once was not, it bothered her more than she realized. "Well, maybe for both our careers, I ought to wear something more appropriate," she said, and then added, "I'll wait up until you get home tonight and model all the fabulous designer gowns I own for you. That ought to take all of two seconds, then maybe we can find something else to do." She let her voice trail off.

"Wow! Can't pass up an offer like that. I've gotta train for this and get some rest. See you in the morning," Michael said and hung up.

Dorel said goodbye to the buzzing line and hung up. She opened her wallet and recounted the cash that Abie had forced on her. Three thousand dollars—not enough for that fresh start he told her to use the money on, but it would certainly go a long way in buying a beautiful dress that would make Michael proud to take her anywhere.

God, she was beautiful. Michael watched Dorel at his side, easily conversing with the TA management and museum patrons. Her red hair was pulled back into an intricate roll, showcasing her long neck and perfect features, with artfully applied makeup hiding the faded bruises she'd suffered during their time together. Her form-fitting black silk sheath with tiny straps rode well above her knees exposing gorgeous legs. She took his breath away. It was all he could do to share her with people tonight when he wanted to be home making love to her.

Michael couldn't imagine her with anyone else—ever. And he knew she never really belonged to anyone but him through all time. He had always loved this woman. Now more than ever. As if the love they'd shared culminated at this moment, in this incarnation to be more than both of them.

She'd said she loved him. To hear her say those words was almost more than he could bear. It had cost her dearly, because he knew that she had feared him. Feared him, and feared for him. He wondered if the love Dorel now expressed was hers alone, or was it the accumulation of all their lives together? It shouldn't matter, but it did. He wanted Dorel's love for himself. To love only him, Michael Gabrielli. He wanted to disregard their pasts together and the love they shared through time.

Just focus on the present, the now.

His soul seemed to hush those thoughts. What did it matter? She loved him. Now and always. He didn't have to be the eternal warrior for her to love him. In fact, that had nearly killed what she felt for him. A thousand years ago, even a hundred years, the Guardian and Defender roles worked well. The Guardian was totally dedicated to protecting and serving the Defender. Now Michael understood why the tempting power no longer worked on her.

Dorel was a strong, independent, brilliant woman. She wouldn't automatically accept such a subservient role. And because she refused it, she'd saved them, freed them both.

We can have children, he suddenly realized.

He would ask her to be his wife tonight. They could drive to Reno tomorrow evening after work. Yes, that's what we'll do. She would say yes because she loved him.

On the way home, Dorel drove her Cherokee because Michael wanted to look at her. Or so he'd said. But she felt it was more. He had something on his mind. She would rather look at him, but consented to drive to make him happy. Making him happy seemed so natural. So right.

"What'd you think?" His voice was a masculine purr that sent thrills down her spine.

"Very nice. Fun even. I thought you were the best looking

man there. So did all the other ladies, I noticed."

"Yeah, they did," he said.

"Watch it, boy, I think I'm about to experience my first jealous fit." She flashed him a smile and took the offramp, merging onto the Valley Freeway.

"Maybe you just ought to go with it. Let's see the green eyed monster. Coming from your gorgeous green eyes, how bad can it be?"

"Hmm, good question. I don't know. I've never been jealous before. I'm not now. Just feeling sort of possessive maybe. It feels . . . unusual."

"Have you been thinking about—well, what you're going to do with the rest of your life?"

Dorel glanced at him with a slight frown. What was he asking? Had he changed his mind? Did he want her to leave? "There's a heavy question out of the blue. Well, like I said our first night back, I'm mostly interested in finding out about you. Have you tell me more little Michael stories of your childhood. I haven't really thought about the future."

"Are you open to a suggestion?"

"About how to spend the rest of my life?" Was a hint of a smile playing at the corners of his mouth? Dorel wondered nervously and hoped it was. Her hands began to itch on the steering wheel. Surely, he wasn't going to ask her to leave. He couldn't look so lovingly at her and want that.

"Yes. But I think I'll wait until we get home, then we'll discuss it."

She almost sideswiped a car beside her at his answer.

"Maybe I ought to drive," he suggested, then kept silent for the remainder of the trip.

Even though she'd learned that Michael was an introspective and deep-thinking man, his silences still troubled her. She wanted to know what he was feeling. Sometimes she felt like she knew, but now she wasn't sure. He hadn't told her that he loved her. She loved him with every ounce of her being, but if Michael couldn't love her, she would leave.

Pulling around to the garage, Dorel punched the door opener button and the door raised on the dark interior. "The light must have burned out." She slowly pulled the Cherokee in beside the rental in the large, deep garage, the headlights pointing yellow circles at the back wall, and turned off the engine.

"Keep the lights on so I can see my way to the door," Michael said and got out, leaving his door open. The dome light illuminated Dorel as Michael pushed the buttons on the alarm's wall pad and unlocked the door.

As Michael pushed the door open and turned sideways to motion for her, a black figure with a sword raised over its head shoved him back into the garage.

Dorel screamed.

Michael scrambled backwards, raising his arms protectively, trying to assume a defensive fighting position to the attacker. But his tight tuxedo pants and slick-bottomed dress shoes hampered his flexibility and timing. He needed to throw off his jacket and shoes, but he could only weave and bob, trying to avoid the flashing sword. His disadvantage was ominously clear.

Michael was losing.

Fumbling hysterically with the key, she restarted the car, but killed the engine trying to jam it in gear to run over the hooded attacker. I would have hit Michael as well, she realized in helpless horror.

Dorel leaped out of the stalled car, her gaze wildly searching the shadows for something she could use against Michael's attacker.

A deep, protracted groan rumbled from Michael as he

staggered backwards into the rental's right headlight, clutching at the sword blade the black-shrouded man jabbed into his chest. He jerked the sword out and Michael reeled, sliding down the front of the car to his knees and fell sideways to the concrete floor.

"Michael!" Dorel screamed and ran to him, oblivious of the sinister man standing over him.

Blood pooled over Michael's white pleated front shirt. A small crimson rivulet flowed from the corner of his mouth as she lifted his head to her lap.

His eyes fluttered open and he tried to smile, but grimaced against the death rattle in his throat. "Dorel," he gasped. "I love you." Michael's head fell to the side as the last breath rushed out of him, and he died in her arms.

"Noooo! Michael, nooo." Dorel hugged his lifeless body to her breast. Her cry of grief echoed off the cold metal surfaces of the garage and, magnified a thousand-fold, blasted her heart apart as she rocked Michael's still warm body in her arms.

"Get up," snarled the man above her as he grabbed her by the hair.

She wouldn't leave Michael. She didn't want to live without him. There would be no point to such an existence. The murderer must kill her, too.

"Get up, Everly," a man's familiar, foreign-accented voice boomed. He jerked her to her feet with such strength that she was forced to release Michael. His body slid silently away, back to the darkness beside the car.

She went limp and closed her eyes, anticipating the stroke that would send her to join Michael. Feeling his presence hovering near, Dorel prayed, wait for me.

The deathblow didn't come.

The man released her hair. With a disgusted snort, he

pulled the hood off his head. A Japanese man sneered at her with cold black eyes. "I, Hiroshi Inada, proclaim that you are not the chosen one. So weak and wanting death. You are not the Guardian of the sword."

The impact of his words was ultimate torture. He had come for the sword. For a useless sword he had murdered Michael and now would finish her. It was so unfair. So senseless.

She'd made Michael destroy the one thing that could have saved him. It was her fault he was dead. In penance, she had to fight Inada. Kill him for Michael.

"Perhaps you are not so weak?" he oozed, carefully watching her face. "Could you be the Guardian after all?"

"You son of a bitch. I'll kill you myself," she growled and shoved him with all her power. He fell back just enough that she could run into the house.

"Katana! Katana," she yelled frantically for the dog and ran to the silent, dark living room with Inada pounding close behind her. Her foot caught and she lurched forward, sprawling across the hardwood floor on her stomach.

Inada flipped the wall switch that turned on display lighting in the bookcases and barely illuminated the large room. Dorel squinted, trying to focus and hastily pulled herself to her knees, her leg brushing wiry fur. She turned her head to see the Airedale lying unmoving on the floor, a large bloody wound on his side.

The monster had killed Katana, too!

Screaming rage exploded within Dorel. She sprang up and charged the murderer.

Chapter Sixteen

"You murdering bastard," shrieked Dorel, ripping at him. "I'll kill you!"

Inada clamped her arms at her sides. Holding her tightly against his body, he dragged her to the center of the room across from the burl coffee table and shoved her to her knees, facedown into the area rug. He rolled her over, put his knee on her chest and pinned her arms down painfully despite her furious struggle.

"He was not the Defender, Everly. You should not have given the sword to him. You have squandered time and perhaps many lives. You have disobeyed. It is I who am the Defender. The sword belongs to me."

"Like hell. The Baroness gave it to my grandfather for me. If it was for you, she'd have given it to you."

"I said you were disobedient. Now and then. Michiko, you knew you must return it to my family where it belonged. But you gave it, and yourself, to him!" The hatred in his voice spit on her.

"It belongs to Fusao. To Michael. Never you. He was your ancestor long ago. Once. That doesn't mean the sword stays in your family. It follows him. Always," she growled, trying to pull her arms out of his hands.

"Quiet!" He grabbed both of her wrists in one hand and clamped his other hand over her mouth and squeezed her nose closed.

Dorel bucked and writhed but her lungs began to burn as precious air was exhausted. She'd thought she wanted to die, but she now knew she wanted to live, if only just to kill him.

"You will be silent?"

Ears ringing and vision blurring, she nodded hysterically.

His knee still on her chest, Inada released her nose and dug his fingers into her cheeks, forcing her to look at him. "Where is it?" His black almond eyes willed her to tell.

"Here, of course." Dorel tried to think rationally of her next move.

"You will bring it to me."

"Why? You can't use it. You are not the Defender."

"You will perform the ritual. I will be the Defender. You will be my Guardian. You know that to be true. You have to go where the sword goes until your death. You will give me the sword and I will help you to meet your death. Releasing you to join your lover."

"I told you, it won't work. It is not for you." She had to stall him. Once he learned the sword had been destroyed he would waste no time killing her.

"I am the Defender," he roared. "I have chosen it. You will do as I say. Get the sword."

He grabbed his sword and pressed the sharp blade under her chin. One quick movement and he would end it for her right now.

"All right," she agreed to his evil face, hating him with all her energy.

Inada lifted his knee off her chest and grabbed her dress by the bodice. He jerked her up with him. The thin straps popped off the front of the dress and she grabbed the thin silk to her breast as she teetered to her feet.

"Where is it?" he hissed.

"In the drawer over there. Under the bonsai."

He shoved her ahead of him to the wall of shelves. Her hand trembling, Dorel pulled the drawer open and started to remove the sword.

"Leave it. I will take it." Inada tossed his own sword aside and picked up the scabbard. "Prepare yourself for the ritual."

Dorel shuddered, rubbing her side. As she turned away, Inada squeezed so close she could feel his breath on her neck. What am I going to do? she worried. She didn't know what ritual he meant and barely remembered giving the sword to Michael the first time. In her mind's eye, she saw his poor lifeless body sprawled at her feet in the garage.

Hatred grew in her, obliterating humanity and compassion. She would kill this monster if it were the last thing she ever did, and it probably would be.

Marching her to the middle of the living room, he held the scabbard out to her. "You will begin."

Dorel stood before the sword, unable to do as he said. Even useless, it was going to get her killed. She hadn't broken the cycle. This was just a horrible new twist. She took hold of the sword and closed her eyes.

Inada sucked in a breath. "Such beauty," he breathed.

His lust made her skin crawl. She turned her back to him, trying to guard the sword from his gaze. Could he see what had happened to it just looking at it? She could actually feel it. That horrified her. Perhaps the sword was not destroyed at all. But getting even with her for trying.

"Begin," he ordered a second time, his voice edged with deadly impatience.

She turned slowly to him, trying to resolve her own approaching death. "There is nothing to begin."

"You refuse me?" He grabbed her hair, jerking her head back painfully. "You will do it."

"I can't. I don't know what to do," she grimaced and held very still.

"Do what you did when you gave the sword to Gabrielli." He released her hair and stepped back, waiting.

She lifted the scabbard by the sword's hilt. Holding it out to him with one hand, she said, "Here. Take the sword that's brought me nothing but misery. May it make your life unlivable forever." She jammed the sheathed sword at his chest. "Die, you son of a bitch."

Inada actually laughed. "Everly, I do not believe that is the exact ritual you performed for Gabrielli. But it will do. You see, all you had to do was willingly present me the sword. You have." He snapped a short bow and raised the scabbard upward, the red cord dangling before his face. "I accept this sword as my divine right."

It wouldn't work, Dorel knew instantly. She watched the red cord sway against the front of his black shirt, wishing it was his blood, but she knew soon it would be hers that would be spilled moments from now when the sword didn't speak to him. It had been for her and Michael only.

Michael was dead, and so was the sword. For now.

Inada closed his eyes and drew the blade slowly from the scabbard. Dorel was rooted in place, mesmerized by the absolute concentrated bliss and expectation on his face.

The sword slipped noiselessly out into the light. His hand dropped as the four-inch blade cleared the scabbard. His eyes popped open and he beheld the defiled sword.

"Arghh!" he screamed, his eyes blazing with fury. "You fool, what have you done?"

"I told you it was not for you. We cut it up. You killed Michael for nothing," she answered quietly as a strange calm eddied across her tense shoulders.

Inada stared unbelievingly at the short, broken blade and upended the scabbard. The remaining pieces slipped out, clinking to the floor in a silver cascade. "There is just enough left to cut your throat," he roared, and tossing aside the scabbard, lunged at her.

Dorel ducked and tore around the couch, keeping it between them. Inada jabbed the blunt-ended blade at her with his long arm. She dodged and crabbed sideways to the end of the couch.

Aggressive peace.

Her grandfather's voice sounded in her ears. So real, so alive she almost looked to see if he were standing near her. The same instant, she realized his physical presence was not important. His words had the power.

First, you must counter all thoughts of killing. Physical defense is not the only way.

Dorel's heart thumped faster and she tried to clear her mind. Inada resolutely pressed her. Help me, Granddaddy, she pleaded silently.

Repel the violent thoughts—of both of you. Think of your love for Michael. Your living love. Demand that love to empower you.

Oh, my darling Michael, she sobbed. She did love him so. "I love Michael," she proclaimed aloud, feeling the positive energy vibrate through her with the words.

Inada stopped and cocked his head, then grinned evilly. "You waste your love on a fatality. He is as dead as you will be."

The profane power of his words almost knocked her down. She stopped and reached out mentally for more positive energy.

Aggression is not the same as violence. It is not wrong. It is a creative, active power. Use it, Dorel. Demand it.

"I demand peace." The mandate flowed from the center of her being. "I call upon all the love and good through all of time and space. Every word of love that was ever felt or spoken, I summon its power now." Dorel stood still, her thoughts and body concentrating like a huge lens bringing into focus the illuminating power from the universe.

She became a glowing, pulsing being full of radiant power. At one with the universe. The positive energy of love palpitating around and through her, spreading from her focused center outward, encompassing the world.

Dorel raised her arm and opened her eyes. She pointed at Inada who stood stiffly at attention. "Go from here in peace. Do not seek further violation. You shall destroy no more."

The sword fell from his hand to the floor with a bang and rolled to the pile of metal shards that was left of its blade. Dorel pulled her gaze from the broken sword to Inada.

"Go in peace," she repeated.

Inada backed away, his demeanor transforming before her eyes. Fury drained from his face and was replaced by smooth, reasonable intelligence; tension left his body, his shoulders settling lower and the stiff malevolence dissolving from his limbs. He strode to the foyer where he turned back to her. Staring into her eyes, he issued a short bow and left the house.

She knew in her heart he would never return.

Dorel exhaled slowly and felt the centered energy transfer out of her. She released it willingly. Slumping to her knees, exhausted and terribly sad, she covered her face and sobbed into her hands in release.

Go to him, Dorel. The silent command intruded on her grief, focusing her on poor Michael. He lay dead in the garage. She should call the police.

Go to him, the command repeated.

She pulled herself to her feet and stumbled to the hallway door leading to the garage. She stood with her hand on the knob, not wanting to see the horror that awaited her.

Weeping quietly, she opened the door. Brightness from the headlights puddled in front of the Cherokee. She squeezed her eyes closed, not wanting to see his body beside the car. Choking down a rough breath, she opened them.

Michael was gone!

Dorel gasped and clamped a hand over her mouth. Inada must have stolen his body. Why? Why? she screamed silently and ran around the garage, searching for any sign of Michael. Not even blood remained as a testimony to his murder.

Of course Inada would get rid of the evidence. He must have had people with him to do it.

I've got to call the police, call Rhett, she decided agitatedly, and turned for the house. She stopped herself. And tell him what? That Inada burst in and killed Michael? Then she ordered him to leave?

Who would believe that?

Oh, Michael, why leave me now, she grieved, not caring about anything else. He loved her, he'd finally told her. Too late.

Dorel retraced her steps into the house and saw the dark lump lying on the floor in the living room. Poor Katana.

She grabbed the wedding-ring quilt off the futon in her room and took it to him. Wrapping it around and under the dog, she pulled his heavy body to the deck door. Inexhaustible tears streamed down her face as she left the dear animal on the deck and returned inside. She searched every room and closet, but found no trace of Michael. In his room, she stared at the big bed that just this afternoon had held their lovemaking. She threw herself down across it and cried until she fell into an exhausted sleep.

Dorel!

"Oh, Granddaddy, he's dead. Michael's dead," *she whimpered.*

Do not be sad, Dorel. You will find each other again.

"*No, I've lost Michael even though the cycle has been broken. How can that be? I didn't know that he would die anyway. If I hadn't listened to you and talked him into destroying the sword, he could have used it to defend himself. It's my fault. I've changed the cycle somehow and killed him. Lost him.*"

You've only lost the Defender, Dorel. That's all. You aren't condemned to those roles any more. You are both free as you planned when you first created the Trust together.

"*Then where is Michael, Granddaddy? Is he with you in heaven?*" She felt his rich good humor and smile.

We aren't in the same group, or you might say consciousness. I'm your guide, your guardian angel, if you like. I always have been. Michael is your soulmate.

"*I want to be with him.*"

You are always together, Dorel. Just as I am always with you. You must believe.

Dorel rolled in bed and fought the comforter wrapping around her. She snapped awake and wiped her tear-chapped cheeks.

It was still dark out when Dorel stumbled into the living room and looked out the windows to the deck. Suddenly, she remembered Benten and ran through the house calling the cat, praying Inada hadn't hurt her too.

She found the Persian curled up on Michael's desk chair, alive and very sleepy. Dorel stroked her and crooned to the disinterested cat. She heard the birds begin to stir in the garden just before sunrise. Unable to face the day, she wanted to hide here among Michael's things and pretend he was still alive.

Dorel rose and moved around the office, touching, caressing his well-worn books, his favorite pen. She slid her hands over the diplomas and awards on his walls, willing any residual energy that was Michael to her fingertips.

Never had she felt so desolated and alone.

The night began to recede beyond the windows. Dorel turned her back on the dawn and walked to the living room. Sinking to the floor next to phone on the end table, she closed her eyes. She had to make the call.

It would start everything all over again, but she didn't have a choice in the matter. Inada could not simply murder Michael and get away with it. She took a deep breath and lifted the phone receiver, focusing on the buttons—nine—one—

Movement on the deck stopped her. Someone was outside. Inada? Not again, please. She couldn't stand anymore. Shaking, she replaced the receiver and walked to the broad expanse of windows. The sun was just lifting its fiery head over the Cascade Mountains.

The first spiking rays of golden light flashed into the sky and across the land. Dorel narrowed her eyes against the radiance. A halo of fuzzy light gathered, taking form on the deck. She turned her head slightly and held up a hand to shade her eyes.

A form dressed in black materialized in the glow and stood facing the rising sun. Dorel's heartbeat paused and her breath caught as she recognized the beloved figure. She dropped her hand and rushed to the door, opening it slowly so as not to disturb the apparition. Stepping out on the deck, she tiptoed forward.

Michael's peaceful, beautiful profile faced the rising sun. He raised his arms deliberately. The sword lay across his palms, whole, unbroken beside the scabbard. He raised the sword to the rising sun, staring unblinking into its radiance.

A bright ray of light separated from the golden orb and arced toward him. It swirled around him and settled upon the sword like a lightning bolt. The sword shined brightly in Michael's hands.

A throbbing hum issued forth, vibrating through her, pulsing like a bloodstream of energy. The sound built in intensity, forming into recognizable words.

"It was not yours to destroy, but to continue the eternal struggle. Now it must pass to another," a disembodied voice droned and became louder, lower in frequency.

Dorel clapped her hands over her ears at the almost painful noise. The light drew in and around the sword, pulsing and humming. It flared out in a flash of blue-white that shot skyward and instantly disappeared.

Dorel blinked against the black spots before her eyes and dropped her hands from her ears in the silence that remained. Michael stood still facing the now completely risen sun, his hands empty.

His chest rose as he sucked in a breath and shook his head as if waking. Dorel reached out toward his apparition, afraid but compelled to make sure he was real. She felt a bump at her knee and reluctantly drew her eyes away from Michael and looked down.

Katana sat beside her legs, grinning up at her. His nose pushed her knee again as if to urge her toward Michael. This can't be possible, she marveled in shocked happiness. Even if this were a vision or dream, she would go with it, savor it. Make it last forever.

Michael turned to her with his arms still outstretched. His face animated with love and rapture as she stepped into his arms and felt the warmth of his body press against hers. She met his lips in a gentle kiss. They were warm and firm. Alive.

Michael was alive!

They held each other for long moments, drawing strength

in their love. She finally drew back a little and looked into his eyes.

"How can this be? You were . . . he killed you."

"I know, Dorel. I know." He pulled her to him again and buried his face in her hair.

"Is this real, Michael? Can you stay? Or have you just come to say goodbye?" Horror turned her heart cold.

"I think I'm supposed to stay."

She led him to a chaise lounge and pulled him to sit beside her on the beige cushion. "Tell me what happened."

Michael took a breath and untied his black bow tie. Dorel looked at his shirt. It was sparkling white where before it had been covered with blood. Had he been only injured and not killed? She glanced at Katana sitting on her feet. He, too, had no evidence of his fatal wound.

Please, don't let me wake up. If this were a dream, Dorel wanted to live here in the dream with them instead of the waking world where she was alone.

Or maybe everything had been a nightmare from the day she walked into the gun show. Perhaps none of it had happened?

"I died, I remember that. It was like you read about. I heard the roaring and saw the light. I hovered above you and Inada." Michael grasped her hand. "I'm so sorry, Dorel, you had to go through that and sorry I withheld my love. It made things doubly difficult for you. Hurt you. I regret that so much."

She clasped his hand to her lips and kissed his warm skin. "Oh, Michael, I do love you and I am so glad that you told me you loved me then. Especially then."

"It wasn't right. I'm sorry. You've saved us. Brought me back. Your love did."

"How could that be possible?"

"When I went to the Light I was met by a being. Someone I've come to know, yet have always known, but not in this lifetime. I met your grandfather. I watched while he helped you. And I helped you. There were so many gathered to help you. You felt it, I know. All that positive energy and love directed to you. You received and used the energy from us. To save us. And you saved Inada, too. He doesn't have to repeat his errors of the past."

"It sounds as if you are forgiving him, Michael. After all he has done to us." She wasn't sure she could ever forgive him.

"That's part of it. We have to forgive if we want to be free. I think you know that. You're feeling the residual negative energy hanging around and coming into your thinking, keeping you from forgiving."

"I can't help it," she protested, feeling hatred for Inada beginning to take hold of her again.

"Let the feelings come. Don't block them. Just let them pass through. They won't stay because you won't block them or stop them. There's nothing wrong with these thoughts. They're just energy. Don't attach any negativity to them. Let them go."

"You know about *aggressive peace,* Michael?" she asked, recognizing the concepts as those her grandfather told her.

"I guess so," he answered with a shrug. "We've experienced its power. Seen it work. I don't know exactly how I'm alive right now, other than I had the choice. I believed I was dead and I was. But since you broke the cycle, I was given the opportunity to return. We've finally learned what we set out to and we can start over with a new trust, a new agreement for ourselves, from this moment on."

He smoothed his fingertips along her cheek. "You did it, Dorel. All by yourself, fighting me every step of the way. I might have been the culmination of all warrior existences I've ever experienced, but the strengths and intelligence of all that you have ever been are centered in you now. And you were born with the desire, a determination to set us free this time. And you remembered."

"Oh, Michael. Is this real? Not a dream?" Dorel asked, searching his handsome face.

He smiled and kissed her forehead. "Sure. Life is a dream. What's real?"

Her face fell and she gasped. "I was afraid of that."

He laughed. "Come on, I was waxing existential. As far as I can tell, I'm not going to disappear in a flash like the sword. We're still stuck together."

"What about Inada? Is he *stuck* with us, too?"

"No, he's changed. Free to get on with his life's plan, like we are."

She looked down at the dog. "And Katana? Explain him."

"Don't know. Maybe if I could come back, unaffected by Inada, perhaps it was the same for him. We changed the present. That goes for Katana and maybe Inada, too."

Dorel stroked the dog's big head and got a quick lick in return. She bent and kissed his rough-furred ear. Whatever the reason or process, she was glad they were all together.

"What about Abie? Is he back, too?" She didn't want to see him again, changed or not.

"Hmm. I don't think so. But I'm not sure. He was so stuck in his belief of violence, violating the spirits of others and greedy for money, I don't think he's back yet. He has a lot to work out, but he'll get his chance to do it again."

"What about us? What do we do now that *we've learned what we set out to* as you said." She frowned at the uncertainty of the future.

"We live and love. I was shown what our lives hold from today, but like when we're born, the memory fades. I don't remember any of it now. And I don't think I have any interest in remote viewing it to find out." He touched the back of his hand to her cheek. She clasped it and kissed his fingers.

"Michael, would you marry me? I want to be your wife in this lifetime as well as your partner and soulmate through eternity."

"I was planning to ask you last night. And I would have this morning, but you beat me to it. Yes, I will marry you."

Dorel caressed his cheek, delighting in the warmth of his skin and reveling in the vast love open to them. "I love you, Michael. We are so lucky to have another chance."

He gently clasped her hand from his cheek, brushing her fingertips with his lips. "I love you, too."

The rising sun warmed the gentle breeze gliding over her skin. A sigh of contentment eased across her lips. "I'm so happy. I know we're safe now, because we've been saved by our love. I hope no one else ever has to go through what we have."

"Don't worry," he assured her, wrapping his arm around her waist and gently guiding her into their house. "If we can break the cycle of fear and greed for power and learn what we came to do, others can, too."

"I hope so," she said, resting her head against his shoulder. She heard the wind chimes softly tinkling an enchanting melody of infinite harmony that promised Dorel was now free to live an Eternal Trust of love with Michael. This lifetime and the next.

Epilogue

Glancing at his watch for the tenth time in as many minutes, Michael strolled to the open garage door and checked the driveway.

Why did he always do this? Spencer used to be on time. Never late. But now . . .

"Michael, are they here yet?" called Dorel, leaning out the door to the house.

He smiled. "Nope. Late as usual."

She led Katana by the collar into the garage and tried to load him into the back of the car. "Come on, jump up there." The dog put his front paws on the bumper and waited. "Oh, all right, I'll help you." She lifted his back end and shoved him into the car, then pushed the door closed.

Michael slipped his arms around her waist as she straightened up, and nuzzled kisses into her neck. "Wanna take a chance that they'll be really late?"

Dorel turned in his hug and dropped a quick kiss on his mouth. "Uh uh, you devil. About the time you got me out of these jeans, they'd coming blazing home and catch us."

He scowled. "Old friends and rotten little kids. They can sure ruin a guy's sex life."

She kissed his frown away. "You liar. You have a fabulous sex life."

He ran his hands down her back over her tight jeans and cupped her bottom. "Yeah, I do," he agreed with a sly grin.

The motorcycle roared into the garage, its handlebars almost grazing the side of Dorel's old Cherokee she refused to get rid of. Spence put his feet out, steadying the Harley and turned off the engine.

"Hi, guys." He pulled off his helmet. "Are we interrupting something?"

"Of course," carped Michael. "Isn't that the way you plan it?"

"Daddy, Uncle Spence raced a policeman," chirped a little voice from under the big helmet.

Dorel rushed over and lifted the boy off the seat in front of Spence. Motherly concern on her face made Michael smile, which he was careful to hide behind his hand.

"Speennnce?" Dorel's voice rose in pitch. "Why do you continue to do that? It's too dangerous." She helped her son out of his helmet and smoothed her hand over his curly strawberry blond hair.

"No, Momma. I like it. It's fun." He smiled charmingly at his mother.

"Martin Everly Gabrielli," Dorel scolded, but a smile lurked in her attempted stern expression, "don't you try to make excuses for Uncle Spence's bad behavior." She turned to Spence, handing him Marty's helmet. "Well?"

"I'm sorry we're late. I was really just making up time so we wouldn't be in trouble." Spence tied the helmet on the rack behind him.

"Where'd you go today?" Michael asked as he buckled Marty into the backseat of his new Range Rover. Dorel scooted into the driver's side and started the engine.

"The gun show, naturally. The kid can't get enough. I tell you, Mike. He's got a real knack for armor. Really knows his stuff. Amazing for a kid his age." Spence strapped his helmet back on.

"He's brilliant like his dad," Michael boasted and closed the car door.

"Could be. But it's more, Mike. I've never seen a kid like

266

him, and I might be a tad prejudiced being his godfather, but he's extraordinary. Knows things he shouldn't." Spence started the bike. "See ya, Marty my bud. Thanks for letting me take the boy, Dorel." He waved to them and turned the motorcycle out of the garage.

Michael climbed in the passenger seat next to his wife, as she backed the Rover out and headed toward Auburn where they were going to take the Beaver for a hop to the San Juan Islands.

Pondering his friend's words, Michael agreed. Yes, his son was talented. People said he showed genius and should be enrolled in special schools where he could reach his real potential. But teachers weren't necessary, because even at nearly four years old, Martin Everly Gabrielli's vast knowledge could teach them all. He was here for a special purpose, Dorel often said.

He glanced over his shoulder and grinned at Marty. His son returned the smile with his strangely wise eyes. Reminded once again of Dorel's grandfather, Michael turned back to the road in front of him and embraced the future.

He reached for Dorel's hand, relishing her warmth and strength, grateful she loved him as much as he loved her. Life was good, and they had each other. For eternity.